The Kidnapped Madonna

Juliann Dorell

To Nikki—
I'm honored to
sign your book.
Love,
Juliann Dorell
"Julie"

This book is a work of fiction. Names, characters, places, and incidents are products of the author's imagination or are used fictitiously. Any resemblance of such incidents, places, or figures to actual events or locales or persons living or dead is entirely coincidental.

The scanning, uploading and distribution of this book via the internet or via any other means without permission of the publisher/author is illegal and punishable by law. Your support of the author's rights is appreciated.

This book is dedicated to my brave and dedicated
warriors: Eric and Brian

And with a grateful heart I thank
Pat, Lynnie, Janet, Marilyn, and
Page Master Louie.
I could never complete my stories without your
help, and life would be so dull without you!

Thank you Darlene for your knowledge and
support.

….and to Marnie

Cover by Marilyn Droz

Prologue.....the Madonna Angel

The young boy proudly pulled his makeshift wagon towards the sleepy Mexican village. He avoided as ruts and rocks on the dusty road as he could, mindful of his delicate cargo: his and Mamacita's chicken eggs. The chickens were precious animals and he guarded them every night by sleeping in or near their enclosure lest the coyotes or other predatory animals try to get them. Because these eggs were very valuable. He sold them to the villagers but mainly, the priest and nuns at his village church bought them. He, Diego, saw that Mamacita, his sister Luisa and he had food to eat. Only ten years old, Diego was head of his household. His father was dead. He died working in the agricultural fields of the local rich patron. That wasn't going to happen to him. Each day he prayed to the Madonna Angel's picture in the church. She brought him luck. After all – it was after he had prayed to her that he found the wooden crate with six chicken hens that had fallen off the truck passing through his village.

Diego had known it was an answer to his prayer that he could feed his mother and sister. His neighbor shared his old rooster with Diego's hens for some eggs, since all his hens had died.

Soon, Diego was in business. Mamacita ground corn kernels into mash and fed them well. More hens and roosters replaced the old ones, which they ate, and Diego was able to buy material for a dress for his sister and a shirt for himself. They were both growing fast now. Mamacita used the old dresses and rags to make a quilt. It was a thin quilt but he loved its warmth when he slept outside with the chickens.

He arrived at the town square fountain near the church. Other people started to arrive and put their wares on the ground. Potatoes, chili peppers, apples, and papayas were put into piles around the fountain. Diego would quickly sell a dozen eggs here and take the rest inside the church for the Father. Then, he could visit his Madonna.

His egg business concluded, Diego reverently approached the picture in the alcove. He had removed his hat and clutched it to his chest. Silently, he stretched his hand up to the beautiful silver haired Madonna. She smiled down on him and he felt her power. He reached out to the painting and stroked her hair, as he said a prayer to her. "My Madonna please keep my family healthy. Give me success at the mission school so that I can make more money to buy a business. Make my body stronger, my fists like rocks so that the other boys fear me. Give me courage to stand against Rogelio who threatens to take my egg money. I must stop him from trying to make me scared." Diego stood up and bowed to the Madonna and made the sign of the cross. He touched her hair one last time before backing away and leaving the church. He felt her smile on his head like a benediction. His breath filled his chest and he stood taller as he walked through the church doors.

1

Deep in the interior of Mexico in a small dusty village, Villa Verde.........Diego stands proudly on his balcony. He can see his workers outside the walls that contain his hacienda. They are busily unloading 'product' he will use in his underground labs. He is now a wealthy man – owner of all he can see. The fields of cotton and grapes flow around him for miles. He is no longer the young man pulling his wagon to and from his home to the village, hungry and worried about taking care of Mamacita and his little sister. Diego is an educated man now. Father Alberto had helped him receive a scholarship to attend university. Because of his math skills, he attained a diploma majoring in business.

His time at the university in Mexico City had been difficult. He was away from his Mamacita and little sister Luisa, and because he had to work for his room and board, he was unable to go home to see them. They were able to keep up his chicken and egg business so they kept eating, but Rogelio, his old nemesis, made their life difficult. His cruelty in killing a chicken while he walked toward Mamacita's door knowing they saw him when he made a surprise visit to their small house, scared them.

Luisa was growing into a beautiful young woman and Rogelio made crude and ugly threats to her. Diego knew this was a score he would settle with that bully. But Diego was a patient man when he needed to be. He would take care of Rogelio when he finished university and returned home to his village. One of his first missions when he eventually returned was the demise and disappearance of Rogelio. With the help of his close friends, Ramon and Jose, Rogelio was never seen or heard from again. This was the first of many acts Diego and his friends would carry out while Diego built his empire.

Diego approached the local drug lord, Raoul Gutierrez for a job. His knowledge of business and a promise to make him even wealthier cemented his services to the drug cartel Gutierrez and his associates controlled. Diego soon became a powerful member and with the large sums of money he earned, began to carry out his dream of making his village a better place for his family, the local people, and for himself. Diego began to build his own private empire.

Acres of land around the hacienda were now tilled and planted with cotton. Higher into the foothills the land was developed into acres of grape vines. Nearer to the hacienda, vats and buildings stood where the wine was produced and prepared for shipping. While underneath the ground, a cavernous underground drug lab was carved out and cemented walls supported areas where methamphetamines, cocaine and marijuana were developed and prepared for distribution. Small cement turrets camouflaged with plants protruded three feet above the ground containing filters and fans which circulated air for the underground workers.

The cotton fields and winery made Diego appear to be a legitimate businessman and a wealthy citizen, but he was so much more. He was a complex man capable of great kindness to his family, employees, and villagers, but he was also a man capable of carrying out severe punishment to those who crossed him or were a threat to his world.

Diego's hacienda was a fortress with an army of personal soldiers whose sole job was to protect Diego, his underground labs, the illegal drug assembly and distribution.

Although twenty years had passed, he still prayed in the village church at the portrait of his Madonna Angel. His generous donations to the church had created a more modern school for the children, a small hospital, a market and butcher shop, and an airport for small airplanes and helicopters.

The villagers he had grown up with were now the recipients of Diego's wealth. Gone were the poor huts that were never adequate for the families who lived there. In their place were small houses with running water and heat. Small corrals, gardens and chicken coops were available for each family on request. Hunger was no longer a problem for the villagers. Most of them worked for Diego either above or below the ground. Not *one* of them would ever think of betraying Diego.

He was their life's blood. Without him they their lives would return to a mere existence; constantly worried about their daily survival. They knew he prayed to the Madonna Angel in the church alcove. She had rewarded him with many blessings and Diego had shared those blessings with them.

The Madonna Angel belonged to all of them now. Many of the villagers prayed to her every day. They believed that she was a source of goodness and strength for their village.

2

Annaliese pulled the brush through her platinum hair with a slight frown. She leaned forward and narrowed her eyes. Yes, she thought, I do have bags under my eyes. She had been tired last night when she went to bed but could not fall asleep. Tossing and turning she had awakened several times thinking each time that the ibuprofen, a glass of water, and the umpteenth potty break would help her finally fall asleep. But nothing had helped. Now, she was feeling achy and very tired. A couple of her friends had come down with the flu and Annalise worried that she could be getting sick. Not that she couldn't fight it off. Oh no! She was as healthy as an ox. She never caught the colds and flu that passed through her office and friends. This was just her body fighting off the flu, if anything. Wait! It could be PMS.....no it wasn't time for that yet. She tossed and turned, punched her pillow into a bump under her aching neck, and tried to go back to sleep. Finally, giving up, she made a cup of tea and prepared to go to work.

She put the brush in the drawer and closed it with a thud. A little more light makeup under her eyes, mascara, some lip gloss and she would be fine. The shopping she was going to do at lunchtime was not beckoning to her as it normally would. Annaliese loved to shop and she really loved buying presents for her friends. She had looked forward to getting something for her boyfriend, Derek – even had her favorite store in mind at Ocean Crest Plaza in Costa Mesa, California.

The Cadwell Cooking Store had all the cookware, utensils and just about anything a budding chef could want and that's where she was going to buy something for her sweet guy. With that happy thought, Annalise turned away from the mirror grabbing a couple of Kleenexes for her runny nose. She looked a little pale with smudges of dark skin under her eyes. Maybe she was just getting a minor cold. She shivered and touched her aching head. That can't be good, she thought, as she felt her warm cheeks. Darn! She refused to let a little cold slow her down.

As a rule, Annaliese spent only a brief time on her makeup and hair. She had never thought she was beautiful no matter how many times she was told. She just believed that she attracted attention wherever she went because of the unusual silver platinum color of her hair (which was natural), her startling silver blue eyes, and her 5'7" height; all because of her Scandinavian ancestors. She believed she was just a tall curiosity. Derek told her she was beautiful, but boyfriends were supposed to tell you that.

As she pulled on her jacket the ache in her shoulders made her realize that today would be a long day. Even though lunch and shopping at Ocean Crest Plaza was always a pleasure, she debated all the way to her car about just staying at her office instead. But she had only a few days before Derek's birthday to buy his gift and there was no way she would not have his gift bought and beautifully wrapped for his special day. So she would just have to 'suck it up,' as her brother would tell her, and go shopping. There. Decision made.

Annaliese loved her job. She was a 'people person' which was perfect for the position she held at the company she and her brother, Mathias, owned and operated. Bergdahl Properties was a large property management company. Annaliese recruited and developed new and current clients and was the main contact person for the business. Mathias preferred to work quietly using his business and law skills to manage the large properties their company represented. They worked well together mainly because of their closeness as brother and sister. Mathias was also her best friend. Since the loss of their parents five years before, their relationship had become even closer. Until recently, they had even shared a large condominium.

Annaliese had taken a big step moving out and living on her own. At twenty-five years old she had just recently become serious about a boyfriend for the first time in her life. Derek had been her friend all through college. Last summer when they decided to take a trip together to Barbados, Derek declared his love for her and his desire to have a relationship dating only each other with marriage in the future. He was a good man, an established lawyer and a person Annaliese felt she could trust. Life was good.

Annaliese settled into her desk, stowing her purse in the bottom drawer while greeting Mary Carlisle, who was secretary to both she and Mathias.

Mary was a good and trusted employee, and former high school classmate of Annaliese. She could run the office for Annaliese when needed and that made it possible for her to take long lunches and
short vacations. If only she could get her brother to take time off. Together, Annaliese and Mary could run the office very efficiently if he would take a vacation.

Mary had been in love with Mathias for years but was too shy to tell him. She had confided in Annaliese but refused to accept her advice and let him know about her feelings. Mathias dated but had no serious relationship. He was more concerned about his career and increasing the business. Annaliese was secretly plotting to bring them together. She was very fond of Mary and thought the competent secretary would be a good match for Mathias. Besides, she was Annaliese's friend. One she spent time with outside of work.

At lunch time Annaliese still had a headache but decided to go shopping and skip eating lunch. Derek's birthday present was important to her. She was sure she would start feeling better soon. She decided to park in the underground parking near the largest store in the mall. It was a safety feature to have a lot of cars and people in the area and it was also near the gourmet kitchen store she wanted to shop for Derek's gift. Grabbing her purse, she got out and locked her door. The mall wasn't too crowded today so she would be in and out fast and would still have time to rest before resuming her office duties.

Annaliese decided to window shop once she was in the main part of the mall. The stores were always so interesting and colorful at Ocean Crest Plaza. She enjoyed being here even if she didn't buy anything, shopping was fun. Slowly, Annaliese strolled along the walkway not paying attention to the looks she was getting from the men she passed. She paused briefly at a clothing store that specialized in lingerie. If she felt a little better she would go in and purchase something to wear to dinner with Derek. Not that she didn't have a lot of pretty underwear, but no girl had too many matching frilly bras and panties – simply impossible!

Diego arrived in southern California and found a flurry of activity at his cousin's home in preparation of her daughter's wedding. He enjoyed shopping in the extravagant stores at Ocean Crest Plaza. He decided to leave the pre-wedding chaos and go there for lunch, and go shopping for a wedding present instead of giving the newlyweds money. He had already bought them a beautiful condo in a gated community. He wanted to give them something elegant and beautifully wrapped.

He had his two bodyguards follow behind him discretely, several paces back. He didn't want to be too obvious but he could not afford to be without their protection. For one, he always carried a lot of cash and secondly, he could not trust that he was safe from harm. He did not trust his cartel partners – never had. It would be a simple thing to get rid of Diego and take over his lands, and his share of the business. There was no trust among any of the people he dealt with on a daily basis. The strongest and smartest stayed on top.

He had been contemplating his future lately. It was time to marry. Time for a family and children of his own. Just then, his eye caught a glimmer of silver hair and an attractive figure on a woman moving ahead of him in the middle of several shoppers. Something --- the silver hair maybe, made him want to see more.

He walked faster to catch up so he could see her up close.

Suddenly, the hair stopped moving and the people moved around so that the woman was exposed to his view. Diego was stunned! She was a beautiful young woman! He could only see her profile as she stared into the store window, but he knew that if she turned to look at him she would be breathtaking. He stopped and waited, silently begging her to turn toward him, but she didn't. She turned and started walking farther away from him rejoining the crowd. Without thinking, Diego quickened his steps to overtake the woman. He was astounded! He had to see her up close. In a quick decision, he rapidly gained on her and bumped into her on purpose knocking her to the side.

"Oh, I am very sorry senorita! I am so clumsy. Please forgive me?" he begged. Diego's hands grabbed her arm as if to steady her, but held her in place. For a moment he stared, speechless. He studied her face and felt his heart pounding as he gazed into her eyes. It was unbelievable! She was so beautiful! But more than that.....he almost couldn't take a breath....she was his Madonna! The exact vision as the picture in his church alcove that he prayed to almost every day! God in heaven!

Annaliese returned his gaze. He was amazed. Ice blue eyes and hair the color of spun silver stood before him. She smiled. She lit the darkest corners of his world. Then she turned and walked away. NO! Where was she going? He wanted to stop her. He had to see her again....talk to her. But he would frighten her if he kept trying to look at her. He could follow discretely at a distance. It was unbelievable! Who was she? She was walking slowly ahead, looking in the store windows. Diego wanted to take her somewhere and talk to her but how could he meet her and ask her name? He couldn't stalk her. She would get scared and summon the police. That he couldn't allow. Besides, he had to purchase a wedding gift and be back at his cousin's home within the hour. She expected him to attend the groom's wedding dinner that evening and he had promised to be there.

Looking over his shoulder, he made eye contact with his guards and jerked his head, summoning them to his side. "Quickly, follow her! Don't let her see you. Get her car license number. Call me with the information and I will make a call to my special contact and give you her address. Then, go to her house without being seen by anyone. Don't let her or her neighbors see you. Watch for security cameras. Juan, figure out what kind of security system is there, if she has one. I will decide what I want you to do and let you know when. But in the meantime, make sure you know where she is and what she is doing every minute. Do you understand?" Diego asked desperately. "I will take a taxi back to my cousin's home."

"Si Patron. We will not let you down." Ernesto and Juan hurried away after the silver-haired woman.

Diego couldn't believe he was letting her walk away. If he were in his village she would be his, locked away in his hacienda forever. A plan was forming in his brain. If he didn't have this damn wedding.....he wouldn't have to trust Ernesto and Juan to watch her.

He wished that his other two body guards, Ramon and Jose, were with him. They were longtime friends and completely trustworthy. Juan had never given him any reason not to trust him, but he wasn't sure about Ernesto. Diego knew he had a reputation for having a bad temper and because of it, had gone to jail. There wasn't enough time to bring in his friends. He would have to make sure Ernesto and Juan knew that he would not tolerate any disobedience. They would do exactly as he ordered – or else!

Whatever it took, that woman was his Madonna and she would belong to him. She was going to disappear from here and forever live in his hacienda in Mexico. He had a plane available. He would somehow get her to the special airport he used to move drugs and weapons between southern California and Mexico. It was almost hidden as the location was out in the middle of the desert in an old deserted airstrip.

Trusting Ernesto and Juan alone with her was something he would have to do, although he would prefer to be with them. A few threats should work to keep her safe. All they would have to do is drug her
long enough to get her on the plane. He couldn't leave the wedding early. His cousin had an entire week planned to celebrate her daughter's wedding. In addition to taking the woman to his hacienda there was a special shipment of weapons he needed to take back with him and make the trip a double bonus.

He was concerned about what drug to use on her. He had no problem getting drugs of any kind. Several doctors in southern California, as well as Mexico, were on his payroll. He didn't want to hurt her or make her sick. Two drugs came to mind: fentanyl and versed which were used by anesthesiologists. He needed to keep her from fighting his men when they took her, as well as, keep her quiet and easy to transport to the plane.

And after that, the journey to his hacienda. The thought of tying her up was distasteful for someone as precious as his Madonna. No, it would be best to make her unaware of what was happening to her until she was safely locked up in her room at his home. It never occurred to Diego that she would never agree to live with him under any circumstances. As palatial as his hacienda was and for all he could give her it would not be her choice. But single-minded Diego never considered anything other than possessing her.

When Annaliese left Cadwell's, after purchasing Derek's gift, she couldn't help but feel uneasy. The two dark-skinned men standing against the railing across from the store were there when she went inside several minutes earlier. She had seen them before when a man had bumped into her and held on to her arm.

They were staring at her, and when she stared back at them they quickly looked away. They gave her an uneasy feeling as though they were watching her. Turning down the aisle she hurried to the parking lot to return to her car and tried to dismiss her unease. It was just this nagging body ache and headache she decided.

She would go home, take a nice hot shower and some aspirin and go to bed with a hot cup of tea. That should have her feeling better in no time. She didn't see the two men who had followed her and were walking down the parking aisle two rows over from her car. Juan ducked down and inched his way toward Annaliese when she stopped at her car. He took out his cell phone and snapped a picture of the front of her car as she backed out to drive out of the parking structure. A phone call later, Ernesto and Juan knew Annaliese' address.

Pulling into her condominium complex she relaxed. Annaliese pushed the button to open her garage door. The door raised up, she pulled in and immediately closed the door. A light clicked on and she gathered her purchases and her purse. After entering her condo she pressed the button activating the alarm system. Mathias had had a state of the art system installed after he heard about some burglaries in her area. Her sweet brother was very protective of his baby sister. More so now that it was only the two of them after the death of their parents. He kidded her that he was protecting his business partner and didn't want to train a new one. But she knew he worried about her and wanted to keep her safe.

3

Outside the complex and down the street a dark sedan pulled to the side of the road and parked. Diego had called Ernesto and had given him all the information on Annaliese' driver's license. They would stay near her condo, ready to follow her if she left either by car or on foot. At ten o'clock, Ernesto told Juan to get some sleep. They would share the watch since it appeared the woman was not leaving her home tonight. At midnight, Juan awoke and told Ernesto to get some sleep while he inspected the woman's home. He also told him to move their car so that no one would become suspicious of them. Ernesto decided he would go get some food and drinks for them as they hadn't eaten since breakfast. After that, he would sleep for a couple of hours.

Juan was grateful that he was dressed mostly in black. He zipped up his jacket hiding his lighter colored shirt. Silently, he moved toward the woman's condo, listening for barking dogs. A noisy dog would be far worse than a security system. He would never get the chance to shut off her system if her neighbors had a dog. He didn't hear any dogs, possibly because they were all inside with their owners. Juan used the shrubs and trees to hide while he moved towards the condo. Each condo was separated by a driveway which led to a garage behind the condo. As Juan moved in the shadows against the wall of Annaliese' condo, he found a gate between her condo and the garage.

Pulling himself up he peered over the gate and saw a small yard with a covered patio and a glass door into the house. Perfect! He could easily access the house from this door! Juan looked up and studied the condo on both sides of this one. The windows were high up on the second story and were wide and narrow making Juan think that they were used for light and not looking outside. If he had it figured right, he and Ernesto would not have to worry about nosey neighbors if they used the back door to take the woman.

Directly behind the back wall of the condos was a roadway so that he didn't have to worry about rear windows of neighboring condos there. Juan felt good. If Diego gave them the word, they could take her tonight before dawn. Juan would have Ernesto drive their car, without lights, down this back road. A small sidewalk with another gate was next to the garage and they could take her out that way.

Juan was thinking as he crept down the walkway to inspect the gate. He could easily break any lock on the gate. They could quickly put her in the car and be out of the complex this way. As Juan approached the gate a light came on in the neighbor's back yard. Juan froze. The neighbor came out and began walking toward the other side of the wall where Juan stood. He held his breath. He heard some rattling noises and realized the neighbor was opening a garbage can on the other side of the wall. Some more rustling noises and soon he could hear the person putting the lid on the can and walking back to the patio door. The door closed and the light went off. Juan hurried to inspect the gate. *Muy facil*! He couldn't wait to tell Ernesto. They could do this fast and be gone before anyone missed her.

Juan returned to the car to wait for Diego to call. Ernesto had been sleeping and was slow to respond when Juan tapped on the window to have him open the door. He had purchased some food and had eaten his half before falling asleep. Luckily, they had disabled the car's interior lights so that it remained dark inside the car when he opened the door. "This will be no problem, mi amigo. We will go in through the back patio door, and be out in no time. Go back to sleep. I will wake you in a couple of hours."

Diego had called and given the word. A man would meet them here and give them two bags. One contained a hypodermic needle with drugs, tape and a soft rope to secure the woman they were going to kidnap. The other bag had a blanket, gloves and knit hats to hide their hair and faces to obscure their identities from the security cameras Juan had seen inside the condo complex.

Ernesto and Juan didn't have the code to open the security gate. They were going to have to wait until a car drove through the gate. They had timed the opening and knew that they had just enough time to get in. Their car license was stolen so the camera would be useless in tracking their car.

Diego's orders were that they would take her, drugged and secured, to the desert landing strip where a plane waited to take them to Mexico. The plane would also have a cargo of weapons that would be their responsibility to off-load and transport to the hacienda along with the woman. After locking her in a room where she could sleep off the drugs, Diego would have his precious Madonna.

Early in the morning, Ernesto and Juan saw their chance. A large SUV had pulled up to the entrance gate and was putting in the code to open the gate. The SUV was starting to pull through the entrance when Ernesto slowly pulled in behind it. Sure enough, their car easily passed through the gate. Ernesto watched the driver ahead of him, seeing if he was being watched through the rear view mirror, but the driver wasn't paying any attention. Quickly Ernesto turned the opposite way from the SUV and drove around the complex.

They pulled next to the back gate of Annaliese' condo and got out. It was now 5 o'clock in the morning and the complex was dark and very quiet. Dressed in hats pulled low over their faces they opened the car doors. They walked toward the back wall of Annaliese' condo looking around to make sure no one was looking out and would become suspicious. Ernesto carried the bag with the drugs they would use to control the woman. Juan would do all the opening of doors and gates. Since they didn't have a cutting tool for the lock,

Juan easily picked it with a small tool he carried. He was always ready to open any doors Diego needed opening or using his electronic skills for whatever job Diego had for him. He was very good at his job.

As they approached the patio, a light came on inside the condo. Both Ernesto and Juan froze against the back wall of the condo. They looked at each other and Juan whispered, "Stay here. I will look inside and see what she is doing." Slowly, Juan moved closer to the glass door. He leaned over and looked inside. The woman was making a cup of tea.

Even though Annaliese was feeling ill, the balmy August morning let her be comfortable with bare feet and sleeveless pajamas. She picked up her cup, turned and started walking toward the patio door. Juan ducked back and pushed Ernesto toward the wall away from the patio. "She's coming outside!" he whispered.

Annaliese felt horrible. She would call in to work and tell Mary that she was staying home today. Right now she would have a hot cup of tea. She enjoyed her patio and liked to sit and watch the sunrise or sunset on her comfortable patio chairs. After talking to Mary, she would go back to bed and watch TV and doze. A couple of aspirins and she would start to feel better, she hoped. She would also call Derek and tell him not to come over tonight. He didn't need to get sick because of her.

Ernesto dropped the bag and squatted down pulling the zipper open. He pulled out the hypodermic needle ready to inject the woman. Juan watched him and nodded. He would quickly grab her when she stepped outside and hold her while Ernesto used the hypo to put her to sleep. He edged toward the door flat against the wall.

The door slowly slid open. Juan waited until she was more than half way out before he stepped forward and grabbed her arm. The cup with hot tea fell to the patio floor breaking the cup and spraying hot water on Annaliese. Before she could scream, Juan had swung her around with her back to him and his arm around her face and mouth muffling her scream. He was stronger than the woman and pushed her against the wall, leaning against her and holding her while Ernesto came forward and quickly injected her arm. Within seconds, Juan could feel her starting to relax. Before she could slump down to the ground he and Ernesto pulled her around, picked her up and laid her down on the chaise lounge. Ernesto took the tape out of the bag, tore a piece off and used it on Annaliese' mouth. Juan took out the soft rope and tied her hands together and then her feet.

Juan then moved to the back gate and looked around listening for sounds of people and dogs. Hearing none, he motioned to Ernesto that it was safe. He returned to the woman and leaned over her and made sure she was breathing. "Okay. Let's get her to the car. Can you carry her alone while I open the gate and car door?"

"Si, mi amigo. Vamos rapidamente." Ernesto picked her up and put her over his shoulder. The two men rushed to the gate and quietly opened it. Juan put his hand up and stopped Ernesto. He looked right and left checking for cars and people. Seeing none he motioned for Ernesto to come out. Juan was grateful that it was not yet light. Dawn was minutes away and the street lights were slowly fading.

Juan opened the car door and ran around to the other back door. After opening the door he leaned in and helped Ernesto place her on the back seat. Juan had a blanket and placed it over the woman, covering her completely.

Ernesto was already in the car with the engine started when Juan got in on the passenger side. Before he got the door closed they were moving down the road heading to the gate. Juan wanted to relax but he was waiting for sirens. This had been too easy. Ernesto was careful not to speed even though Juan knew he would love to get out of the complex fast.

The gate needed a code! They were trapped until someone drove through the gate. Just as Juan was going to tell Ernesto to back up and pull over to the side and await a car coming in or going out of the gate-----the gate slowly pulled open! A car was coming into the complex! Ernesto waited and as soon as the car was through he gunned the engine, raced around the car and through the gate. Squealing the tires as he turned left out on to the main street, Ernesto took a big breath, "Amigo, we did it!" He smiled at Juan and slowed the car down. It wouldn't do to get stopped by the police. The large bump on the back seat covered by the blanket couldn't be seen from the outside but if they got stopped, a police officer could see that it was a body back there.

Ernesto wanted a cup of coffee and some breakfast but he and Juan had to drive to the desert without stopping. Diego was waiting for them to call him. Juan had his cell phone out and was dialing right now.

Diego answered on the second ring. "Tell me it is done," he ordered.

"Si, Patron. We are driving to the airport right now." Juan was so relieved.

"She is not injured? Did you check her and make sure she is breathing and not injured?" Diego barked.

Juan leaned over the seat and pulled the blanket off the woman's face. She was pale. He pulled the blanket down farther and saw that her chest was rising with each breath she took. "She is fine, Patron. Don't worry."

"If she is injured in any way you both will be very sorry." Diego growled.

"I understand." Juan knew Diego would severely punish them if they had hurt her. "We will remove the tape and ropes when we put her on the plane, Patron."

"See that you do. Don't touch her except to remove the ropes. Do you understand?" he said with steel in his voice.

"Si, Patron." The phone went dead. Ernesto and Juan exchanged looks. "I hope that I didn't tie her too tight." Juan looked back at Annaliese. "Should we stop and look?"

"No. We can't take the chance that someone could see her. We will drive to the airport, when we get to the desert, we can stop somewhere if there are no cars." He looked angry. "You are too afraid of Diego. We have done what he wanted. She will be his. We will probably receive a reward for bringing his Madonna to him," he sneered. "Now relax. I will drive for a while and. when we get out in the desert, I will pull over and you can check her and drive the rest of the way."

It was done. Juan and Ernesto had kidnapped an innocent woman for their boss. Juan felt a little sympathy for the beautiful woman lying on the back seat. They had taken her away from her life. No one would ever know where she was. They wouldn't even know where to look for her. Such power! Diego always got what he wanted.

Two hours later, and Ernesto stopped the car on a side road he had entered from the freeway. It was a deserted road with an abandoned gas station. He drove around to the back side where the car couldn't be seen and parked. Juan sensing something had changed awoke with a start.

"Where are we?" Juan rubbed his eyes and stretched his arms above his head. Then he remembered the woman and swiftly turned to lean over to the back seat, putting his hand on her chest. He sighed with relief. Just then she moved. "We'd better get going to the plane. She's going to wake up any time now," he looked at Ernesto with concern.

Ernesto spoke in Spanish, "Oh I think she is already awake. She has been moving for some time now. Perhaps she thinks we don't know she is awake. She may be uncomfortable with the ropes being tied up for so long." He leered, "I could untie her and make her very comfortable. Diego would never know the difference." He watched her for a moment and then looked at Juan his eyes filled with question.

Juan knew what he was asking. "NO WAY, Ernesto," he said firmly. "We will do exactly as Diego has ordered us. Nothing more, do you hear? She belongs to him --- not us! And, she is not some woman of the streets to be treated without respect. Now drive quickly to the airport. It's not far from here. I know because I have been here many times before for Diego."

Juan turned forward and crossed his arms waiting for Ernesto to start driving. He turned his head eyeing Ernesto with concern, "You will get yourself in more trouble than you can handle, amigo. You have had problems with your temper and your lust for women before."

Juan knew that Ernesto had served time in prison for attacking and abusing a woman. She had been his girlfriend and Ernesto had caught her cheating on him. He had almost killed the man she had been with and then had gone after the woman who tried to run from him. Diego must not know of Ernesto's past. He would never have trusted him with this woman if he knew. It was up to Juan to protect her. He could never dishonor his Patron. Diego had helped his family and he paid Juan well for all the jobs he had done for him. He looked at Ernesto and shook his head, "No, Ernesto. We will do just as Diego has told us. Nothing more or less."

"You are a coward, amigo. I did not know that about you. Diego thinks he can order the world to do his business. And you jump and run for him never thinking for yourself. I know for a fact that his partners are getting tired of his superior attitude," he said with a smirk. "I know many things you do not. I do not fear Diego." Ernesto pulled back onto the freeway.

Juan said nothing. His mind was churning. Ernesto was up to something. He was not to be trusted. That was clear now. Juan would inform Diego about him and his behavior as soon as Diego returned to the hacienda. In the meantime, he would watch over the woman more closely now. He would say nothing more to Ernesto. The faster they reached the safety of Mexico, the better.

Annaliese was awake. She had heard the men speaking Spanish and only understood a few words. One word gave her chills: airport. Her headache was worse than when she awoke this morning. At least she thought it was still the same day. She tried not to move but her feet were numb and her hands chafed against the rope. Her whole body felt like someone had beaten her. She felt sick to her stomach and hoped that what little was in there would not come up into her mouth. The tape was firmly in place and nothing there could come out so she had to keep from throwing up. She couldn't panic. Even though she felt so ill, she was still a big strong girl.

Annaliese took stock of herself: she was still wearing her pajamas with nothing on underneath and her feet were bare – no socks or slippers. It would be difficult to run if she got loose. But run she would, screaming like a banshee. Again, the word airport came to mind. If they put her on an airplane she would be far away from any chance of someone helping her unless she could escape. She opened her eyes. It was broad daylight now. All she could see was bright blue sky.

The car slowed down and turned to the right and sped up. Again, the men spoke to each other in Spanish. They sounded angry. Annaliese wondered what they were angry about. The car turned again and stopped. The two men opened the car doors to get out and she felt very hot air flow over her. Could they be in the desert? Would they release her now? Surely they had to realize that she would need to relieve herself. If they gave her food she would need the tape removed, too. Annaliese said a prayer asking the Lord for help.

Juan opened the back door and he and Ernesto pulled Annaliese out never letting her feet touch the ground. She opened her eyes and looked at the two men. They were not looking at her. She memorized their faces so that she could identify them later when she escaped.

Annaliese was in the desert. It was very hot, not surprising for a typical June day. The men were carrying her to a plane that was sitting nearby on a crumbling asphalt road. They passed an old building that looked abandoned. She struggled and one of the men spoke to her.

"I am sorry for your discomfort, senorita. We will remove the tape on your mouth and the ropes once the airplane takes off." Juan spoke kindly to Annaliese.

If that was said to make her calm, it had the opposite effect. She fought with more strength now. She couldn't get on that plane! Her struggle forced the men to put her down. The other man who hadn't spoken to her grabbed her roughly by the neck, "Your fighting us will do you no good, senorita. You are our prisoner. Don't make me hurt you." He put his face close to hers, "I might enjoy making you behave." He tightened his hold on her throat and Annaliese felt faint.

"Stop it, Ernesto! She can't breathe! Now bruises will be on her throat for Diego to see. You are a fool!" Juan grabbed Ernesto's hand and pulled. Ernesto let her go and pushed her against Juan.

"Then we'd better drug her again. It's obvious she's going to be a problem," he said with disgust.

"Let's just get her on the plane, then she won't have anywhere to go."

Juan and Ernesto picked up Annaliese and started up the stairs. Another man looked out from inside of the plane, "What's this? I didn't sign on for a kidnapping. Who is she?"

Ernesto shouted, "Get back in your seat and start the plane. This isn't your business, you're getting paid to fly. That's all. Has the cargo for Senor Diego been loaded and tied down in back?"

The pilot hesitated, "Yes, everything has been done," then he turned back inside and sat down, strapping himself in and putting on his head phones, mumbling to himself. The engines started and Annaliese was placed on a couch inside the airplane. The two men had returned to the car and brought several bags on board. Ernesto, who had grabbed her throat opened one of the bags and brought out a hypodermic needle. Annaliese cringed and tried to pull away. She knew what he was going to do. He took her arm and pushed it down on the couch. "Hold her so she can't move while I inject her," he said to Juan.

"Sit on her if you have to," he said roughly. He looked at Juan nodded then plunged the needle into Annaliese' arm.

She felt the prick of the needle and within a few seconds she felt a heaviness in her body. She tried not to close her eyes, but couldn't stop it from happening. Maybe it was better to be unconscious. Annaliese would think about escaping later. Her last thought was a brief prayer again begging for help.

Hours later, Annaliese became aware of voices speaking Spanish. She tried not to move so the men wouldn't notice her if they were close by. Instead, she took stock of what she could feel: a soft bed - she must still be on the couch in the airplane, her hands were still bound, but the rope felt a little looser, and her feet were still bound together. The voices were farther away now. Annaliese slowly opened her eyes. It was dark outside. She could see out the airplane door which was completely open. There was no guard inside the plane. Maybe there wasn't one outside either.

Annaliese tried to sit up. Immediately, her head started pounding and her stomach turned over.

Fighting back the urge to vomit, she took huge breaths of air. She wished she had a jacket or a blanket because she felt shaky and very cold. Thinking she probably had only a few minutes before they would come for her,

Annaliese forced herself to concentrate on getting the ropes off of her hands. She relaxed and made her hand go limp and rolled the rope as far down her hand as she could. It was working! The rope was moving off her hand! One last pull and the rope fell away.

Pushing herself up, Annaliese felt the nausea come back with a vengeance. Breathing deeply, she leaned over her knees and threw up on the carpet by her bare feet. Luckily, she had only had a cup of tea and a bite of her toast. These people deserved to have her throw up on their plane. She didn't even care.

Rapidly pulling on the rope around her feet, Annaliese released them and tried to stand up. She swayed so much that she quickly sat back down. This wouldn't do. At this rate she wouldn't be able to run down the plane stairs and hide. Slowly, she stood up and held onto the arm of couch. She realized that she wasn't going to feel any better no matter how long she stayed here. Her only option was to get as far away as she could and find help.

Annaliese slowly approached the open door. She leaned forward and saw several men unloading boxes from the back of the plane. A truck was close by and blocked most of her view. That was good. That meant they wouldn't see her right away if she could get down the stairs and start running.

She looked out to see if there were any buildings. Nothing. She looked further out and could see lights in the distance and the steeple of a church. That was her only hope. To get to that church and beg the people there to help her.

Annaliese hurried down the stairs and started running toward the lights. Once she was away from the plane the night would conceal her. The only light here was from the truck's headlights, and it was pointed away from where she was running. She concentrated on every step she took. The ground was getting rougher with each step and she knew she would have painful, bloody feet but that was not important now. Whatever it took – she was going to reach that church.

The lights were closer now. Annaliese had not heard any noise from behind her at the plane. That meant that they hadn't discovered she was gone yet. She stared at the steeple, her only focus, and kept putting one foot in front of the other. No longer running, Annaliese tried for a fast jog but wasn't doing much more than a stagger. She was breathing so hard she thought the men could hear her back at the plane.

At last, Annaliese approached small houses. Dogs started barking but she didn't stop. She couldn't trust these people to defend her from thugs. She had to get to the church. The road was better now but the pain in her feet was terrible. More houses and more dogs barking, but no one came out to look.   Annaliese felt sweat running down her face into her eyes.   She wiped her arm across her forehead and fisted her hands determined to keep going.

Up ahead, she saw bigger buildings and realized she was approaching the town.   The church couldn't be far now. She was so thirsty, her throat was so parched. It would be difficult to talk once she found people to help her. They would give her water - if only she could get to the church.   She could see a fountain now. It would have water but she shouldn't stop there. Her decision to stop was taken from her when she heard a vehicle rapidly approaching.   It sounded like a truck! Oh no! They were coming for her!

Ernesto was driving like a mad man. He had gone into the plane to put her in the truck and she was gone! He and Juan searched everywhere near the plane. They couldn't believe that she could have run away. He had given her enough of the drug that she should still be sleepy. The men who had been loading the truck had helped them look for the woman and one of them had seen something shining in the distance, moving toward the village. Ernesto knew immediately that the shining was the hair of Diego's woman.

She had just reached the fountain when the truck slid to a halt and the men jumped out running for Annaliese. The angry man who had shouted at her had caught up to her. She screamed as he grabbed her hair pulling her to the ground.

I've got to get up those stairs, she thought. "Holy Mary, mother of God, save me," she whispered.

"You bitch," he screamed into her face, "you would run from me? I will make you sorry." Ernesto was furious. No one ever escaped from him, he thought, as he removed his belt from his trousers. His anger had ignited like a flame to gasoline. He would teach her a lesson.

Annaliese struggled to her feet and lurched forward toward the church stairs she saw ahead of her. After only a few steps strong hands pushed her roughly to the ground. She heard the man screaming at her in Spanish and didn't understand what he was saying but heard the word 'puta' and knew that was a bad name for a woman. She didn't care what he was saying. She would get up those stairs somehow.

Juan tried to grab Ernesto's hand holding the belt, but he was enraged and didn't hear him and pulled away. He shoved Annaliese again and she hit her head on the fountain.

Juan pulled him away from her. They fought over the belt. Ernesto was stronger than Juan, but he had to stop him from hurting the woman. She was up again, blood trickled down her forehead. She had made it to the church and was crawling up the church steps.

It was now early morning and the dawn made it easy to see her. Their loud voices brought several people out of their shops. Many more would be coming to early mass.

Juan had to get Ernesto under control and get the woman in the truck before anyone could interfere. She had started up the steps again. Ernesto hit Juan, knocked him to the ground and stormed after the woman.

The first slap of Ernesto's belt felt like fire on Annaliese' back. He kept hitting her again and again down her back, her buttocks and legs. She screamed in agony and dragged herself forward toward the church door. A scented draft of air moved over her face as the church door suddenly opened. The lashing stopped and Annaliese lunged toward the long black robe in front of her.

"Ernesto, stop! Diego will kill you for beating her you idiot!" Juan hollered. Ernesto dropped the belt and stepped back. Annaliese pushed past the man in the robe and holding on to the backs of the church pews, she staggered down the church aisle toward the altar lit with candles, her bloody feet leaving a trail.

A side door on the altar opened and Annaliese saw a nun enter. She hurried toward Annaliese with open arms. The man in the black robe at the door, Father Ambrose, had followed her down the aisle and now helped her up the three stairs. Annaliese collapsed into the nun's arms, clinging to her like a child. The weight of her body forced them to the floor in front of the cross. Annaliese laid her head on her lap.

"Father, who is this poor creature?" Sister Beatrice asked in shock.

Before he could answer, he heard Ernesto's angry voice as he ran down the church aisle. "Give her to me Father. She belongs to Diego. I'm taking her to the hacienda!"

Ernesto bent over to grab Annaliese. She shrank back trying to escape his hands. "Please help me, Father," she croaked, "He kidnapped me!"

Ernesto stood still and looked down on the woman and what he'd done. The side of her face was dirty and bloody. He reached again to pick her up and Sister Beatrice slapped his hand.

Father Ambrose looked at him with disgust, "You disgrace our church and our Lord! How dare you bring your violence here?"

Ernesto staggered and gasped, panting loudly. He groaned and wiped his sweaty face with his hands. He realized his temper had just cost him his job with Diego and maybe his life. Turning, he fled up the aisle pushing past Juan and the villagers who were filing into the church – curious to see what had caused so much commotion. He had to get to the hacienda and gather up his things to escape before Diego returned from California. The villagers were whispering and pointing at the woman in Sister Beatrice's arms.

Slowly, they came forward, their voices getting louder. Father Ambrose looked perplexed. Before he could question them, a loud voice said, "Madre de Dios! It's a miracle! Look! She glows from heaven's light!" All the villagers crossed themselves and kneeled down.

Sunrise through the stained glass windows on the altar made the disturbed dust motes around Annaliese' glow in her silver hair. Sunlight glimmered through the dust causing a halo effect around her head. Father Ambrose stepped back and without thinking, crossed himself. She looks just like the Madonna Angel, he thought. No wonder Diego had to have her.

The aura around Annaliese lingered. She was unconscious now. The villagers grew more excited, calling for more people to come and see her. They all knew. She *was* the Madonna Angel and had come to them, they exclaimed.

Sister Beatrice smoothed Annaliese' hair with reverence. "Father we must take her to the hospital at once."

Father Ambrose looked into the crowd. He chose two men who were big and strong. "You and you," he pointed. "Come and help carry this woman to the hospital."

The two men removed their hats and stepped forward.

4

Dr. Hermosa was on his way to the village hospital when a young boy ran to him and grabbed his coat sleeve and pulled. "Hurry, hurry doctor!" he pleaded. "You must help her!" he cried and pulled harder. "Our Madonna Angel is hurt and bleeding on the church altar!" The boy tightened his hold on the doctor's arm. Dr. Hermosa picked up his medical bag and released the boy's hold on him.

He started running toward the church and saw many people crowded around the church doors. The young boy grabbed his arm, again, and pushed through the people, urging him to hurry faster. The sun was shining through the mosaic windows and on the altar he saw something silver shining near Sister Beatrice. As he approached the altar he saw that it was the silver blond hair of a young woman in Sister's lap.

"You see, doctor? She has a halo like her picture in the alcove! She is our Madonna Angel!" the boy said in awe.

Father Ambrose ordered the two men to pick up the woman. "Dr. Hermosa, these men will carry her to the hospital. Tell them where to put her for your examination. I will send Sister Beatrice along to help you." He moved down the aisle, urging people to step back and make way. Dr. Hermosa followed behind the men and watched the people they passed who were crossing themselves and whispering.

Who is this woman, he wondered? And how did she come to be injured and placed on the church altar? He was amazed! She did look like the Madonna Angel.

When they reached the hospital, Annaliese was placed on a gurney and rolled into the examination room used for emergencies. Dr. Hermosa ushered the men out and called for a nurse who closed the door of the room. He noticed that people were silently filing in to the hospital. "You must go about your business now. There is nothing to see. I will take care of the woman and will let Father Ambrose know about her condition, later this morning." When the people didn't move, he said in a stronger voice, "Go now! I can't have you crowding my hospital. This place is for the sick and injured. If you must stay, you have to wait outside." A nurse started pushing people toward the doors. Several people made the sign of the cross and turned to leave. Others followed and soon the room was empty. Dr. Hermosa shook his head and entered the room with the silver haired woman. Sister Beatrice had covered her with a blanket while a nurse was preparing a table with medical supplies for him.

Gently he touched her cheek, "Can you hear me?" Annaliese moaned and opened her eyes. "Who are you? Do you know where you are?" he asked as he motioned for the nurse to place the moveable table with supplies closer to the gurney.

Annaliese' throat was so parched and sore she croaked, "Ana...." and then let the darkness take over. Two hours later, the doctor had treated her badly abused body with medication, and bandages, which covered both of her feet. Sister Beatrice had washed her body and face, and Annaliese never regained consciousness.

Dr. Hermosa was concerned. Her temperature was high. It was clear she was ill as well as injured. He had a tube for intravenous fluids attached to her arm to treat dehydration. Another tube flowed through her other arm with antibiotics. He had drawn blood and would know more about her system when the report came back. In the meantime, he was afraid she also had a concussion. Hopefully, not severe. The poor woman had taken quite a beating. Father Ambrose had told him about how she had run into the church while being chased and beaten by Ernesto Garcia. It was a good thing that he had run away. If she was Diego's woman, as Father said, he was a dead man as soon as Diego saw him.

Father Ambrose also told him that she had been Ernesto's prisoner. Juan Carrera was sitting in the waiting room. He had been with the woman and Ernesto, too. He told Father that Diego had told them to kidnap the woman from California and bring her here to his hacienda. If that was a fact, they had committed a crime against this woman. He wasn't in a position to deny Diego if he wanted this woman. Juan told Father that Diego saw her and thought that she was his Madonna Angel. Dr. Hermosa would take good care of her. She would have to stay in the hospital even if Diego didn't agree, and wanted to take her to his home. He didn't look forward to Diego's visit when he returned from California.

A few days had passed when Diego stormed into the hospital, roaring for Dr. Hermosa. Annaliese had finally awakened the evening of the day she arrived at the hospital, but was still weak and very ill. She hadn't been able to stand due to her injured feet, but she could help lift herself into a wheelchair for brief rides to the bathroom.

"Where is she?" he roared, striding down the corridor. Dr. Hermosa heard him before he saw him.

"Senior Diego. Please, she is doing better. I urge you to quiet your voice. Please, you will frighten her and she has been through enough terror."

"Where is she? I want to see her ----NOW!" Diego shouted with his hands on his hips.

"I will take you to her. But she is very ill, Senor, as well as injured from the beating."

"Arrrgh! I heard and I will deal with Ernesto as soon as my men catch him!" he growled. Juan had waited at the hacienda and told him the entire story, only escaping death because he tried to stop Ernesto, and he didn't run away like that miserable coward. Diego's bodyguards had beaten him, but he would recover.

"I'm sorry, Dr. Hermosa, I will calm down. I don't want to scare my Madonna."

Quiet now, Diego walked softly into Annaliese' room. She was awake and sitting in her bed, eyes wide with fear.

"It's YOU!" she cried. "The man from Ocean Crest!" She cringed and looked anxiously at Dr. Hermosa.

"You must not be afraid, my Madonna," Diego said softly as he approached the bed. "I will not hurt you." He reached out to take her hand and she jerked back, holding her hands up so he couldn't hold them.

"Go away! You are the reason I am here! Call the police, doctor! I have been kidnapped by this man and his thugs!" Annaliese cried. She looked at Dr. Hermosa pleading with her eyes.

Dr. Hermosa said nothing, just looked at Diego. Diego returned his look and jerked his head to the side, silently telling the doctor to leave the room. Without looking at Annaliese, the doctor left the room and closed the door.

"I am sorry, Madonna, my men were to bring you to my hacienda only. Nothing bad was supposed to happen to you. I will punish all who are responsible for your injuries, I promise."

"I didn't ask to be taken anywhere! How dare you even think that you can just take me without my permission! I have a job and people will be frantic when I don't call or show up for work! AND --- my name is NOT Madonna!" she shouted.

"You are my guest now. No one knows where you are. You are my Madonna. I found you and now you are mine." Diego said as if he didn't hear her talking. "You must rest now and get well. I will visit you every day until you can be moved to my hacienda."

He reached out and grasped her hand before she could pull back again. Smiling into her angry eyes, he leaned forward and placed a kiss on her hand while holding it tightly. Annaliese briefly wondered if he was crazy but his eyes were clear and he looked like a normal man. Diego was handsome; tall and lean, with muscled arms filling out his long-sleeved shirt. He was clean-shaven with light olive skin and long-lashed black eyes. But Annaliese was not fooled. He was not a nice man. He had had her kidnapped for himself. She dreaded what he wanted, feeling she already knew. But why have her taken all the way to Mexico? And, why was he calling her Madonna?

Diego reluctantly left his Madonna in the hospital after warning Dr. Hermosa to take good care of her and guard her safety. While making stern eye contact with him, Diego made sure the doctor understood that she could not leave with anyone except himself under unspoken penalty of severe injury. Dr. Hermosa knew better than to disobey him. Diego had done many good things for him, their village and the people. But he also knew about Diego's reputation for violence when he was crossed….and, there was no way he would cross Diego Garcia Vasquez.

After a week of mostly sleeping, Annaliese awoke late one afternoon to the banging of a drum! What was that? She tried to get up, but fell back in too much pain. Sounds of people and music had her listening and wondering if they were coming in where she was! A nurse came into her room, smiling as she saw that Annaliese had awakened.

The nurse greeted her in Spanish, "Buenos noches, Madonna." Then in broken English, "You hear people, si? They are happy and make a parade. It is Dia de la Independencia. Our freedom from Espana.

You understand?" She fussed with Annaliese' pillows and covers. "You must have food and water, now. Don Diego will be angry if you are not eating."

She left and the outside door must have opened because the noise was very loud now. Annaliese groaned, her head was pounding, her body ached so badly she could hardly move. She hoped the noise and people would all go away, soon. A drink of water sounded so good. She hoped the nurse brought only water and no food. Just the thought of eating made her stomach heave.

Diego came to the hospital to visit his Madonna every day. Dr. Hermosa knew she dreaded his visits and she watched anxiously until he arrived. He read her hospital chart, thoroughly, and sternly warned the staff to make sure she ate. Annaliese had very little appetite and refused to be forced to eat. She was rapidly becoming a difficult patient and did not care that she made the nurses very nervous because they all feared Diego. Her fever had ceased, but she was weak and her feet were still too sore to bear her full weight. The headaches were less frequent and she could now lean back without too much discomfort. The day she would be forced to leave the hospital was looming closer and Annaliese was scared.

Diego seemed oblivious to Annaliese' discomfort when he visited her room. His presence filled her room; people scurrying around him, avoiding eye contact but rushing to comply with his every command. He was king and this was his kingdom.

Annaliese had pleaded and begged the nurses and Dr. Hermosa to help her. She knew they were aware that she had been kidnapped, but they refused to contact her brother, the police or anyone who could her get back home. Even Father Ambrose turned a deaf ear saying that the Lord would protect her and she just had to allow Him his way ---- whatever that meant!

She was a prisoner. She had prayed for help and no longer bothered hoping God would hear her plea. Her prayers were not going to be answered. Her name was never used. It was Madonna now.

When she asked for some clothes she received a white nun's robe to wear. She had lost count of how many times the nurses had crossed themselves when they entered her room. Even though Dr. Hermosa talked to her, he never said her name. He hadn't called her Madonna, but he never addressed her as Annaliese either.

As a result, Annaliese retreated inside herself and refused to talk or eat. After two days of rebellion, Diego arrived early in the morning on the third day. He calmly walked in without speaking or making eye contact with Annaliese, closed the door and moved a chair close to her bed. Diego sat down and grabbed her hand and pulled her toward him so that her face was close enough she could feel his breath on her face.

"Let me be perfectly clear, my Madonna. You will eat starting this morning. I don't care if you talk. But, you will eat when food is presented to you. And you will obey me when I tell you do to something – do you understand, hmm?" His voice was steel and his eyes were hard black orbs. Annaliese said nothing. Diego waited without releasing her hand. "If you do not do as I ask, someone will suffer. Are you prepared to let that happen, Madonna? Because if you are, you will see that happen right before your eyes. I am not a man to make idle threats, my dear. I have injured people before. I have killed before. Do not make me prove myself to you."

Diego got up, released her hand and moved the chair back against the wall. He turned and looked at Annaliese, holding her eyes to his. "I'm waiting, Madonna."

Annaliese sat still, weighing his threat in her mind. She had seen everyone obey him. They treated him with utter respect. Should she test him? The thought of seeing him punish someone because of her was detestable. She wanted to defy him so much she raged inside knowing she was going to relent and eat. BUT – she would NOT talk! Slowly, she nodded her head.

"Is that a yes that you will eat?" he smirked.

Annaliese slowly nodded again. "Very well. I will not hear or read in your chart that you are refusing food, again, yes?"

Diego continued to look at her as if she was a naughty child. If she could stand she would be tempted to slap his smug handsome face. She felt real, true hatred for this man who controlled everything and everyone. She would try to escape as soon as possible. If she had to eat, it would be to become strong enough to run as far as she could.

"And let me make this clear as well, Madonna," Diego enunciated each word slowly as if he had heard her thoughts. "If you attempt to escape, I will kill anyone who helps you or gives you any ideas of how to leave this hospital or my hacienda. Do we understand each other?" He stood tall and imposing while he waited for her answer.

With a deep sigh, Annaliese nodded her head affirmatively while keeping her eyes on Diego. She hoped he could see the hatred in her eyes and feel her disgust. In all her life, she had never thought of doing harm to anyone or anything. But at that moment, she knew without a doubt, that she could fight this man, even hurt him, maybe even kill him, and never look back with regret for as long as she lived.

5

While Annaliese was lying unconscious in Diego's airplane and about to land in central Mexico, far away from her home in California, Mathias is late locking up the office. He still took great pride and smiled each time he saw their logo on the door – his and Annaliese', Bergdahl Properties logo. They had spent so much time designing it. It was very special because of their joint effort. He couldn't take as much credit for the design as his sister. Annaliese had done most of the work, but insisted on their sharing it. As always, she never needed to shine alone. It was one of the many reasons he loved her. She was such a good and fair person.

He was a little concerned about his sister. She had gone home early yesterday, according to their secretary, Mary, because she felt unwell. That wasn't like her at all. According to Mary, she had gone shopping during her lunch time but had felt worse, so she didn't return to the office. When she called Mary, she said she was going to go straight home and to bed. He had let her sleep last night and didn't call her, but he hadn't heard from her all day today. Since she lived near him he decided to stop by on his way home. Perhaps he could fix her something to eat if she hadn't had dinner yet. Although he didn't want to get sick, it was more important to see to her needs. They only had each other and were very close.

Mathias checked his cell phone. He had sent Annaliese a text message earlier in the afternoon but had gotten busy with a property management issue and hadn't checked his cell phone. Now when he looked, his phone showed no answer from her. That, too, was not like his sister. Maybe he would take her to an 'after hours medical clinic' for medication. His concern inched up another notch, and he hurried to his car and started to drive to her condo complex. He called her cell phone while enroute. Maybe he could stop on his way there and pick up whatever she needed and make some soup for her. If she needed him, he would spend the night at her condo. There was no answer, and her cell went to voice mail. He told her he was on his way and would go back to the store if she needed him to get some things for her.

When Mathias pulled into Annaliese' driveway, he noticed there were no lights on in her condo. Quickly, he got out of his car and hurried up the walkway to her door. She still hadn't responded to his voice mail or text message. He opened the door with his key and entered the dark living room. "Hey, Annaliese! What's up with you? I'm here for a soup and med run if you need me," he said as he walked to her stairway. Suddenly, he heard a cell phone ringing. He turned and in the dim light he saw her purse where she always left it on a table near the front door. A shopping bag from the Cadwell Cooking Store sat next to it, and her keys were there, too. She was home but not answering her cell phone or his greeting.

Mathias was really concerned now. He turned on the lights as he went up the stairs. She always left a light on both downstairs and upstairs during the night. But no light was on in either place. She must be really sick.

Her bedroom door was open and Mathias quietly approached her bed without turning on the light in case it would wake her up. Even in the dark room he could tell that the bed was empty nor had it been slept in. Her closet door was open and the shoes and jacket she wore to work yesterday were on a chair by the door.

This behavior just wasn't like his sister. Mathias searched the other bedrooms and bathroom upstairs and found nothing disturbed. Pulling out his cell phone as he went back downstairs, he called Derek. Just as Mathias reached the kitchen, Derek answered the phone.

"Hey, Mathias. Glad you called. What's up with your sister? I haven't heard from her all day, man!"

Mathias stood staring at the open patio door, afraid to walk out onto the patio. Afraid he might see something….. Slowly, he walked across the kitchen, touching the top of the chair where Annaliese usually sat and ate her meals. The patio was dark, too, but he was afraid to turn on the light. His sister would never leave an open door unless she was sitting on her patio enjoying the evening. But the lights would be on. He could hear Derek's voice talking to him but he couldn't talk back.

At the doorway he stopped and leaned forward not touching the doorframe. First looking as far right as he could, then he slowly panned to his left. No Annaliese. One of her flower pots had fallen off the small patio table and lay broken on its side, the clump of flowers and dirt half out of the pot. One of her tea cups was also on the patio floor, broken.

"Call 911 Derek. Please call 911 and come over." Mathias ended the call and put the cell phone back in his pants pocket. Carefully, he backed into the kitchen and walked to the front door where he would wait for Derek and the police. He took a deep breath, his heart was pounding and he felt sick to his stomach. He exhaled and looked up at the night sky and said a prayer for his sister.

Taking out his cell phone again, he thumbed through his contacts, found Mary Carlisle's cell number and pressed the call button. Mary answered on the second ring.

"Hi Mathias. How is Annaliese feeling?" Mary's voice sounded so good. He wanted her to come over now, too.

"She's gone, Mary. Can you come over to her condo right now, please?" Mathias' voice cracked. He was close to crying – something he hadn't done since he lost his parents five years ago.

"What do you mean she's gone, Mathias?" Her voice went up in concern.

"I came by to check on her. She hasn't answered my text or calls and Derek's either. Did she call you this afternoon?"

"NO! Not since she called and told me she was going home and going to bed. She went to Ocean Crest Plaza to shop for Derek's birthday present. Could she have car trouble or something?" Mary's voice was shaky. He could tell she was walking while she was talking. "I'm on my way, Mathias. I'll be there in ten minutes." Mary ended the phone call and Mathias still held his phone. He was bewildered and confused. Where could she be? What was he going to do without his sister?

A police car pulled up in front of Annaliese' condo at the same time as a very upset Derek arrived. Mathias greeted him, and addressed the officer as he approached the porch. "Thank you for coming so soon, officer." Mathias continued talking to the officer, telling him everything about his sister's day while holding on to Derek's shoulder. He was glad Derek was there. He needed his support. He felt a soft hand take hold of his other hand and gently squeeze. Mathias didn't need to look down. He knew it was Mary – friend, secretary and one of the nicest women he knew. She, too would be a comfort. A second police officer arrived and told Mathias that they should all wait on the porch while the condo was searched.

Several minutes passed and the officers returned to the front door. They turned on the living room light and beckoned Mathias, Derek and Mary into the condo. "We need to take an official missing persons' report. You will need to make a statement of your whereabouts today for the report, as well as anything you can think of that might help us."

Mary immediately volunteered to make coffee. She was familiar with Annaliese' condo as they were friends who frequented each other's homes regularly. Derek sat down and was very quiet. As he gave his account of the day, tears slid down his cheeks and he wiped them away with his hands and sniffled. Mary had a Kleenex box and handed him several tissues. She was so quietly competent and such a comfort. Mathias smiled his thanks for her presence and thoughtfulness.

"We've searched the premises. There were signs of a struggle on the patio. We think it's a good possibility that your sister's been abducted. Can you think of anyone who might want to harm your sister?" The officer looked from Mathias to Derek to Mary. Each shrugged and said no.

"Anyone she has had a problem with at work or in her personal life?"

"We will continue our search of the neighborhood and talk to the neighbors. There are security cameras in the area and we will access those as well. Make sure we have all your contact information. Someone will contact you in the next day or so and take your statements. We will do our best to find your sister. I'm sorry, that's all I can tell you for now." The officers finished their coffee and left the condo. The silence in Annaliese' living room was heavy. None of them moved.

Mary was the first to get up. "We probably should lock up and go home. I could fix us all something to eat at my house if you'd like?" Derek shook his head no.

"Thanks, Mary, but I think I'll just go to my house." He turned to Mathias.

"Will you let me know anything you hear? I mean - anything – as soon as you know, okay?" He sniffled again and turned to leave, then swirled around and grabbed Mathias and hugged him. "I really love her, man! She just can't be gone!" He rushed out the door and ran to his car. He started his car engine and laid his head on his steering wheel for a brief moment before pulling away.

Mathias sighed, "Well I guess it's just you and me, Mary." He looked at her, his face pale and drawn. "I don't know how much sleep I'll get tonight or how much work I'll get done tomorrow. Would you mind, if I camped out on your couch tonight?" He looked at Mary with a silent plea.

Mary loved this man….had loved him for a long time. It pleased her that he needed her now. She also loved Annaliese. She would do whatever it took to comfort Mathias and stay by his side until they found Annaliese. It would be a long night. "I'll drive, Mathias. We can leave your car here and pick it up in the morning. Do you want me to take you to your house for a change of clothing?" Mathias looked bleak and pale. He stared sightlessly out at the street.

"Come on, Mathias. I'll take you home, then to my house. They will find her. I will stay with you until they do." Mary took his arm and guided him to her car. Opening the door, she hugged him before he sat down in the passenger's seat. His arms suddenly tightened around her and he buried his face in her neck. His body shook and he sobbed, "I'm afraid I might never see her again, Mary. What am I going to do?"

"They will find her, Mathias. You have to believe that. Until then, I will not leave you alone unless you want me to. We will get through this together, I promise." Mary said a silent prayer as she walked around the car after closing the door for Mathias. She had always wanted to tell Mathias how she felt about him. She had loved him for years. Annaliese had urged her to tell him as well. Now, she had an opportunity to show him how she felt. He needed her and she needed him. She could wait to tell him. He needed her support. If anything came from their need, then it was destiny.

They would wait a long time for word about Annaliese. Their world would change, but not as much as Annaliese' world. In just a few hours' time, all of their lives had changed forever.

6

The hacienda of Diego Garcia Vasquez was a large fortress with thick walls and court yards inside them. A long driveway lined with trees and shrubs and paved with tiles led to ornate heavy metal gates. Bright red, pink and yellow hibiscus flowers grew around the brick pillars holding the gates in place. As the car with Diego and Annaliese arrived, the gates slowly opened revealing several armed soldiers in black uniforms waiting for his car to approach. As the car passed them, they nodded their heads in deference to Diego. He acknowledged them with a quick nod back. Inside the grounds of the hacienda, a cadre of workers were trimming the flowers, shrubs, and cleaning the giant fountain in front of the marble stairs leading to the metal-grilled dark wood front doors. It was a grand entrance, worthy of a king.

As the car drew to a stop and the doors opened, the workers stopped and waited. Diego got out and turned to help Annaliese out of the back seat. She heard a murmur of voices and looked at the workers who were in awe of this new visitor. Annaliese knew what they were saying. She was used to the looks and whispers now. They all thought she was the Madonna Angel of the picture in the alcove in the church. It was tiresome. She wasn't pleased.

Diego had taken her to the church so that she could see the picture. It was true. She did look a little like the Madonna, but only a little. The peoplewere desperate for a miracle. But Diego was absolutely positive that she was the Madonna who had come down from heaven for him. He told her he prayed to the Madonna Angel several times each week. She answered his prayers, that's why he was so successful. It was laughable! But she didn't dare laugh. Diego was not a man with a sense of humor.

Diego took Annaliese' arm and helped her up the stairs to the entry doors which were opening as they walked. Even though she had been hospitalized for over a week, it was still very difficult to put weight on her injured feet. But with special pads in her socks she was able to hobble with help.

At the door stood a pretty woman wearing black pants and blouse. She smiled at Diego, "Welcome home, Senor Diego. Welcome home, Madonna Angel."

Annaliese frowned as the woman turned her smile on her. "I hope you are feeling better," she inquired. Annaliese just kept walking, doing her best not to limp too much but failing. Already she was tired just from her walk to the car from the hospital, the ride here and the walk up the stairs. She still was not talking to anyone.

Diego smiled and pulled Annaliese to a stop. "Thank you Juanita. I fear that my Madonna is not well yet and is tired from her journey here. Can you follow us to her rooms and assist her into bed?"

"Perhaps a nice cup of tea would help soothe her and then she can sleep." Diego walked away from the massive staircase in the middle of the large entry room toward an elaborate wooden door and pressed a button. The door opened revealing an elevator. Annaliese was so relieved. She doubted that she could have walked up the giant staircase. She was too big for Diego to carry even though he was a large man.

Juanita closed the door and pressed another button and the elevator began to rise. "You have rooms on the third floor. I'm sure you will be pleased. They have been completely re-done for you. I hope you will be comfortable," he smiled.

Juanita looked at Annaliese for her reply. Annaliese narrowed her eyes and frowned deeper than before and turned away from Diego. Juanita looked surprised. Diego ignored her and looked straight ahead as the elevator came to a stop. The door opened to a hallway decorated with dark bronze wallpaper covered in leaves with beige and brown muted flowers highlighted with gold. The floor was a beautiful dark brown wood plank floor, highly polished.

Juanita led her to double doors which were edged with gold filigree. She pushed and both doors swung open to a beautiful room. Annaliese couldn't help it, she gasped before she could catch herself.

The room was a dream anyone could admire. A beautiful crystal chandelier hung in the middle of the ceiling, the top surrounded by an intricate wood mounting trimmed in gold. The walls were covered in light yellow silk complementing the light pecan wood furniture which had light yellow accents and white and yellow porcelain handles and knobs.

The floor was covered with a lush light brown carpet with pale yellow flowers and light green petals. Large windows along the back wall were covered with antique glass that shimmered with sunlight. Intricate bars inside the glass made the windows look like diamonds linked together. Silk and satin drapes were drawn back and a large valance went across the entire wall. To the left was the largest bed Annaliese had ever seen. It was bigger than a king bed and had to have been specially made. A silk padded headboard was imbedded with gold hob-nails and the bed was covered in embroidered satin and filled with accent pillows.

To the right, was a large open door leading to a walk-in closet larger than Annaliese' bedroom at her home. She could see several empty hangers inside the closet. Farther to the right was another doorway. She could see a tiled bathroom that would have pleased Cleopatra. Next to the door was a heavily padded chaise lounge which matched the bed with satin and pillows. Annaliese scanned the room, then scanned again. There was no telephone or television.

She would be trapped in paradise. There was no outside door, either. The bedroom doors had a large deadbolt which Annaliese knew would be used any time she was in this room.

"You will have a full wardrobe complete with underthings and night wear. Juanita will be your full time assistant. There is a button on the night stand you can use to summon her day or night." Diego waited for Annaliese to respond. She pulled her arm away and hobbled, painfully to the bathroom. She slammed the door closed but noticed there was no lock. What a surprise!

Diego turned to Juanita, "She refuses to talk. Perhaps you can convince her to communicate."

He frowned and turned to leave. He wouldn't stay and wait for her to come out. She was being difficult. He would wait her out. Besides, there was another way to make her talk if he had to, but he would rather she would just start talking again without threats.

The first few days Annaliese spent in the hacienda, she was bedridden with only trips to the bathroom. One morning, Juanita arrived with a wheelchair and took her down to have breakfast on the patio. On her way there, Annaliese studied the hacienda. Juanita told her that Diego's rooms consisted of the entire second floor. She said they were safe here.

The whole hacienda was an impenetrable fortress. All the glass was bullet proof and the doors were lead-lined. Annaliese thought he had to have a lot of enemies to live like this. Unfortunately, with the hacienda being so safe, it would be more difficult for her to escape. She would bide her time and watch and get stronger.

The patio was a lovely place filled with ferns, orchids and other exotic plants underneath an elaborate slatted roof which allowed a gentle breeze and soft sunlight to filter through. Thick padded chairs with ottomans and settees were scattered about and a large dining table with six chairs sat in the middle. A four-tiered fountain bubbled water into an oyster covered pond filled with brightly colored koi fish.

It was a lush oasis inviting one to relax and become a part of nature. The high walls of brick and wrought iron had thick glass in between and topped with sharp spikes for security, surrounded the patio. Ceiling fans shaped like giant leaves turned gently, moving the air and flowers like a scented island breeze.

Juanita pulled a chair next to Annaliese' wheelchair at the table. Two male servants dressed in black like Juanita, brought trays filled with an array of eggs, toast and fruit. A small pot of strong smelling coffee was placed next to Annaliese. With a huff, she moved the coffee away and sat back with her arms folded.

"You don't like coffee, Madonna?" she inquired.

Annaliese hated that she didn't use her name. She frowned her displeasure and shook her head.

"Do you prefer fruit juice, or perhaps something else?"

Juanita only had a slight accent. Annaliese thought she must have spent a lot of time in the U.S. She wondered if perhaps Diego had taken her here by force, too. But, she wasn't going to ask or try to become friends. She had listened to Diego's threat about hurting people.

Juanita put a little spoonful of each food from the tray onto a lovely china plate and placed it in front of Annaliese. The food smelled heavenly! Annaliese felt her stomach grumble. She wasn't going to get stronger unless she ate, so she had to give in and it really made her so. Damn. MAD, she thought.

Annaliese reached to pour a glass of orange juice, but Juanita stopped her and poured it for her. Picking up her fork she stabbed a piece of pineapple with a vengeance making a scraping noise on the delicate plate. Juanita noticed and smiled at Annaliese, "You might as well give in, Madonna. Act like a child if you want, but Diego always wins…." She bent down closer to Annaliese' face, "Believe me. He *always* gets what he wants. You belong to him now. The sooner you live with that, the better for us all. Do you understand me? WE make him happy and we are ALL happy." Juanita relaxed and began to fill another plate for herself.

"We will be spending a lot of time together. I will dress your hair, do your nails and pedicures, see to your clothes and anything else you require," she said, as if this was just a normal state of affairs.

Annaliese looked at her with raised eyebrows. Juanita continued, "I have been here with Diego for many years, and yes, I belong to him, too." She kept eating and didn't look at Annaliese, "…and yes, I sleep with him, cut his hair, his nails, fix his clothes and anything else he needs me to do --- whenever he asks – without question. This is my life. And before you think to feel sorry for me, my life here is far better than than anything I could have hoped for in the United States. I was one of ten children living in a slum when Diego saw me on a street corner. He took me home, gave my mother a wad of cash and brought me here to live. I want for nothing."

"So, you see, I will never help you to escape. You understand? NEVER! I will not hesitate to tell him if you step out of line or try to convince anyone to help you do anything you are not supposed to do," she said in an even tone. "If you just do what you are told, life can be very good for you. The people already adore you and are begging Diego to take you to the church so that they can see you and ask for benedictions. You are a celebrity! Enjoy it and, please, make my life easier. We can live together as though we are friends, or I can be your worst enemy without Diego knowing a thing – your choice. So, what do you say? Easy or difficult?" Juanita calmly looked at Annaliese with a tight smile on her full red lips. She reminded her of a fox sizing up a rather nice fat hen for supper. Well, she would play this game for now and bide her time. She had a lot to learn and a lot of time to do it. Now she knew it would take longer for her to make her escape. But escape she would.

"I understand….and I prefer hot tea," Annaliese said with a superior nod of her head.

Juanita's eye widened in surprise! "So! You can talk," she chuckled. "Diego will be pleased to know. Now eat and I will take you back to your room for a nap. I have work to do."

When they returned to Annaliese' room, Juanita helped her into bed. They had not spoken to each other after Juanita's little speech. As far as Annaliese was concerned the less said the better. Juanita was her enemy.

Annaliese watched as Juanita picked up a large brown paper package in the huge walk-in closet, came out and placed it on a table. She opened it with a small knife she had on her belt. The package was yards of white silk material. The same material as the white silk robe Annaliese was now wearing. This was all the clothing she had. Of course, the ripped and blood-stained pajamas she had been wearing when she was kidnapped were long gone. She hadn't been wearing a bra or panties so she wore nothing under this robe. Somehow, she had to get some pants, a blouse and jacket to wear. Juanita was several inches shorter than she and a little heavier, so they couldn't be expected to share clothes. She clenched her teeth and decided she would have to talk to Diego. He had said she would have a wardrobe. She would ask for some clothes to wear.

Juanita came out of the closet with another package – more white silk material. Gathering up the material and packaging, she carefully unlocked the bedroom door and exited, re-locking the door. A few minutes later she returned with a tape measure, pencil and tablet.

"Stand up for a minute," she ordered.

Juanita pulled back the covers and helped Annaliese stand by the bed. She took the tape measure and started measuring Annaliese from head to toe, making notes on the tablet. "Okay, I'm done. Get back in bed, now." Then she went through the process of unlocking and locking the door, and was gone.

Annaliese fell asleep wondering what she was going to do so she wouldn't go crazy. She had a college education, a full time job, friends and activities in her old life. Now she was an ornament in a room with no books, TV, radio.....nothing! Perhaps there would be something for her to do after she had completely recovered and could walk and wear shoes again.

Dr. Hermosa came to see Annaliese each week. He was always kind, but distant. He, too, didn't want to be friends. She was finally declared to be healed, concussion gone and she could now walk without pain and could wear shoes. Except, she didn't have any to wear!

Juanita was always with Annaliese when Dr. Hermosa came to examine her. After he left, she told Annaliese that it was time for a surprise.

She went into the closet and came back with several shoe boxes. Inside were white sandals, white ballet slippers and white bedroom slippers. Annaliese looked at Juanita with surprise. "These are my size! How did you know?"

"Try them all on to be sure, but I took a guess on your size and ordered them a few days ago. If they're too small I can get new ones tomorrow, special delivery."

"Why are they all white?" Annaliese asked as she tried the sandals on.

"Because that's the only color you need." Juanita said in a flat voice.

"What? Why only white?" But it suddenly occurred to Annaliese that she knew the answer and dread filled her chest.

"Because you will wear only white silk robes and white shoes, Madonna. Just like in the picture in the church alcove. The Madonna wears white." Juanita strode over to the closet and opened the door. Hanging in a long row were several white silk robes Annaliese hadn't seen before.

"These were made for you. This is what you will wear. Every day." Juanita's voice was devoid of feeling. She was waiting for Annaliese to explode her response.

Annaliese decided she wouldn't give her that satisfaction. Calmly, she walked over to the closet and touched the robes while walking down the row.

"They're beautifully made."

Then she walked back out of the closet, turned into the bathroom and slammed the door. She could hear Juanita laughing as she exited the bedroom and locked the door behind her.

7

Diego came to Annaliese' room every day. She had abandoned her silence, but there wasn't much for her to talk to him about as he kept his questions to simple ones about her health, her day, the food she ate, and if she needed anything. His eyes watched her hungrily and he continually touched her when they were together: holding her hand, placing his hand on her shoulder or, and this made her angry, hugging her hello and goodbye. She held herself still and stiff when he got too close. She refused to share any affection with him. She made her hand completely limp without any pressure when he held it, sometimes against his chest. She turned her face as far away from his as possible. Diego pretended not to notice, but Annaliese could tell he wanted more from her. Well, he wasn't going to get it!

A few weeks after she started wearing the new robes and shoes, Diego appeared all excited in her room. "We will go into the village this morning, Madonna. The people want to see you!" he said rubbing his hands together.

"Why do they want to see me?" she softly inquired, dreading the answer.

"Because you are our miracle!" Diego grabbed her hand and led her down the stairs.

Annaliese could see a car waiting at the bottom of the entry stairs. His two guards who were always nearby were standing at attention with the car doors open. They were dressed in the black uniforms and had gun belts making them look like soldiers.

"Why do you have guards? Are you in danger?" Annaliese inquired.

Diego frowned, "I am a rich and powerful man, Madonna. People envy me. And I protect what is mine."

Annaliese was glad to be out of the house and going somewhere, anywhere would do. But the closer they got to the village she began to dread where they were going. "What am I expected to do?"

"You will go into the church, greet Father Ambrose and Sister Beatrice, and sit in a special chair. The villagers will come and you will listen to them and give them benediction."

"But I don't speak Spanish! How can I possibly talk to them or understand what they are saying?" she cried.

"Father Ambrose will be at your side. He will tell you what to do. You will not need to speak, just smile, nod your head and perhaps, touch them. All this you will do with grace, Madonna. I will not tolerate your acting up or trying to run away. You understand, of course, Madonna?" Diego leaned close to her face and pulled her closer to his lips.

Annaliese tried to pull back, but he held her chin and cheek. She was afraid he was going to kiss her! He laid his forehead against hers and inhaled. Annaliese was afraid to move. Finally, Diego dropped his hand and leaned back in his seat. His face was a mask with no emotion showing, but his hands were fists on his lap. She let out her breath not knowing she had been holding it while he had been close to her face.

When they arrived at the church, a line of villagers stood there waiting for her. They smiled and clapped their hands when she got out of the car. Father Ambrose and Sister Beatrice were waiting for them at the top of the church stairs. Ugly memories filled Annaliese' mind as she walked up with Diego holding her arm. She hadn't been here since she had been beaten. Her memories were a bit vague, but she remembered the pain as she practically crawled up these stairs.

Father Ambrose and Sister greeted her warmly. They were kind, gentle people who had given her great care when she had been in the hospital. Annaliese was surprised they were buying into this "Madonna thing" of Diego's. How could they think that she was worthy of giving benedictions to these people? Surely they had to know she wasn't the Madonna Angel of the picture? But they guided her down the aisle to a special red velvet chair that resembled a throne! The villagers had been held back from entering the church.

Diego stood in front of her as she settled herself in the chair. He reached down and lifted her face up, "Remember your duty, my Madonna," he whispered and squeezed her hand just a little to emphasize his words.

Annaliese nodded and avoided returning his gaze. Diego stepped back and spoke to the priest, "I will be in the back of the church. Madonna will remain in this chair until I come back up to get her, understand Father?" he said with a voice as smooth as steel.

"Si, Senor Diego, I understand."

Diego opened his arm sweeping around to the church aisle, "Then let us begin." One of his guards opened the doors and soon a long line of villagers with heads bowed and hands clasped in front of them as if in prayer, proceeded up the aisle toward Annaliese. Another guard stopped them, allowing only one at a time to go up the altar steps to Annaliese.

Annaliese quickly lost count of how many villagers came up the aisle asking for her favor. The blessings they asked for were a wide range: prayers for sick family members or animals, for strong crops, better weather and, help to get pregnant. The most difficult one was a frail old woman who was assisted by two strong sons who asked to live long enough to see her first grandchild born in three months. Annaliese wanted to weep and scream, "I am not your Madonna Angel!" The sweetest

sweetest one was a little boy who reminded her of a young Diego, who presented her with a circle of flowers and had her bend down so he could place it on her head. He just wanted to tell her of his thanks and love for coming to his village. Annaliese bit her tongue so she would not cry out in frustration. She managed a weak smile and reached out to touch the dark curly head of the young boy.

At last there were no more villagers. Annaliese was alone with Father Ambrose and before Diego could get up the aisle she asked in hushed tones, "Father, how can you pretend I am the Madonna? This is so cruel of you to let them believe I am some sort of miracle!"

Father replied as Diego stepped up to hear, "My dear Madonna, you have been a miracle since you first reached this altar in pain and bleeding. You did not see the halo around your head or the aura surrounding Sister Beatrice as she held you in her arms." He looked beseechingly at Diego. "Is it not true, Senor Diego, since you began praying to the Madonna our village has been blessed?"

"Yes, it is true, Father." He turned to Annaliese, "YOU ARE OUR MADONNA ANGEL! There is no doubt." Diego grabbed her arm and pulled her up and down the stairs. "Thank you, Father. Our Madonna is tired now and needs to rest. We will return in a few days for the villagers. I will let you know when."

The ride back to the hacienda was quiet. Diego hadn't spoken to her. She could feel his displeasure so she remained silent. When the car stopped at the stairway to the hacienda, before he got out of the car, Diego leaned over and said, "This is the only time you will question who you are. There will be no doubt voiced to Father Ambrose or Sister Beatrice or anyone else again. Do you understand me, Madonna? I'll allow you this one time. But no more."

Diego pulled her out of the car and held on to her arm all the way through the house, up the stairs and into her bedroom. Before he let her go he pulled her close and kissed her at the corner of her mouth.

He held her a moment longer as if waiting for her to respond. Annaliese stood still and waited. Finally, Diego expelled his breath, and left the room. She heard the lock being turned and sighed with relief. She was exhausted!

8

A routine was established. Each week the villagers were waiting and each week she issued benedictions. It was easier now. She never questioned Father again, or hardly spoke to him or Sister. She did her duty like a machine.

Her days were a monotony until one day when they returned from the village, three large black Humvees with several guards were waiting at the gates to the hacienda when they arrived. Diego quickly got out his cell phone and barked rapid orders in Spanish. He looked at Annaliese and said, "Do not get out of the car unless I order you to do so, and do not talk to these men unless I nod my head. Understand?" Diego was very tense. The guards in the front seat had both withdrawn their weapons and were very tense as well. Annaliese could see more guards with their weapons drawn on top of the wall.

"What is it? Who are these men?"

Diego didn't answer. He got out of the car as the doors to the Humvees opened and one man got out from each car and approached Diego. Annaliese could not hear them speaking. One of them looked over at her car and motioned with his hand. Diego said something to him but the man started walking toward her car. Both of Diego's guards had gotten out with him so Annaliese was alone. Something was going on and she thought it had to do with her. She could tell that Diego was angry. The man was almost to the car when Diego stopped him and they exchanged a few strong words Annaliese couldn't understand.

The hacienda gates were opened and the man returned to his car. Diego got back in the front seat of the car. One guard started the car and drove through the gates and as Annaliese turned to look out the back window, she saw the three Humvees follow behind. The guards walked along the cars like the secret service officers do with the president's car. How strange, she thought.

Diego turned to Annaliese, "These are very dangerous men. They have heard about you and have come to meet you. You will say as little as possible. I will only let you stay in the room with them for a few moments, then I will dismiss you and you will go upstairs and into your room. Do not smile at them or encourage them in any way." The car stopped at the stairs and Diego's guard opened the door. Diego got out and opened Annaliese' door and took her arm, pulling her close to his side as they started up the stairs. Behind her she heard the men following them speaking to each other in Spanish.

As soon as they were inside the hacienda, Diego shouted orders and several servants scrambled though the hallway and disappeared. In English Diego said, "Come into the living room. We will have some refreshments and I will introduce you to my friends, Madonna."

Annaliese was perplexed. His friends? After warning her about how dangerous they were he was inviting them in for refreshments? How odd!

Each man was dressed in colorful silk shirts and dark slacks. One guard stood near each man. Their weapons were back on their waists and they stood at attention.

"Please my friends, have a seat and I will introduce you." Diego hadn't let go of her arm so he pulled her back farther away from the men. "May I present my Madonna Angel?"

Diego said their names as they approached: Don Raoul Gutierrez, Don Victor Jimenez, and Don Juan Contreras. Each man stepped forward, bowed and offered his hand. Diego lifted her arm and let her hand be held by them. In Spanish Don Raoul said, "I am charmed to meet you, Madonna. I have heard so much about you. My friend, Diego, has been remiss in not bringing you to my hacienda. I am inviting you to attend our party tonight to celebrate Dia de los Muertos." He leaned forward and kissed her knuckles. Diego pulled her hand way.

Annaliese looked at Diego, eyebrows raised. "It's a celebration to honor our dead." Diego turned to Don Raoul, "We will celebrate here with our villagers, but I thank you for your invitation, my friend."

The next two men echoed almost the same sentiments as Don Raoul, when they were introduced. Diego never released her arm. When they had all been introduced they took a seat and were served wine, cheese and fruit. Diego escorted Annaliese to the doorway and motioned her to leave. One of the men stood and in English said, "Wait, Diego, we want to talk to her. Why don't you let her stay? Come my beautiful one, sit by me," he beckoned to Annaliese.

Diego blocked Annaliese and quietly said, "Go to your room *now*." He turned to the men, "My friends, Madonna is tired and will go to her room to rest. Perhaps another time."

Before she turned away she saw that the men were clearly displeased with Diego. She wished she could listen to their conversation but she went to her room as she was told.

The living room was quiet as the men poured more wine and drank. Don Raoul rose and walked to the front of the room and stood in front of the huge fireplace. "Why did you not tell us about her, Diego?" He looked around at each of the other men, "We had to hear about her from our people?" he said sarcastically. The other men murmured their agreement.

"She came only to me, my friends. For years I have prayed to her, never thinking that she could possibly be a real woman. When I found her, it was a miracle! She is mine. I cannot share something so precious." Diego was firm in his statement. The men knew they would not see her again except by accident.

"Diego, if she has brought so much good fortune and blessings to you and your people, how can you not share her with us. Aren't we partners? Don't we share our wealth? Such a beautiful woman should be enjoyed by all. Don't you agree my friends?" he looked at the other men and they nodded in agreement.

"Are you suggesting that I pass her around like a whore, Don Raoul?" he growled. More kindly he added, "She is not that kind of woman and has no meaning for you as she does for me. We have all had great fortune. We are all wealthy and powerful men. What more can you ask? You must find your own blessings. I will *not* share her." His voice was final.

The men exchanged looks. Don Victor stood, "Diego, be honest now. You have benefitted more than we. You have the gift of knowing how and what investments to make to increase your wealth. You share only a part of that knowledge with us. We are in business together, but your fields grow stronger, your labs produce more product, and your vineyards and cotton fields are very profitable. Now, someone who has brought you so much luck cannot be shared?" He looked at each man with question in his eyes.

"We started together to run this cartel as partners. We are here to meet your Madonna, but we also bring our concerns that you are becoming wealthier and more powerful than us. Is this fair, we ask?" asked Don Juan turned to the other men who nodded in agreement.

Diego looked at each of the men. "Can I be blamed for doing what I do, the same as you, but doing it better? You make no sense. I give you constant advice. I send men to your fields and labs to help when needed. I take as much risk as you when we ship our product around the world. Each shipment is divided in four equal shares every time, is it not?" With his hands out, Diego asked, "What more can I do? I can't make you spend less or stop using our product." The men looked guiltily at each other and then looked angrily at Diego.

"You are becoming a dangerous man, Diego!" Don Victor said loudly.

"You are wrong, Don Victor. I am as I have always been. It's the drugs talking, nothing more. I am tired of this conversation. It is getting us nowhere. I am not sharing my Madonna with you.
Find your own. Now, unless we have other business, please excuse me."

The men walked toward the door together. Clearly, nothing had been settled with this visit. In fact, Diego was thinking, things had just gotten much worse. Their concerns about his wealth and power had already been voiced in previous meetings. Their greed was becoming more of a problem. Diego had become more of a problem now because he had his Madonna and wouldn't share her. He had seen the partner's eyes devouring her. That was why he rushed her out of the room before they could be even more attracted to her. She was his – now and forever.

At least two of the men who just left were using their own drug products which could only lead to failure and danger to the others. They could end up killing each other in their own personal war. It was time to get out. Time for his plan to be put in motion. Diego had been secretly creating a plan to end his life here in Ville Verde. The village, hospital, school, church, cotton fields and vineyard were all strong entities. The villagers who worked in each of these areas could continue without him. He had trained supervisors who knew how to run each business and train the workers. He had put in place a bank account to continuously support them even in the event that he was no longer in control.

He would disappear with his Madonna and set everyone else free. The cartel members would try to take over the production of the drug fields, drug products, and the labs. They wouldn't have a chance, and would not be able to touch the villagers' bank account. For the drugs and labs he had another plan. A plan steeped in danger.

In her room, Annaliese nervously paced back and forth on the soft rug. She knew she was being discussed by the men. The lecherous looks the men had given her made her worry about their conversation with Diego. Would he pass her around if they wanted her? She didn't think that Diego would share her, but if they thought she brought good luck or good fortune to them would they overpower him and force him to share her? She'd die first.

The way those men had looked at her was with sexual favors in their minds. They probably thought that she was sleeping with Diego. Which brought another thought to her mind: was Diego starting to become more affectionate with her? That kiss the other day had made her uncomfortable. It was almost on her mouth. Afterward, he had fisted his hands as though he was holding back. His eyes were not just looking at her, watching her. He looked at her with longing. He wanted more. She had seen that look before in the eyes of her dates who wanted more, even Derek before they started sleeping together. It was just a matter of time before he demanded it.

9

After dinner, a beautiful platter was brought in to the dining room filled with what looked like shiny bread. Juanita explained that it was a sweet egg bead, a tradition for celebrating the Day of the Dead. Diego informed them that they would all go outside after dinner because they were going to enjoy the music and people dancing. Annaliese heard the lovely guitars and singing and couldn't help herself, she was going to enjoy this celebration. Once outside she could hear a clinking and shushing when the people danced. She looked at the men and women and could see white things hanging in belts and dangling from skirts. "What are those white things?" she asked Diego.

"The people wear shells so they make noise when they walk and dance. This celebration will go on for three days."

"And the church will stay decorated the whole time with the flowers and skulls, and photos?" she asked. "Is this your sort of Halloween?"

Diego chuckled. "No, we celebrate and honor our deceased relatives with decorations in the church, with music, dancing, and special food. Not door to door trick or treating." He frowned. He raised his hand

and turned to the crowd. The music stopped and Diego said, "Good night. Please enjoy the music and food." Like he was a king, the people nodded and waited until she and he were inside the hacienda before the music and dancing started up again.

The meeting the next morning with Dr. Hermosa began abruptly, "Can you contact your nephew who works for the United States Strategic Operations Unit today or tomorrow?"

Dr. Hermosa's mouth dropped open and he fell into the chair behind him. He slowly took out his handkerchief and mopped his brow. Heaving a sigh which he was afraid could be his last, he looked at Diego with despair. "How long have you known about my nephew?"

"For over a year. Answer my question. How long?" Diego demanded.

"Why do you want me to contact him? I have never given him any information about Villa Verde, you, or anything else. This I say on my honor to you, Senor Diego."

"I have need of his help and if you don't want to die, you will help me," he said sternly.

Dr. Hermosa cringed thinking of his wife and three children who could not survive without his salary and did not hesitate. "If you allow me to use my phone, I can call him now." He had begun to sweat as Diego nodded his head to make the call. Taking out his handkerchief and cell phone he swallowed, wiped his face and hands and held his phone ready to dial.

"What is it you want me to tell him, Senor Diego?"

"I want you to set up a meeting with either him or an operative as soon as possible. All haste should be made. I will not discuss anything over the phone. I am in need of their help. There is extreme danger because of the cartel partners. This information I am telling you has just put a noose around your neck, or worse, unless you keep this between you and me. Your wife and children are now as vulnerable as you are. Now, dial your nephew." Diego put his hands behind his back and stood waiting.

Dr. Hermosa called his nephew and was told he would be contacted by an operative sometime in the next week or two. It was done. He and Diego parted ways both swearing their cooperation and secrecy. The doctor would contact Diego as soon as he had word from his nephew or the operative.

It was time to educate Madonna about how to leave here in secret and show her the hidden passages. There was much he needed to show her that no one, not even his close friends or Juanita knew about. Once he showed her the secret passages he had to make sure that she couldn't leave without him.

Diego would give Madonna a tour of the hacienda and the grounds and stress to her that it was too dangerous for her to leave the hacienda without his protection. Even more so now that the partners had seen her.

he saw how much they wanted her and not just for the good fortune she could bring them. She was breathtakingly beautiful. Her silver hair and ice blue eyes were in stark contrast to their dark skin, hair and eyes. Her tall, graceful body seemed to glide when she walked in the white silk robe and slippers.

Annaliese' tour began on the main floor. The foyer was as large as her entire condominium! The room was as wide as it was long ending with a long office closed off with heavy ironclad doors with three locks. Inside, an entire wall housed TV and computer screens. Each screen showed different views of the grounds and the area surrounding the hacienda, as well as, some type of information she couldn't decipher. Some of the screens showed white rooms with people wearing white uniforms and masks. It looked like some kind of lab. Other screens showed the inside of the hacienda including her room!

With shocked eyes Annaliese turned and looked at Diego, "My room! They can watch me get dressed and sleep! How dare you!" she shrieked.

Diego smiled, "No, no, Madonna. The cameras are activated when you leave the room. Your robe has a tiny chip that is activated when you exit the room. I know where you are at all times"

Annaliese was angry. She had absolutely no privacy here!

Diego's tour continued outside the hacienda. "All the doors in this hacienda can be sealed with one switch in this room. The walls are two feet thick and all the windows are bullet proof. You saw my partners. I have never trusted them. By now you know part of my business is in the drug trade. That business doesn't breed close friendships. And now those men are becoming more dangerous to me."

"Today, I will take you around and show you some things that even Juanita doesn't know. But I am asking you not to share this information with anyone, even Juanita. I have a very good reason for this; please trust me to keep you safe." Diego guided her to the rear of the hacienda, still inside the walls. But these outside walls were at least twenty feet high and topped with spikes that looked like they were another foot tall at least. A wire connected the spikes. Diego pointed at the wall spikes and said, "The wall is electrified and programmed to explode if a certain amount of weight touches anywhere near the top starting with the top block. None of my workers even lean on the wall. They don't trust it," he smiled.

Annaliese thought it was a very dangerous place, especially now that she had seen the cameras which showed soldiers with large, frightening-looking weapons patrolling the grounds both inside and outside the walls.

Even Diego was armed but not as much as the two men who were always at his side. Ramon and Jose were very dangerous looking men. They never smiled or acknowledged Annaliese when she was with Diego. He had told them he wanted to be alone with Madonna. They were excused to their own devices and they smiled. They looked like sharks.

Diego leaned over and whispered in her ear, "Do you see that large plant with red flowers at the end of the dirt road to my right? It's quite far out there, can you see it?" Annaliese nodded her head, yes. "Keep that position in mind until later. Look carefully, remember exactly where it is." He kissed her cheek. The guards had turned and were walking away, giving them privacy.

When they re-entered the hacienda, Diego took her into the kitchen. Annaliese had never, ever seen such a state of the art kitchen! Several workers in white uniforms with black-striped aprons were preparing a feast. Food was everywhere with workers chopping, stirring and mixing various ingredients. Four ovens were in operation and two large gas ranges were filled with pots bubbling and steaming. Annaliese was very impressed! "We feed a lot of people four times each day, seven days a week. It's smells good in here, no?" He pulled her arm, "Let's go. I have more to show you."

Diego walked back to the main entryway of the house. "Do you want to take the elevator or the stairs up to my suite of rooms?" he asked.

Annaliese was shocked! He was taking her to his rooms! She stood staring at him. He returned her stare waiting for her answer.

He raised his eyebrows, "Well?"

"The stairs," she whispered. That way it would take longer to get there and she could think about what she would do once they entered his rooms.

"Very well," Diego put out his arm inviting her to precede him up the stairs.

Annaliese was curious to see Diego's rooms, but a sense of dread grew as she climbed the ornate stairs. When they reached the top and walked to the double doors, Annaliese was impressed with their grandeur.

Intricate wood carvings covered the heavy, dark mahogany doors. Large brass fittings matched both doors and keyholes awaited Diego's key. But what he used to open the door was a remote control device. With a smooth click, the doors opened to reveal a breathtaking room. Dark burgundy and navy blue were the color palette used in silk, satin and the tapestries hanging on the walls.

The bed was yet another huge king-sized specially-made monster filled with lush pillows on top of the heavy brocade bedspread. This room also had a large walk-in closet, larger than Annaliese' room. Diego's was filled with three rows of bars with suits, shirts, pants, casual clothes, ties, and then open box shelves for shoes and other accompaniments for his wardrobe.

At the very back of the room, Annaliese could see a large wall unit with a paned-glass door. Inside, she saw rows of weapons and boxes of bullets. There were large guns, like rifles, only they looked more complicated. She walked to the closet door and stopped just inside. A comfortable looking circular couch sat in the middle. It was covered in heavy tapestry-like fabric. A set of soldier's camouflage clothing lay folded on the couch with socks and boots on the floor nearby. The boots looked too small for Diego.

"Yes, those clothes are for you, my Madonna," he smiled. "We will go out around the estate from time to time. I have a lot to show you and you cannot wear your gowns and white slippers or sandals." Diego didn't tell her she would not have to wear her robes after they left here. He would buy her another wardrobe when their new life began.

"I have more to show you." Diego pulled her forward and closed the closet door and locked it. Diego turned her to look directly at him, "What I am about to show you only three people know about. Ramon, Jose, and myself….now you. You must NOT tell anyone about what I am going to show you. Understand, my Madonna?"

He pulled her into his arms, held her close and whispered in her ear, "I must trust you with some secrets, Madonna. I am new at this 'trust thing,' but I have to reveal some secrets now because things around me are changing. When you leave my rooms, a plan will be in effect that no one but us can know." Diego held her closer. Annaliese could feel his heart pounding. His cologne filled her senses with a subtle blend of exotic spice and bergamot. She relaxed and he sighed. This was crazy. She was actually enjoying being held!

Annaliese stiffened. He was a mad man! What was she thinking? Her hands were at his waist and she pushed firmly against Diego. He let her push, but only released her until he could see her eyes. "You are mine, Madonna. We were meant to be together."

Before she could reply he pulled her over to the back wall at the end of the rows of clothing. There was a shelf unit framed with brass. Several shelves had wood dividers which held matching baskets full of socks, and underwear. On the far side of the unit, an elaborate hanger held several belts. The bottom part of the unit was three drawers with brass pulls.

"Watch me." Diego pulled back the top drawer and reached inside the opening. "Give me your hand," he ordered, grabbing her hand and putting it inside the drawer. "Do you feel this button way back here on the side?" Annaliese nodded her head, yes.

"Now, reach up here," and Diego pointed to the bottom shelf. There is another button on the side of the last divided cubby. Remove the basket and you can see it." She removed the basket and saw the button. "Now push both buttons at the same time."

Immediately, the entire unit of shelves and drawers opened to reveal a door made of heavy metal bars. A key hole was in the middle of the door. Annaliese looked at it and then at Diego. "The key is here." He pointed to the front of the shelf unit. On the top shelf, underneath the basket on the far left. Annaliese lifted the basket and found a flat pocket attached to the underside. Inside was a key. "Open the door, Madonna."

Annaliese used the key and opened the door. She could barely see into the gloom. "There is a flashlight just to your right on the floor. Don't step forward until you find it and turn it on." Annaliese bent down and felt around and found the light. She turned it on and gasped! A narrow staircase went down at least twenty feet into a tunnel.

She couldn't see too far, but the walls she could see were damp. "Is it safe?" she asked.

"It's made of stone and concrete over a foot thick. It hasn't been used for a long time, but it's very safe. There is no water to flood it and the walls and ceiling are lined with heavy timbers and iron rebar. Come."

Diego took her hand and led her down the staircase. He had a flashlight, too. Down, down they went. Diego went slow because of Annaliese' long gown.

"Do you remember the large red flower at the end of the dirt road, Madonna?"

Annaliese whispered yes. Diego laughed "No one can hear you. We are way below the surface and these walls are thick. Even my drug labs start about ten feet away, and they too, are thick and insulated."

The steps ended and the tunnel continued another thirty feet or so ending at another metal-bar door.

"You need the key again. This door can only be opened in an extreme emergency and then only with great care." Diego pointed to the other side of the metal door. Can you see there is a wooden hatch in the ceiling there?"

Annaliese could see a hatch. "How can you climb up? It's too high!"

"Point your flashlight to the back of the wall." Annaliese pointed the light and saw a metal ladder hanging on a hook. "There, is the way out. Place it against the wall to your right and you can reach a latch. Pull the latch and release the top hatch, but push slowly when you push it up. You will be inside a round cement pipe. It's wide enough for one person at a time to climb out. The red flowers are on a large plant that surrounds the pipe so you cannot be seen. It will be difficult to climb through the plant, but we should be able to get out without being seen."

"Why?" Annaliese asked.

"We are going to leave here in a few weeks. We will go out this way and leave everything behind except what I will pack in two backpacks. One for you and one for me. I will explain the papers and contents before we go, alright?"

"There will be enough room for one change of clothes, only. You will dress in the clothes and boots you saw in my closet." He pulled her close again. "But don't worry. I have enough bank accounts, cash, and jewels to last a life time….ten lifetimes even."

Annaliese' head was swimming with all this information. They were leaving in a week! She could be free! She pushed back to look into Diego's eyes. "Where are we going? And, why are you running away?"

Diego hesitated. "I will give you all the details later. Nothing is settled yet." He kissed her hand, "You'll have to trust me. I'll keep you safe. I promise. Now, let's go back."

Annaliese turned and started back down the tunnel. Diego was close behind her. When they reached the stairs he took hold of her arm again and helped her up the stairs. At the top, he opened the metal door and they went through. After locking the door, he closed the unit making sure it clicked in place. He gave the key to Annaliese and nodded toward the basket. She pulled it out and put the key back in the envelope, replacing the basket in the cubby. She turned and they made eye contact.

Diego placed his hands on each side of Annaliese' face. She knew what he was going to do, and knew she wouldn't fight him. He lowered his face to hers, touching forehead to forehead.

Diego lifted her chin and placed his lips on hers. Gradually, he increased the pressure and pulled her closer, wrapping his arms around her.

Annalise was trapped in his embrace. Her arms hung down at her sides. She found herself returning his kiss. His lips were soft and he was a good kisser. Derek's face appeared in her mind and she stopped returning Diego's kiss. He pulled back and looked with questioning eyes. "What?" His voice was husky with desire.

Annaliese shook her head. "I have a boyfriend." She tried to pull away.

"No, that was your other life," he said sternly. "You're with me now." He started to pull her back.

Annaliese put her hand on his chest, "My name is Annaliese Marie Bergdahl!" She pounded her chest, "My name is Annaliese Bergdahl!" she hollered.

Diego shook her. "Enough! You are my Madonna!" He shook her again, waiting for an answer.

"I want to go to my room now." Annaliese pushed him away. She started walking to the closet door. Diego reached out and grabbed her, turned her to face him, and shoved her up against the door.

"You are here with me! Don't defy me - you know I will not allow that!" Diego kissed her, hard. Annaliese didn't return the kiss but she didn't fight him.

He released her and stepped back. "You need me right now. You are not safe without me.

You have to cooperate with me. We will leave together.

Until that time, you will obey me, understand?" He pulled her into his arms again and held her tightly against his chest. He buried his face in her hair and breathed in her scent. He rocked her from side to side as though he was soothing her.

Annaliese waited for him to let her go. He stopped rocking her and then removed his hands, sliding them up her arms and smoothing them over her hair. Stepping back he spoke in a gravelly voice, "Alright, open the door. I'll walk you to your room. Don't tell Juanita anything about what you have seen."

Annaliese waited for Diego to unlock the door and open it. She walked straight through his room and paused in front of his bedroom door. He clicked the remote control and the door released. Annaliese opened the door, passed through and without looking back she walked up the stairs to her room. Diego stayed behind her all the way.

At her door, she paused, knowing it was locked. Diego had his keys out and reached around her to unlock the door. Annaliese stepped through and shoved the door closed behind her. Stopping in the middle of the room, she waited for Diego to come in. Several seconds later, she heard the lock click. She heaved a sigh of relief. Not tonight. He would leave her alone tonight. She shuddered with relief.

10

Diego often visited Dr. Hermosa. He had built the hospital and hired a competent staff to make sure it was stocked with all the medical supplies they needed to care for his village and the surrounding area. Today was no different. He told Ramon and Jose to wait outside while he talked to the doctor. They were accustomed to waiting for their boss and made themselves comfortable with coffee from the nurses' mini-kitchen.

Diego seated himself in the doctor's office and waited. Minutes later, the doctor arrived and was not surprised to see him. "Good morning, Senor Diego." He closed his office door and took his seat behind his desk. He leaned forward, "I have news for you," he said quietly. "Do you want to discuss this information here or somewhere else?" Dr. Hermosa was very tense.

"Time is of much importance, doctor." Leaning forward, Diego whispered, "We can conduct our business here if we are quiet. What have you learned?"

"A man will arrive sometime in the next few weeks. In disguise, he will come to the hospital with an injury. I will treat him and contact you for a time and place to meet him." Dr. Hermosa wiped the sweat above his mouth with a shaky hand.

Diego had thought about this. He couldn't have Ramon and Jose aware of what he was doing. They would be left behind when he departed. The only privacy he could have without them was the church when he prayed. He would have to use the church to meet this man.

Hopefully, Father Ambrose would give him his usual privacy as well. Diego knew this was his only chance. "Very well. Tell him we will meet at the church when you give me the time. The small room near the Madonna Angel is where I pray. He should wait for me there, inside the room. Father Ambrose never uses the room. I have the only keys."

He removed a key as he spoke to the doctor. Putting his hand out with the key, Diego grabbed his other hand, "He must wait here in complete silence. I trust this will work and you have not betrayed me, Dr. Hermosa." Diego eyes burned into the doctor's.

"Senor Diego, I have as much to lose as you if we are found out," He whispered, his voice strained. "I have a wife and children. I would never jeopardize their safety."

"Good. I have one more important duty for you, Doctor." Diego let go of his hand and sat back. "I have a microchip that I need implanted in someone."

Dr. Hermosa blinked with surprise. "A microchip? And you want it implanted," he gulped, "In you?"

"No, the Madonna…can you do it?"

Dr. Hermosa was shocked, but he considered the situation for a moment. "Yes, I can do that. When do you need it done?"

Diego thought for a moment, "Tomorrow I will bring my Madonna to you for a checkup and you can do the implant then. Can you do it privately, without any nurses?"

For a moment the doctor was speechless! The Madonna! "Well! I will make sure that I do it alone. It should only take a few minutes. Just a small incision and a stitch or two to close it up."

"Good! It's settled then. The Madonna will come for a checkup while I say my prayers in the church." Diego look pleased.

Considering the risks they were taking, Dr. Hermosa thought it amazing that Diego could look so relaxed.

"Thank you, Doctor. I will see you tomorrow," Diego said in his normal voice. Dr. Hermosa was very tense. He watched Diego carefully. They could soon be dead men. Diego's partners and Diego himself were not people one took chances with. Dr. Hermosa knew that Diego was going to sell his partners out. This could be a bad situation.

Diego got up and walked to the door. As he opened it he said loudly, "Thank you for your time, Dr. Hermosa. I will bring the Madonna in tomorrow for her check-up." He turned, nodded at the nurse outside at the desk, and walked out to greet his men and go on with his duties like nothing was amiss.

Dr. Hermosa heaved a sigh. He was sweating and it wasn't hot. He hoped he was doing the right thing. It was too late now. He couldn't tell his wife what he was doing. Everything was in motion. Life in Ville Verde was about t to change forever. He only hoped he would live to see the changes.

Dinner at the hacienda was a quiet affair. Diego was tired after his long day. After his visit with Dr. Hermosa he made it a point to visit all the areas of his entire estate, from the vineyard to the underground labs. He felt driven to make sure all was well and functioning at full speed. He was a master of control. His people were accustomed to seeing him where they worked. Each supervisor reported directly to Diego on a weekly basis. If you valued your life, you did your job and gave a report to Senor Diego - anytime it was requested.

Diego had accomplished all he had dreamed about doing when he was a small child; for his village, for the people, his beloved church and school. All that he had accomplished would mean nothing for him if he stayed much longer. It would end in disaster for him.   Already the clock was ticking.   He knew how his cartel partner's greedy minds worked. They had made it very plain to Diego that they believed he had more than they did in a partnership that was supposed to be an equal split, four ways. Diego knew it was an equal split when it came to the drugs, but he invested more in other areas and wasn't foolish about using drug products.   His choice to use the land he personally owned, for vineyards and cotton fields gave him a wider profit.

The partners chose not to venture into anything other than growing marijuana and developing drugs in their underground labs. That business was the four-way split.   They constantly pent money on lavish toys, jewelry, and parties where guests mistreated their estate homes and squandered the partnership's drugs. Diego had no patience for their lazy behavior or for their complaints that he had more and they wanted a bigger share. So, he knew it was only a matter of time before they would make a move to get rid of him and take over.

Diego waited until after dinner, when he was alone with Madonna in her room, to tell her she was going to have a microchip implanted in her body at Dr. Hermosa's office. He feared that she would not want to cooperate, but he would give her no choice – he couldn't. The microchip was the only way of escaping his cartel partners, and the only way to save his life. He was going to make a deal with the U.S. Strategic Operations Unit. The information on the microchip was going to bring down an entire drug cartel, as well as, some very important people in Mexico and the United States. But he would only give the operatives this information when he and Madonna were in a safe location of his choosing. He was not going to tell them where the information was until he was ready. He had to control when and where the information was revealed in order to guarantee their survival.

At the end of dinner, Diego told Juanita that she could retire for the night. He would take care of Annaliese. Juanita nodded her head and smiled at him. She knew he was making a move on Madonna.

Something was different. All manner of thoughts were going through Annaliese' brain as they made the long walk through the hacienda and up the stairs to her room. Maybe he was going to talk about the tour, the secret passage, or maybe they would be leaving soon. Annaliese was excited by that thought. Escape was near!

Diego looked serious as he closed the bedroom door, "I need you to do something for me that is more important than anything you will ever do in your life." His face was strained and he looked very stern. Annaliese had a sense of dread.

"What is it you want me to do?" she whispered.

"Tomorrow I will take you to see Dr. Hermosa for a checkup. He will be alone with you while I go to the church. When you are in his office, Dr. Hermosa will implant a microchip in your body." He took a deep breath, "No one, I repeat – NO ONE," he said fiercely, "can know that he has done this. Only you and I will know. The microchip contains about five billion dollars' worth of information. When we get to the United States, and we are safe, I will have the microchip removed. In exchange for this information, you and I will disappear forever." Diego waited for Annaliese' reaction.

Her mouth was open, her lips formed a large 'O' and her eyes were wide with shock. She was speechless! Her first thought was, would it hurt? Then, ---- IN HER BODY? "Five billion dollars?" she shrieked.

Diego took hold of Annaliese' shoulders, "Madonna-----listen to me! You will do this for us. Can't you understand how important this is?"

Annaliese reached for his hands and tried to break free, "If it's so important – YOU DO IT!" She bristled with outrage, "I've NEVER even had stitches or any kind of an operation….and I'm not about to have one now!" Shaking her head, "This doesn't concern me. This is your deal with the government! I won't do it!"

Diego wasn't really surprised by her reaction. Although, it was clear she was more frightened than she was outraged. It didn't matter. The amount of information he had compiled and transferred to the microchip would fill several file boxes. They had to travel light. No one would expect an implanted microchip, especially in the Madonna Angel. He would never tell her that he was squeamish and could never tolerate having something implanted in his body, then extracted a week or two later. She would do it even if he had to drug her to make her cooperate.

"Madonna, listen to me. I am trading information for my freedom! We would have to carry many boxes of information when we make our escape. We cannot do that! We will have two backpacks. Nothing else! There can be no papers – no information! If any of the partners survive and find us, we can tell them the soldiers surprised us as they did them. I can honestly tell them I left everything behind. You have no idea what is about to happen when I make my deal with the American soldiers." he pleaded.

"My power over them is that only you and I will know where the information is. I have a doctor in the U.S. who will take the microchip out of you, but not until we are safe.

They will never expect that it is on a microchip in your body. We will not tell them where the information is until then. Please, help me --- help us, Madonna!" Diego hoped he could convince her. If he couldn't, he would drug her tomorrow at the doctor's office.

Annaliese was deep in thought, watching Diego who still held her arms. The soldiers would take them to America. But she would control the information now. Implanting the chip in her gave her all the power! As soon as she was on American soil, she would scream bloody murder that Diego had kidnapped her and put a microchip in her! This was her chance!! She didn't care what was on the microchip only that it was a way to get what SHE wanted. There was no way she could do this on her own. She knew that now. She didn't even know where she was except the name of the town, Ville Verde. She had no money and no friends to help her. But she wanted to get back to the United States and her life. Months had gone by, Mathias and Derek probably thought she was dead. Poor Mathias. They had never been separated from each other for very long, even when they attended different colleges miles apart.

Thank God this horrible nightmare was going to end soon. So much had happened to her. She wasn't the same woman that lived a happy life in Southern California. She had nightmares now.

She had become the Madonna; a picture on the wall in an old church deep in Mexico. Annaliese Marie Bergdahl had slipped away and was now a ghost. Could she really go back to her old life and just pick up where she had been? Annaliese had hardly thought about Derek in months.

"Yes." She said quietly, watching Diego's eyes. "I will do it. If it keeps us safe."

Diego was relieved. She was going to cooperate. His ego didn't let him see farther than that. He didn't consider that she would want to betray him and escape.

The next day, when Annaliese went for a checkup with Dr. Hermosa, he was alone in his office. No nurse was there to help her undress for his examination. Diego walked in behind Annaliese, closed and locked the door. He reached into his pocket and brought out the microchip. Holding his hand out with the microchip toward Dr. Hermosa he said, "You hold our life in your hand when you take this."

Dr. Hermosa's hand was sweaty. He took the microchip and turned to Annaliese, "Are you ready, Madonna? There will be no pain. Only a little discomfort afterwards." he smiled.

"I will leave you now. I will return within an hour. You will be done by then." It wasn't a question but an order. Dr. Hermosa nodded and turned to Annaliese. Diego unlocked the door and left the room.

Waiting just a few moments, he sighed, "Good. We can get this over with quickly without Diego here." He was so relieved now that Diego had left.

Annaliese moved with the doctor into the side room. It was prepared for the surgery. A gown was draped over a screen in the corner of the room. She moved towards it passed behind and removed her clothes and put on the gown. Dr. Hermosa was waiting for her standing next to the examination table. A tray stood next to it with several medical instruments including a curved needle and string.

"Lay down on your stomach. I will insert the microchip into your upper buttock. There will be more tissue there and you will not feel the chip after it is inserted. I will inject you and deaden the area, wait a moment, then make a small incision to insert the chip. I will close the opening with two stitches which will dissolve. You will keep the area clean and dry for at least five days, changing the bandage daily. After that, you may permanently remove the bandage. A small scar will show the next doctor where the chip is when it is time for removal.

Dr. Hermosa completed the process in less than an hour. Annaliese relaxed on her stomach and allowed the local anesthetic to wear off. Her butt felt weird. She thought it would probably hurt her later.

When Diego returned to the doctor's office he immediately came into the room where Annaliese was waiting. Without asking he pulled up her gown and bared her butt. With a big smile he touched the bandage, "You have done well, my Madonna!" He leaned over and kissed the bandage. Annaliese grabbed the gown and twisted away from him.

"Get back, it's starting to hurt!" she glowered.

"Has the doctor told you how to care for your beautiful behind, Madonna?" he laughed.

"Yes, just give me some privacy and I will change into my clothes and we can leave." She got up and walked stiffly behind the screen.

"I have seen all of you my beauty. Let me enjoy this moment," again he laughed.

Diego was really enjoying himself she thought with disgust. He stood there and watched her dress. She ignored him. When she was ready, she strode past him and out the door, trying not to limp. It was done, she thought. She was now worth five billion dollars!

11

Thanksgiving and Christmas were approaching. Mathias dreaded the holidays because it would be the first time in his life he had no family to be thankful for, to shop for, or to celebrate the joyous season. He had no reason to make a toast for a happy new year. The last five months had been hell. He and Annaliese normally decked out the office, as well as each other's homes, with lots of colorful lights and decorations. He had no desire to get out the boxes they had carefully put away last year. Sadness crept into everything he did every day.

Bergdahl Properties was a business he and Annaliese had developed together. Mary Carlisle had taken on Annaliese' duties and was doing a very good job. He had hired a new secretary for Mary's former responsibilities. Because of Mary, the office was running efficiently but each time Mathias saw Annaliese' desk he felt a great loss.

The police didn't call anymore with updates on her disappearance. They had gotten busy with other cases now, and people no longer thought about the beautiful woman from southern California who had been taken from her home and was never heard from again. Even Annaliese' boyfriend, Derek, had moved on. He was dating a new girl and no longer called Mathias for news about Annaliese. But Mathias thought about her and worried about what had happened to her every single day and night.

Anger and frustration dimmed all the happiness in Mathias' life. The only time he smiled was when Mary Carlisle was around. If it wasn't for Mary, his days would be empty shells. She encouraged him to keep going and not to give up hope of seeing Annaliese again. He depended on her in the office and more and more in his life. He could talk about Annaliese because Mary loved her, too. She cooked for him, shopped with him, and in the cold dark first days and nights of Annaliese' disappearance, she held his hand and let him cry. He had always appreciated Mary before as a close friend of his sister and a great employee. But, he had a new appreciation for her now that he knew her better.

A few days before Thanksgiving weekend one of his clients entered the outer office. He could hear him talking to Mary and could hear her laughter as he teased her. Mathias bristled. The man was here for business. Why was he bothering Mary?

Mathias got up from his desk and stalked to his office door, "Hey, Clark, Mary's busy right now and we've got some business to discuss," he barked. He stalked back to his desk.

Mary exchanged an astonished look with Clark. "What was that all about?" he whispered.

"I haven't the vaguest idea." She sighed. Mathias had been struggling with depression and was moody since his sister disappeared, but he hadn't been so cranky. She would see if she could cheer him up after Clark left.

She went back to her office – Annaliese' office, and sat down in her chair. Mathias insisted she move her things in here since taking over her job. She still felt uncomfortable using her friend's office and only put a few personal things on the desk. Everything was ready for Annaliese to take over as soon as she returned.

Clark entered Mathias' office and sat down in the chair facing him in front of his desk. "I've been asking her out for months, and no go," he laughed. "Is she seeing someone?" he asked.

Mathias paused, "Well, we've been spending time together since my sister disappeared, so I guess you can say, yeah, she's seeing me." He stared at Clark.

"Okay, then. She's out of circulation, as they say," and he smiled at Mathias.

"Yes, she is out of circulation," but he didn't return Clark's smile.

Mathias finished his business with Clark. He surprised himself. His sharpness with Clark was unusual behavior. He sat and thought for a moment. He realized after Clark left, that he had been jealous of him. Mary had devoted most of her free time to him since he lost Annaliese, and never complained. He looked forward to seeing her every morning and had spent so much time at her apartment, he knew where things were kept in her kitchen. They had cooked together and most Friday and Saturday nights they spent together.......Sundays, too, watching television, playing games or reading in comfortable silence. Mathias decided to ask her out for a special dinner date.

The restaurant he chose was a favorite of Mary's and Annaliese'. While talking to her as she sat across from him, he realized that he hadn't noticed what a pretty girl she was, until that evening. She leaned toward him, to make a point during a discussion about a client, and her auburn hair and big beautiful hazel eyes just took his breath away! What a surprise! She had been in his office for several years and he just had not paid her much attention. When he told her he was sorry for taking advantage of her kindness, her eyes flashed with anger. She told him he was blind, deaf and dumb if he didn't realize that she was there for him because she cared about him, for heaven's sake! The silence that followed that statement was filled with wonder by Mathias as he stared at her and truly saw her for the first time.

Since then, their friendship had become a deeper relationship. He was falling in love with her but as yet, hadn't told her. The only thing about the upcoming Thanksgiving weekend that he looked forward to, was telling her this news. She would help get him through the holidays. Perhaps he would think about marriage in the New Year. Somehow, life would go on with or without his precious Annaliese. But he would never stop searching for her.

Mathias had hired a private detective to continue investigating Annaliese' abduction. The man was a former FBI agent with a lot of contacts and a way of getting more information than the local police. He had used his contacts to get film from the security camera at the Ocean Crest Plaza.

It was taking a long time, but he was scanning each one used on the day Annaliese had gone there to shop for Derek's birthday present. Somehow the film had to help find his sister. It was his only hope.

Mathias smiled, he was spending the weekend with Mary and her family. They would shop together tonight for the food which Mary and her mother would prepare for

Thanksgiving dinner. Her grandparents, two aunts, an uncle, and several cousins would arrive to join them. He would substitute this large and boisterous family for a solitary dinner. Mary would make sure he enjoyed himself. His sister would be there, silently, in his heart.

Mary was waiting for him when he closed his office door. She smiled and took his hand and turned to walk to the door. Mathias pulled her back, "What?" she smiled.

"Thank you for this weekend." He smiled.

"It hasn't started yet, silly." Mathias didn't move and she looked at him and cocked her head to the side. "Is everything okay, Mathias?" she asked.

"Because of you everything is far better than it would have been without you. You have helped me live through these difficult months and I am so grateful. I realized how much you mean to me. I was going to tell you this weekend, but I want to tell you now ----- I love you, Mary. Not just because you kept me going, but because you are sweet, kind, intelligent and someone I want to spend my life with." Mathias pulled her into his arms and smiled at her surprised expression as he bent his head and closed his lips over hers.

When the kiss ended they separated a few inches. Mary's smile was brilliant. "You aren't tired of me, yet?" she teased.

"Not happening, sweetheart." He kissed her nose. "I'm stuck on you and I'm not going to let you get away."

"There is no danger of that, my dear. I'm in for the long run." She quipped. Her smile dimmed, "Seriously Mathias, I love you. I'm prepared to do everything in my power to make you happy."

"Mary, just being with you makes me happy." He quickly kissed her again. "Let's get going. We've got a lot of food to buy. I hope my car is big enough to hold it all," he laughed. Mathias closed the office door and as he put the key in the lock, he looked at the logo: Bergdahl Properties. Would he ever see it without feeling such a sense of loss? Would the pain of his loss lessen with time? He wouldn't give up looking for Annaliese, but because of Mary he could move forward with his life, one day at a time. He would celebrate Thanksgiving and thank God for having found Mary. She had been there for him and brought him sweet sunshine on his darkest days.

He put a smile on his face and held out his hand for Mary's. She took it with both of hers and brought it to her lips. "Let's start the celebration!" she said as she kissed his hand.

12

Diego couldn't sleep. He rose from his bed deep in thought, as he put on his robe and slippers. This wasn't an unusual occurrence, his awakening during the night. Most of his serious thinking and planning was done in the dead of night. But this night, his thoughts bothered him, because they were about his Madonna. She consumed him. He thought about her constantly. She was here, in his hacienda -- all his, but he wanted more. He wanted to totally possess her.

This flesh and blood Madonna was much more to him than worshipping a portrait in his church. He was in love with her as a man loves a woman, not a saint. It was no longer enough to have her in his hacienda. He wanted her in his bed. Diego could have any woman he desired. That had never been a problem for him --- getting a woman. But this was so much more! He wanted the ultimate with her: marriage, children, forever!

What would she think if she knew how vulnerable he was because of her? He would sacrifice anything to keep her. Any woman would want him. He was Midas; all his gold safely tucked away in banks in the Caribbean just waiting for him. What woman wouldn't want him?

His thoughts had led him to her door. Quietly he used his key to open the door. The room was dark, the curtains drawn against the moonlight. A small night light in her bathroom was the only light in her large bedroom.

Diego moved silently toward the bed. He could see her hair even in the darkened room. The silver glistened against her pillow. She was asleep on her side facing him. Her lips slightly parted, were pink and soft. Long dark gray lashes lay against her perfect cheek bones. Diego yearned to touch her. He fisted his hands in his robe pockets. He didn't want to frighten her. This was the first time he admitted to himself that he wanted her physically.

He made up his mind, it was certain now. He would possess all of her. At first, she might resist him, he knew. But she would relent, and soon she would want him as he wanted her. Why not? He was Diego Vasquez, a powerful, rich landowner and businessman. He could give her anything she could possibly desire. How could she not want to be his wife and the mother of his children?

Annaliese awoke to a darkened room. She smelled the exotic spicy cologne before she felt Diego's hand on her face. "I know you are awake, Madonna. Open your beautiful silver blue eyes," he commanded.

Diego softly caressed her cheek and dragged his fingers down to her mouth and stroked her lips. "Ahhh, you are so soft and beautiful, my Madonna," he crooned.

Annaliese turned her head toward Diego and opened her eyes. She could barely see his face in the darkness. He was sitting next to her leaning over her with one arm under her pillow.

When she started to pull back he firmly cupped her face and leaned forward. He sighed then fastened his mouth to hers.

Annaliese started to struggle, "Do not fight me. We were meant to be together. You know I will not tolerate it if you fight me. Do you want me to punish someone because you will not cooperate? It's your choice, Madonna," he waited.

She was screaming in her head. She wanted to fight him; gouging and hitting until she couldn't move. Could she challenge him? Juanita told her about the beating Juan had received because he didn't protect her from Ernesto, including his broken arm. Was she brave enough to fight or brave enough to lay here and submit to Diego? He would possess all of her now. This would be her final humiliation.

How could she tell her brother and her friends about all that had happened to her? And, why was she so ashamed? It wasn't her shame to feel. Being a prisoner, losing her identity was not her fault. But she felt sick with her helplessness. She was a coward. But how would she feel if some poor person was punished because of her?

Diego saw her body relax. He knew she would cooperate. He stood and quickly shed his robe and laid down beside her. She turned away from him, her body straight and rigid, waiting. Diego's hands gently started to explore her body. "You must relax, my Madonna. We will both enjoy our time together. I can make you very happy."

Annaliese gritted her teeth. I will not respond no matter what he does, she thought. Please God, take me away. If she thought of something else she would survive. She tried to remember special times with her family. Her brother Mathias and she playing in the backyard of her parent's home. Silently, tears rolled down her cheeks. She forced her body to relax as Diego removed her nightgown. I will not raise a hand to participate, I will not respond, she thought with contempt.

It seemed like forever before Diego was finally through. "It will get better for us. You will return my affection and you will enjoy my nights with you, you will see," he said, as a matter of fact as he stood up and put on his robe. Annaliese lay without looking at him. Tears still raining down her cheeks. Diego opened the door and turned to look at her. "I do not like your tears. Do not cry tomorrow night when I come to you. I don't like it." He closed the door with a thud. Annaliese rolled over to face the closed door. She had survived.

Rolling and tossing the covers, Annaliese couldn't get back to sleep. How many nights would she have to endure this before they escaped? What if she started to respond to Diego? She lay there thinking. Anger started smoldering within her, like a fire begins with a puff of smoke and builds to an inferno. She was pissed! I will survive. I can let him have his way for now, even if I start to respond to him, but soon ---- I will have my revenge.

Thinking about that time suddenly made Annaliese feel strong! I can do this, I can, she thought. She rearranged the covers and heaved a big sigh. Go to sleep, Annaliese. One day at a time. Soon, you will get your revenge.

Breakfast the next morning was tense. Annaliese entered the room with Juanita and started to take a seat several chairs away from Diego. "NO, sit here," he half stood and pulled out the chair next to him.

Annaliese made no comment and sat down. Diego took her napkin, snapped it open and placed it on her lap. Juanita put a filled plate down in front of her, then filled her own plate and sat across from her and Diego. Curiously she watched them both, waiting for one of them to explode. She could feel their tension.

"I am not a child. Are you going to feed me, too?" she asked petulantly.

"I know what you are, Madonna, and I will do this because I wish to do things for you." Diego reached for her hand and firmly brought it to his mouth for a kiss. He smiled like a crocodile with his shiny white teeth, "I hope you slept well, my Madonna."

Annaliese sighed with frustration. She decided to remain silent. She had no appetite, but knew he would force her to eat. Her fork stabbed a piece of fruit. The pineapple made her mouth water with its sweetness. After several stabs and bites, she lowered her fork. "Please excuse me," she began to rise.

"No, you are not excused! You will remain while I finish my breakfast." Diego looked at Annaliese, challenging her to resist his order. Slowly, he finished eating. She knew that he was enjoying trying her patience. Annaliese refused to look at him. She kept her hands in her lap and waited.

Juanita enjoyed watching this duel between Diego and Madonna. She wasn't jealous. She had shared other beds here in the hacienda – not just Diego's. She wasn't in love with him.

When he was finally finished eating, Diego pushed his plate forward. Juanita quickly jumped up and cleared away his dishes. "Leave us," he exclaimed. He put his hand on Annaliese' head and stroked her hair. "Did you sleep well, my dear?"

Annaliese refused to let him know about her anger and humiliation. "Yes, very well, thank you."

Diego chuckled, "You are strong, my Madonna. But try not to be too strong, my dear. You will only cause problems for others, you understand?"

Always threats, she thought. He lived his life commanding others and making threats to get his way. She had to become a ghost to survive. She had to stop thinking, too. She would do anything to survive and to escape.

Diego stood up and pulled her chair back as she rose. "I have a busy morning. We will go to the church this afternoon. The villagers will be waiting." Quietly he whispered in her ear, "We will maintain our normal days until we leave."

Annaliese pulled away and started walking. "I am going out to the patio," she said without turning. "I will wait for you there." Her head held high she seemed to glide away from him with such grace. She was so beautiful….and mine, he thought. Diego smiled. He enjoyed her challenges.

His smile dimmed when he remembered last night. She refused to respond to his love making. That would change. Yes, that would change starting with tonight.

Night after night, Diego came to her room. Annaliese tried not to wait for him. Her anguish increased with each hour she waited. He never came at the same time.

His possession was complete. She had started to respond to him. She cursed herself. He told her he was like a moth to her flame, as if that would make her proud. She loathed him and herself! No one even knew her name. She was the people's angel by day and Diego's whore by night. She knew she had lost her identity. It had gradually slipped away into nothing. Even time was lost to her; she had only the sun and the moon. She had no calendar. She had lost track of the birthdays and anniversaries of her friends. Had Mathias and Derek given up on her? She tried not to think about that. Survive, she told herself constantly. Do anything to survive.

Annaliese feared for her sanity. She knew she was depressed. It made her tired and she slept poorly. During the day she existed like a zombie.

Lately, her stomach was constantly queasy. She never smiled, even at the poor villagers who still worshipped at her feet. When would this end? One night while waiting for Diego, she had even considered killing herself, but couldn't figure out how to do it. She had nothing to use; no razor for shaving, no nail files or scissors. Then she stopped herself from thinking about death and forced steel back into her mind. She would survive and get free. Diego be damned!

Annaliese no longer said her prayers; for herself, Mathias or Derek. What for? They hadn't worked when she was first taken or since. She was now an atheist. She believed in nothing but herself. No one was going to help her.

But, Annaliese was wrong. Help was already on the way to Villa Verde.

13

The dark night hid the helicopter flying low over the green valleys and hills of central Mexico. The wind muted the rotation of the giant blades as they cruised at high speed. The men sat silently awaiting orders to disembark. Suddenly, the helicopter lowered to the ground, the order was given, and ten heavily armed soldiers disembarked and rapidly disappeared into the dense growth of trees and bushes.

Each soldier became almost invisible as he blended into the blacks and grays of the night. Their faces made indistinguishable by the dull kaleidoscope of green and black matching the same colors as their uniforms. Even the weapons they carried were silent. Long-nosed guns, each one lacking shiny pride of ownership was as disguised as much as the professional man who carried it: both deadly weapons.

The wind is less violent as the helicopter lifts higher above the ground and almost silently disappeared into the sky. If he believed in omens, the night was perfect for a mission, Kendrick thought. The beat of the helicopter blended with the wind. The landing site was a perfect small clearing in the middle of the jungle like forest and they had no enemy on the ground shooting at them. But, his men were highly trained soldiers on this mission. They didn't rely on omens or superstitions. Their creed was to train, complete the mission, and leave no man behind.

Major Jackson Kendrick was proud of his men. They had been together for three years and worked as a fine tuned machine. He knew that they were ready for this very important and perilous mission. Each soldier was armed with an automatic weapon, a pistol, and backpacks with enough ammunition, equipment and supplies for two weeks. After that, if they had not evacuated out, they were trained to feast on the land and what they secretly stole from villagers. Two soldiers also carried small suitcases filled with special explosives.

Kendrick signaled the men to remain still and silent – waiting, listening to the night sounds. After being assured that they had not been seen, he signaled for them to start hiking out to the village of Villa Verde. The soldiers each had earpieces which allowed them to be in voice contact with each other. Two men would be left behind to act as lookouts from the highest points above the village. The rest would change into clothes they would wear to blend in with the villagers who lived and worked at the hacienda. Each soldier had a preassigned job.

Kendrick would meet with the contact. He would then decide the timeline for the destruction of the drug labs, the fields, and extraction of the man who was bringing down a powerful drug cartel. They would hide their weapons until they needed them to complete the mission.

Kendrick's soldiers infiltrated the village. One worked in the underground lab, one watched the church and another worked in the buildings within the walls of the hacienda. Four soldiers were close by and watched for any chance that those inside the walls of the hacienda had been compromised.

Without anyone being aware, Kendrick had come inside the hacienda and like a shadow, had explored the entire house. He had even stolen away inside Annaliese' bedroom. He had watched her and Diego. It was important for him to know as much as possible about Don Diego Garcia Vasquez. He didn't care about the woman. She had nothing to do with his mission.

One week later, Diego and Annaliese prepared to exit the church. Father Ambrose walked with them to the doorway at the top of the stairs. "Thank you father, for all you do for our people," Diego said as he held the priest's hand.

Father Ambrose was surprised. Diego rarely gave him compliments. "You have done much for our people, too, Senor Diego." he smiled. Father smiled down at Annaliese. "And our Madonna brings much happiness to our people as well. You give them a gift each time you are with them. They have much hope and believe your blessings to them are real."

Annaliese inwardly cringed. She avoided eye contact with the priest and turned to look outside the church. He was there! A man she had seen several times by the church steps. She made eye contact. He wasn't one of the villagers who lingered by the church. He was dressed as a field worker, but had the body of a soldier.

His gaze beneath his broad-brimmed hat had been steely, not soft with shyness or longing like the people who came to see her.

She had an odd sensation as he turned away. He hadn't come to her in the long lines of villagers, but lately was always here by the steps or by the fountain. As she watched him, he faded away into the shadows and turned down a side street. She hesitated, almost told Diego about the man. No, she didn't care. Diego had guards to protect them.

After that afternoon, Annaliese started being more aware of the people around her.

Once or twice she noticed men, hard bodied men like the one at the church, watching her and Diego, but they always seemed to melt into their surroundings when she made eye contact. She never told Diego.

Each day while she was on the patio, she used her time watching the workers below her going in and out of the buildings, loading trucks and patrolling the walls. She knew one building was a barracks for Diego's soldiers, another building held large bundles of dark green that were loaded onto trucks. Each truck had several guards inside the back where the bundles were and soldiers inside the cab when the truck drove through the iron gates and left the hacienda. She knew these were bundles of drugs being moved for sale. A door in the ground took two men to open, which led to a staircase going underground.

This was the main door to the drug labs, she knew. Two guards were always nearby, their weapons always ready. She started recognizing faces because the men had the same jobs every day.

Diego's world was a fine machine and he would soon leave it all behind. All that power, she wondered. What would he do without it?

A truck pulled in the back entrance to the hacienda grounds. A large tree was on the flat trailer being towed. It was a pine tree!

What in the world! Annaliese leapt up from her chair and ran to the patio wall. The men were unloading the tree and walking to the back door. They were bringing a tree into the house!

Diego came in the front door and called to Annaliese. "Come, Madonna! I have a surprise for you. You will be very pleased with me! Come!" he called. He was so pleased with himself he made Annaliese smile.

"Is that a PINE tree, Diego?" she asked.

"It is for Las Posadas! My people celebrate the days before Christmas when Joseph and Mary searched for their stable where the Christ child was born." He pulled her forward as the men came in to the large entry way. "Shall we put our tree here in the middle of the room under the chandelier?" Diego motioned the men where to put the tree. Another man came forward with a heavy metal stand for the tree. It was a huge tree and was already filling the whole area with pungent pine scent. Annaliese couldn't help herself. She was thrilled with the tree. Diego was watching her and knew he had scored a winner.

"We will decorate it together, if you like – when everyone has gone to bed?" he asked softly.

Christmas, Annaliese thought. I can't believe it's already Christmas. I have never, in all my life celebrated without Mathias. She looked at Diego in horror, picked up her gown and ran up the stairs to her room, sobbing.

Diego ran after her and caught her before she entered her room. "Stop it, Madonna! Do you hear me? You are here and we will enjoy the holiday together. The people will expect you to attend all the celebrations with me." He leaned in and against her ear he said quietly, "It will be my last time to be with them and celebrate Christmas. Please, do this. If you allow yourself to enjoy the celebrations I promise you will not be sorry."

Annaliese stopped crying and looked at Diego. He so far from home – I was kidnapped was almost begging, she thought. How ridiculous! "I'm!! I have no friends, no one! And you expect me to celebrate? I won't do it! I will not celebrate someone who refuses to listen to my prayers and refuses to help me!" she screamed. She wrenched away from Diego and ran into the bathroom, slamming the door.

Diego stood for a moment. She was so ungrateful. He had brought the tree for her! How could she refuse to celebrate? He would give her one hour, then he would come and get her and they would go to the church and watch the people celebrate. Later, they would decorate the tree together, then he would take her back here to her room and make love. He smiled and walked out of the room. No one disobeyed Diego.

Annaliese wanted to throw something, break something. She was furious! How could he think she wouldn't miss her life! She was NOT going to go with him to the village. She sat down on the toilet and pouted.

An hour later, Diego came back into Annaliese' room. "Come out now, Madonna! We are leaving for the village and I don't want to be late." He paced in front of the bathroom door. Annaliese refused to come out and didn't answer him. "I am not a patient man, Madonna, let's go!" he ordered.

Diego waited for a few seconds, then walked over to the table next to the bed. He punched one of the buttons and waited. Within minutes, Juanita came in. Surprised, she asked, "Can I help you Senor Diego?"

In a loud voice Diego ordered, "Tell Ramon to bring me one of the men working outside. Now!"

"Si, I will be right back." Juanita hurried away.

Annaliese was listening inside the bathroom. Fear made her hands icy cold. Diego was calling her bluff. She opened the bathroom door. Diego was standing like a statue, watching her. His face was a stern mask. "Come here!" he demanded.

Annaliese hesitated, then stepped forward a few steps. "You push me too far, Madonna. Now someone will pay the price," he said calmly.

She heard footsteps on the stairs, then Ramon and another man he was pulling with his arm twisted up his back, came into the room. "Is this man all right for you, Don Diego?"

Annaliese gasped and looked at each man. The poor fellow Ramon had dragged in was terrified. Diego had his hands clasped behind his back and stood very tall. "When I tell you, I want you to take out your pistol and shoot this man." He calmly looked at Annaliese.

"You're crazy!" she hollered. "I can't believe you are such a purely evil man! How can you live like this? These people love you!" She walked forward and stood in front of the man, staring at Diego and Ramon. "I cannot let you hurt him. You've won, Diego!" She looked down, "You've won." She sighed.

"Very well. Take this man outside. Give him some money." Ramon let go of the man's arm and pushed him toward the door. He closed the door and Annaliese looked up at Diego with scorn.

"Doesn't it bother you that I hate the sight of you?"

"You are mine, Madonna. Eventually, you will understand me and we will be happy together. Now comb your hair and do whatever it is that you do before we go to the church. I want to leave." He walked to the door and took hold of the door handle, "I will be waiting for you. Don't take long."

Annaliese walked into the bathroom. She took out her brush and pulled it through her hair, looking at herself in the mirror. "I am surprised that I can see myself," she said to the mirror. Even if she was able to escape, it was too late. She was slowly slipping into oblivion. She felt sick to her stomach. Falling to her knees she vomited into the toilet. Laying her head on the toilet seat she felt tears sliding down her cheeks. I am sick to my soul, she mused. I will never be me again.

Diego smiled as if nothing was wrong as he watched Annaliese walk down the stairs. "There she is, my beautiful Madonna," he crowed.

Annaliese avoided looking at Diego and walked to the door. Diego opened it and she walked down the stairs and into the car. "Am I getting the silent treatment?" he asked.

Without looking at him, Annaliese replied, "I will talk to you when I have to. I will watch the parade and whatever else you want me to see. Isn't that enough? But, I will not enjoy anything! There is nothing left inside of me. I died ten minutes ago when you almost killed a man because I disobeyed you. I have nothing left inside of me, Diego. You have destroyed me." She sat up straight and stared outside the window. Tears slid down her face, but she didn't wipe them away.

Diego took out his handkerchief, took her face and turned it toward him. He gently wiped away her tears, "Your life has changed and you are feeling the stress of it. You are not dead inside, only pouting because I am in charge and have taken away your independence."

Annaliese shook her head. "You live in your own world, Diego. You have no understanding of right and wrong. It's going to be difficult for you in the real world. You cannot be king when you leave here. I won't feel sorry for you. I will enjoy watching you brought to your knees."

She turned toward the window, "Sooner or later someone will be stronger than you." Annaliese turned back to look at Diego, "Maybe they will even kill you."

Diego smirked, "Never. I am too smart and my plans are perfect. We will disappear and live our lives like royalty. You will see." He sat back and took Annaliese' hand, "Now let me tell you about tonight." He spoke like nothing had happened just moments ago. Annaliese felt numb.

Diego kept talking, but he was talking to himself. She couldn't concentrate and his words ran together. "Tonight the people will parade through the village with candles shining brightly.

They will go to the church where Father Ambrose will help them set up a nativity scene. They will parade each night until Nochebuena. That is for you, Christmas Eve, Madonna. We will celebrate by eating bunuelos, tamales and colored gelatin. I will have my men set up giant pinatas filled with candy for the children to take turns hitting until they explode on the ground. The bands will play and there will be lots of music and dancing."

14

Christmas was over. The holidays had been celebrated with lots of good food and music. The children had been given gifts and the church had never looked better. Diego was strangely sad. He knew he would soon be leaving forever. But it hadn't seemed to matter before. Now that it was going to be soon, he realized that he would miss his people. He had taken many things for granted. His power had become such a part of him that he forgot how important the people were. He knew where he was going, but hadn't thought much about how he would be starting over without his closest friends, Ramon and Jose. Everything would be new. He had lived in Villa Verdi his entire life. Now, he would leave everything including his sister, mother, and cousins in California behind, never to see them again. Madonna was cooperating, but just barely. She was sullen and sulky.

Dr. Hermosa had set up the meeting for Diego with the soldier. Diego was not a nervous man, but he was today. Madonna was with the doctor and he was entering the church to keep his monumental appointment which would change his world.

Diego stopped inside and let his eyes adjust to the soft light of the church, stalling to see if he could see if the soldier was already here. Father Ambrose came in through the altar door and waved at him. Diego nodded his head toward the private little room he used for prayer and walked to the door. He entered and was immediately pushed face first into the wall, his hand pulled up painfully against his back.

"What the hell!" Diego sputtered. "What are you doing?" Whoever it was, smashed him against the wall, and proceeded to pat him down like a criminal!

"Major Jackson Kendrick is my name, Vasquez. I'm here to get some information and destroy your drug labs and fields. I'm checking you for weapons." Kendrick gave him one last pat and pushed away.

Diego turned around and sized up the soldier with a sneer. "Do you know who you are manhandling, Major? One word from me and you are dead and all your men with you. Don't ever touch me again. Do you understand?" Diego was tall, but this soldier was taller and more muscled.

Major Kendrick sneered back at Diego. "Let's face the facts here, Vasquez. My men and I are the only way you're getting out of here in one piece. Hand over the information and we can begin to rid this area of the filthy drug labs and fields that made you a rich man. We want to get out of here as quick as possible." He met Diego's stare and dared him to look away.

Diego didn't hesitate to reply with disdain. "The information that I have to give you is in a secret place. You will not get it until I am safely on American soil and ready to leave for my new home, and not a moment sooner. That is the deal.
I have information that will take down a five billion dollar business and some powerful politicians. If you don't want to cooperate, then you can go back and tell your superiors that you screwed up!" Diego struggled to keep his voice down.

Kendrick scowled back at Diego. He wasn't going to intimidate this man. He would have to play the game his way. "All right. I have men in position to take this place down. Just say the word and we're ready." He started to open the door, but Diego stopped him.

"You are to destroy only the underground labs, the marijuana and poppy fields. Nothing else. You need access to the lab. I can tell you how to get in by using an outside tunnel. It's an old air duct that was used to get down there before I had the staircase built. It hasn't been used for several years but should be okay. How will I contact you or should we set the date now?"

"You won't need to contact me after this meeting. Tell me now where the old entrance is located." Kendrick pulled him away from the door so that they wouldn't be heard.

"You go to the end of the cotton field. Do you know where I am talking about?" Kendrick nodded, yes. "There is a dirt road, not much more than a path. About a mile down you will see a hedge of oleander bushes, and a large pipe about three feet above the ground.

That's the way down, there's a ladder built into the wall – it's about twenty feet to the bottom. Then you'll see a small door which goes into a supply room. I will go into the lab tomorrow on an inspection and check out the room. If there is a problem inside I will need to contact you to let you know. Otherwise you won't hear from me." Diego waited as Kendrick thought.

Kendrick didn't want to be seen in dangerous areas more than was necessary. But this sounded like the only way to get in the lab without losing his men. If there was something blocking the way, that would be a problem.

"I will be here two days from now, same time." He went to the door, then turned back, "I saw your woman. She's very beautiful, the Madonna." He pointed his finger at Diego, "She's not part of the deal and won't be going."

Diego reached out and slammed the door closed. Leaning in to Kendrick he snarled, "She's going or the deal is off." He grabbed the door and pulled it open, pushing Kendrick back and stormed out of the room never looking back.

The next day started as always with coffee and breakfast with Madonna and Juanita. Ramon and Jose came to get him, but Diego could tell that they needed to talk to him. They paced, nervously, by the front door. When Diego approached them they told him they had heard a rumor about Ernesto. Diego took the men into his office and closed the door. "Where is he?"

"That's the problem, Don Diego, he's working for Don Raoul now. We can't get to him." Ramon looked at Jose then at Diego. "This can't be good. He knows too much about the hacienda. We need to get the word out to our men that Ernesto is not allowed inside the hacienda for any reason."

Diego was thinking. Raoul could use Ernesto to invade the hacienda. It may already be too late. He needed to warn the soldier, Major Kendrick. Although, they might leave before anything happens. But he didn't want a war to start before his final plans took place.

"What do you want us to do, Don Diego?" Jose asked.

"Nothing. We will keep vigilant. But we will do nothing unless you catch him alone away from Don Raoul's men. Then you will bring him here to me. Come, let's start our morning at the drug lab." He started to walk away, but Ramon didn't open the door. He stopped and looked at Diego. Concern was in his eyes.

"He has friends here, Don Diego. I am worried that they may help him."

Diego considered this, "Yes, you may be right. Have people you trust keep their ears open. Any suspicions ---- any, and you will let me know."

Ramon opened the front door and he and Jose looked outside before allowing Diego to step out. They would guard him even more carefully than usual now.

15

Diego started his rounds by visiting his fields and the lab. He climbed down the stairs and put on a protective mask when he entered the lab. Anyone entering the lab had to put on a mask and gloves. The workers who were there all day had full body suits as well. The drugs and chemicals were dangerous in large quantities. The lab was enormous and filled with hundreds of pounds of drugs being produced and packaged for shipment. Diego casually strolled around the lab, gradually getting closer to the old outside entrance. Most everyone had forgotten about the door.

The back of the lab had stacks of boxes filled with plastic sheeting used to wrap the finished drugs for shipping. It would be easy to move aside a stack to gain entry. Diego was relieved. Everything would fall in place now. He would use Ano Nueva Vispera –New Year's Eve, to escape from Villa Verde. It was the perfect time because no workers would be underground, the lab would be closed. The fields would be empty of workers as well. Everyone would be celebrating by having special dinners with their families. The fireworks would start at 8 p.m. Diego and his Madonna would disappear amid the excitement. He would be outside the complex heading for a helicopter when the really loud explosions would take place. He hoped that no one would be near any danger. But he couldn't worry about that now. All the arrangements were made. It was time to leave.

Sgt. Cole Grenville and Sgt. Ken Solomon hurried down the old wood ladder inside the cement pipe. The small door was easily pried open, and they pushed aside the one stack of boxes outside the door of the giant drug lab. They were in --- and all alone. Splitting up, they quickly attached the C4 plastic explosives, to the legs of several tables throughout the massive room used for manufacturing the illegal drugs. Each C4 charge had a timer with a key ring. Before they left they would pull the key ring and set off the timer to explode and destroy the lab. They would also place a charge in the stairway to the grounds of the hacienda so that would be destroyed as well. The timers were delayed to explode after their team and Don Diego were on the way to the helicopter for extraction. They would all meet up at an agreed upon site near the end of the cotton field. That is, if everything happened on schedule with no complications.

Sgt. Gary Crandall and Sgt. John Bowden and two of the soldiers who had stayed outside the hacienda, carefully placed the incendiary bombs in the poppy and marijuana fields and set the timers. The heavy web covering lay only three and a half feet above the plants and made it difficult for the heavily armed soldiers to move through the fields. They had to do a low crawl to get through the rows. They, too, were hoping everything went as planned. The group had to get far away from the fields before the fiery inferno from the flames of the incendiary bombs covered the plants. Major Kendrick was still fuming about Diego's demand that his woman would also be extracted with him. When the time was right, she would be left behind. His soldiers would separate Diego Vasquez from her and leave no possibility that she would go with them. The man was too arrogant and thought he held the strong hand in this deal he had made to hand over information about the drug cartel. Kendrick didn't know all the details, but did know that he was in charge and would run this mission as he saw fit.

It was H-3, or three hours prior to the time at which the attack was scheduled to begin. The operations order had been disseminated. Back briefs and formal rehearsals were complete. Despite that, those who were not pulling security were still rehearsing, going over their individual tasks according to their orders and the concept of the operation in every detail. Others were conducting final checks of their weapons and equipment or prepping demolitions for breaching doorways or other barriers that may stand between them and the accomplishment of their objective.

Major Kendrick was actively engaged as well. He had positioned two 2-man LP/OPs (listening posts/observation posts) to watch the objective. OP1 was in a hide site about 12 kilometers from the team's patrol base. This gave them a clear view of the hacienda, while providing adequate over and concealment to prevent detection. Their orders were to report any change of the target area that could impact their operation. OP2 was located along the main route between the hacienda and the team's patrol base nearby. While they didn't have eyes on the objective, Diego Vasquez, they were to report all movement on the road to and from the target site.

Meanwhile, Kendrick was reviewing the OPSCHED – the operations schedule that included line items and call signs for every task in the operation from the moment at which the lead elements would cross the line of departure, to the final call that signaled when the mission was completed and they were successfully extracted. The call signs served two purposes: they were simple monikers that were easy for the men to recall during operations that allowed him and higher headquarters to monitor the progress of any operation from the radio, and they allowed for one-word communication to keep the radio net free of lengthy chatter.

Kendrick usually chose the subject that all the call signs would follow and his team sergeant, MSG Coleman, would fill in the OPSCHED accordingly.

Typically they would follow teams in the NFL or NBA. Occasionally he would choose a topic to add some levity to an otherwise grave mission – recently he used words from his favorite movie, Forrest Gump. The men enjoyed rehearsing radio calls for "phase line Jenny" and "Dr. Pepper". But this mission was different. The stakes were too high and the operation too important. The call signs took a more ominous tone – tonight they would be using words found in the Book of Revelation – The Apocalypse.

"Six K to Field 1, Six K to Field 1, armed soldiers on the main road to the hacienda, over."

Kendrick was deep in thought, imagining the men in their assault positions – the last covered and concealed position before reaching the objective. Call sign Pale Horse."

Suddenly, the radio came to life, snapping Kendrick back to the present, "Sabre 6, OP2. Three victors moving west from the hacienda, over." Victor, was short for vehicle; used for clarity and simplicity.

Kendrick, who had met up with Lt. Gardner, had to assume they were hostile and his immediate reaction was to lay in a prone position in his clandestine patrol base. Even as he did so he knew it was silly, for he had carefully selected the location for the patrol base to avoid detection... off natural lines of drift... defensible and undesirable terrain. Even still he understood his natural response emphasized the gravity of the situation, they could not afford to be compromised.

"OP2, Sabre 6. Copy, three victors. How many personnel, over?"

Crouching down, Kendrick replied, "Field 1 to Six K, how many approaching, over?"

"One SUV with eight armed men. Approximately two miles behind I see two trucks with ten men in each truck, fully armed. Not sure they are friendlies, sir."

Kendrick felt a chill of foreboding. This was a problem. None of Vasquez' men had left in trucks or an SUV. This convoy could very well be an eminent attack. "OP2, how much time do we have, over?"

"Not more than ten minutes, sir."

Kendrick barely heard the response. He had been mentally reviewing the OPSCHED since the initial report came in from OP2. Every contingency planned for, every enemy action anticipated. He knew the abort criteria and the call sign designated to notify the men to either disengage or to evade contact and link up at the rally point for extraction. This was the one call sign he did not want to issue. RED DRAGON. The beast in the Apocalypse that threatened the heavens. The beast that would signal the undoing of this mission.

"All stations this net, this is Sabre 6...RED DRAGON. I say again, RED DRAGON, over."

Everyone knew what that meant. Immediately came acknowledgements across the net, "Sabre 1, copy RED DRAGON," "Sabre 2, Copy RED DRAGON, over," and on. Instantly, there was a flurry of activity in the patrol base, a deliberate and methodical, albeit hasty consolidation of personal equipment, the slinging of rucksacks, and the quick sweep to ensure their presence would never be discovered. No doubt the same activity was occurring at the LP/OP locations. Each man worked quickly and silently until they made their way to a loose wedge formation to move to the rally point, ready for any contact to their front.

Six K knew that 'scramble mode' meant the mission was over and all members of the team were to finish their task and meet at the extraction area as soon as possible.

Kendrick contacted the rest of the team and passed the info from Six K to them ordering 'scramble mode' immediately. His mind turned to the next order of business. He had to find Diego Vasquez and get him ready to leave the hacienda without being seen.

Four soldiers were now enroute to the hacienda. Kendrick hoped he could locate Diego and get out before they arrived and the invasion began. It would be so much easier if it was dark, but they couldn't wait until then, the clock was ticking.

The two soldiers who were positioned just outside the village, moved closer to the hacienda. Kendrick ordered them to stand by for help outside the gates when Kendrick, Vasquez, and Lt. Gardner exited the hacienda. As far as Kendrick could see, the only advantage they had now was the fact that most of the people who lived and worked within the walls of the hacienda were busy preparing the New Year's Eve celebration. When Kendrick and Gardner entered the kitchen, they noted that most of the staff had left to go into the village as well. Kendrick wished he had time to camouflage Diego Vasquez. He worried about Vasquez' closest staff: Ramon, Jose and Juanita. They might pose a problem. Because they were closest to Vasquez it appeared that Kendrick and Lt. Gardner would have to sequester them; tie them up and hide them away.

While inside the kitchen, Kendrick contacted the four soldiers who were preparing the destruction of the fields and lab and told them to join the two soldiers outside the gates of the hacienda. Kendrick and Gardner were about to exit the kitchen and head for Diego's bedroom when he heard a loud explosion in front of the hacienda. The invasion had begun.

Diego was just walking in the front door of the hacienda with Ramon and Jose when he heard the blast at the front gate. Ramon and Jose shoved him inside and drew their weapons.

"There's not enough men to protect you, Senor Diego. Jose and I will join the ones left at the gate. You must get inside and summon help from the village," screamed Ramon. He and Jose slammed the door shouting, "Bolt the door!" and ran toward the blown gate as the SUV started driving up the driveway to the front door of the hacienda. Diego could see it was full of men.

Kendrick and Gardner ran toward Diego and grabbed hold of him, "Let's go now!" he ordered. "My men are outside the gates. Is there another way out of here?" Diego struggled.

"Yes! We have to go through my bedroom. There is a secret door. I must get my backpack and Madonna," he said as he started running up the stairs. Kendrick was going to prevent the woman from going, but didn't take the time to tell Diego. Rapidly, he and Gardner followed Diego up the stairs.

Kendrick contacted the four soldiers outside the hacienda gates. He could hear automatic weapons firing. "Team 2, we have alternative exit here. Leave immediately, RED DRAGON, over!"

"Team 2 to Field 1, affirmative! Kendrick could hear the chaos by the gate and knew they were out of time.

Madonna had her ear to the door. She could barely hear anything through the thick wood, but had heard what she thought might be an explosion.

She was frightened. No one had come to get her. She was trapped in her room! Just in case Diego was coming, she ran to the closet and pulled off the white robe and her slippers. Grabbing the uniform Diego had given her she quickly donned the shirt and pants. One pair of thick socks rested on the boots and she sat down to put them on. A thin jacket hung next to the uniform and she grabbed it and the backpack Diego had prepared for her. A zipper with a small lock sealed it shut so that she had no idea what was inside. As Annaliese finished tying her boots, she heard the door opening and looked up to see Diego and two soldiers. She recognized the tall one as the face she had seen by the church and outside the patio.

Diego rushed toward her, "Good, you are ready to go. We must hurry. One of the partners sent his men. They have blown up the gate, and there are not enough men to guard us. We will take the secret door. Hurry!" Diego was about to take her hand when a huge explosion rocked the hacienda. Kendrick and Gardner ran to the bedroom door, weapons drawn.

"They've blown the front door!" Gardner shouted. He and Kendrick fired their weapon hitting three men who were entering the opening where the doors had been.

Kendrick looked back at Diego, "Is there another way to reach your rooms," he hollered over the gun shots.

"No, we have to go back down the stairs to the second floor. There's an elevator, but that would never work!" Diego took out his pistol and grabbed Madonna's hand, pulling her out into the hallway behind Kendrick and Gardner who were rapidly firing toward the downstairs.

Ernesto had lagged behind the five men who entered the hacienda after the blast. Someone was shooting at them. He had seen Ramon and Jose down by the gate. He thought Diego was alone because both men had been killed. Diego must be using more protection since he left. Three of the men Ernesto came with were injured or dead inside the opening where the door had been. He could see movement on the stairs and pushed past a dead body to gain entrance. He had miscalculated Diego. He and the Madonna were being guarded by two well-armed soldiers as they ran down the stairs.

Ernesto saw his chance to kill Diego and took off running. He stayed against the wall and passed under the archway opening to the kitchen and dining room, continuing to hug the wall. As soon as he could, he started up the stairs hoping the soldiers thought no one was left to pursue them. He was lucky. They were stuck outside Diego's doors as he fumbled to get the remote control out of his pocket and push the button. Ernesto fired his gun, hitting Diego two times. Before he could take cover, the two soldiers returned fire and Ernesto fell down the stairs, dead.

Annaliese started screaming! Quickly, Kendrick and Gardner picked up Diego and pushed through the doors. Kendrick reached back and grabbed Annaliese, pulling her into the room and slamming the door shut. The lock clicked and he sighed with relief. He grabbed Annaliese again and shook her, "Is there a first aid kit?" She stared at him with a blank expression.

Kendrick shook her harder and hollered in her face, "Dammit! Is there a first aid kit in here?"

Annaliese stared at Diego on the floor. Gardner was unbuttoning his shirt. Blood was rapidly covering his hands as he worked to get the buttons free. She looked up at Kendrick, "I don't know. I've only been in here once."

Kendrick grabbed her neck, "That's bullshit and you know it! You're his whore and you're telling me you've only been in here once?" He dragged her toward the bathroom and threw her inside. Annaliese fell down and hit her head on the sink cupboard. The pain almost made her pass out. Instead she felt her stomach heave and she pulled herself to the toilet and vomited.

Gardner looked up at Kendrick, "We'd need a skilled medic for him. He's not gonna' make it major."

Kendrick kneeled down next to Diego's face. "Where is the information, Vasquez? I need the papers before we go to the helicopter." He leaned close to Diego's mouth.

"The Madonna knows," he whispered. He coughed and blood oozed out of his mouth. "You must take her with you."

Kendrick turned with astonished eyes and looked at Annaliese. She wiped her mouth with her sleeve, pushed up from the toilet, and started walking toward Diego.

"Where is the information?" he hollered. "We don't have a lot of time!" Pointing down at Diego, he said, "He's not gonna' make it. You cooperate and we will get you out of here." The woman wasn't listening to him.

Kendrick put his hands on his hips and blew out his breath. He'd have to take her with them. Anger boiled in his chest. He had not planned on this.

Annaliese was watching Diego's face. He was whispering to her. She crept closer and kneeled down. He took her hand and pulled her closer to his mouth. "Go with them. Don't tell them anything until you are safe, Madonna. Take my watch," he looked down at their hands. "Inside my watch is the key to the backpacks. Take both packs. You will be a very rich woman. Make them let you keep it all, my Madonna." Diego coughed up more blood; he was dying. He reached his bloody hand out and held her cheek, "You are my Madonna. I have loved you since I was a little boy, starving in my village. You saved me, Madonna." His hand fell away and he closed his eyes. Another bloody cough and he stopped breathing. Diego was dead.

Annaliese felt so confused. She hadn't wanted to leave Diego bleeding on the floor. This man who had kidnapped her, kept her against her will and made her into a pretend saint. She thought she hated him so much, but she had wanted to help him. Quickly, she removed his watch and placed it on her own wrist. Kendrick watched her with disgust. "It figures. You're like a scavenger. I hope it's worth it!" he snarled. "If you're going with us you better put on a hat. Your head will shine like a beacon outside!" He turned away in disgust.

Annaliese ignored him, bent down and whispered into Diego's ear. "I forgive you, Diego." She kissed his cheek, then stood up pulling his backpack out from underneath his arm. The side of her face was smeared with blood. She put it on her back, then wrapped the straps of her own pack around her arm. "Come with me." She ran to Diego's closet and put into motion the release for the entrance to the tunnel that would get them out of the hacienda.

Kendrick and Gardner looked at each other. "If you've only been in here once, how do you know about the secret passage?" He watched with amazement as she pushed and pressed the buttons.

"Diego showed me this passage only one time." She opened the small door to the tunnel. "There are flashlights here." She gave one to Kendrick and kept the other one. They turned them on and Kendrick saw the damp stairwell and dark tunnel below. "The tunnel will take us out to the far end of the property. We are only about ten or so feet from the underground lab."

"Is it safe?"

"Diego says it is." They started descending the stairs.

"Major," Gardner stopped Kendrick. "If this tunnel is only about ten or so feet from the lab, we'd better run like hell!" he hollered.

"You're right, lieutenant, we have about a half hour to get out of here."

Annaliese staggered and almost fell. She felt faint and was still nauseous. Just then, she felt a strong hand grab her upper arm. When she looked back, it was Lt. Gardner holding her up. "You okay?" he asked quietly.

Annaliese nodded yes.

"Let's go." He pulled her close to his side and hurried down the stairs behind Kendrick.

When they reached the bottom of the stairs, Kendrick looked around, then looked at Annaliese. "What now?"

"There's a trap door above. You need this key to open the lock. Then push really hard, it hasn't been opened for years." She opened her hand and showed Kendrick the key. He grabbed it. "How in hell do I get up there?" he growled.

"There is a metal ladder, there," she pointed.

Gardner released her arm to get the ladder and Annaliese swayed forward. He grabbed her again and looked at her face. "You're bleeding." He leaned her against the wall.

"No, it's from Diego."

"Your head is bleeding. You'll need a bandage." He looked at Kendrick then back at Annaliese with concern as he handed the ladder to Kendrick. Kendrick looked over at Annaliese and shrugged.

"I'm okay, let's just get out of here!" she cried.

The two men stepped on each side of the ladder and together they reached the hatch. Kendrick opened the lock and they pushed. Nothing. They pushed again and the hatch barely moved. Dirt cascaded down on them.

Both men heaved with all their might and the hatch slid half way open. They could see branches right above the opening.

"Looks like we're going up inside a large bush. Get out your knife and we'll use it to cut away the branches." They pushed once more and the hatch lifted into the growth above.

Branches covered the opening. Both Kendrick and Gardner quickly used their knives to cut away the branches, throwing them down where Annaliese was standing. They tried not to make noise as they cut away an opening.

"You go first, Lieutenant, take a look around, then I'll come up. The woman goes last. I don't want her running away."

Lt. Gardner looked at Annaliese' white face, "I don't think she's gonna' do any running looking like she is now, do you, Major?" he asked. He didn't approve of Kendrick's handling of Annaliese.

Kendrick looked at her and back at Gardner. "She made her choice. She's on her own. I take her back with us, get the information she - supposedly – has, then cut her loose." He looked at Annaliese, "Until then she has to keep up and behave." He moved over so that Gardner could climb up the ladder.

Lt. Gardner slowly pushed up into the bush. It was very large, with big leaves and white blossoms. It covered the pipe and an area of about six feet. Gardner paused and listened. It was quiet so he motioned for Kendrick to climb up. Once he was up, Kendrick turned and looked at Annaliese. "Are you coming or not?" he snarled.

Annaliese looked up at the opening and inwardly groaned. She was feeling so ill. It seemed like the ladder went up forever. Gritting her teeth, Annaliese grabbed the ladder and started climbing up, pausing for a breath every other step. "Hurry up!"

The lab is gonna' blow any minute!" As soon as she was above the opening, Kendrick reached down and grabbed her upper arm and pulled. Annaliese groaned, "Ahhh! You're hurting me! Let go!"

Lt. Gardner stopped cutting branches and looked back at Major Kendrick then Annaliese. Kendrick frowned and Gardner turned away. She was up and grabbed hold of the bush to keep from falling. The men finished making a path, then paused. Hearing no sounds they stepped out of the bush, Kendrick pulling Annaliese with him."

"Check your GPS and give us directions."

Lt. Gardner did as he was told, then pointed and they all started walking, keeping to the trees and other bushes that would hide their progress. Suddenly, the ground shook knocking them all down to their knees. "There go the labs," Kendrick crowed. Then, one after the other several explosions could be heard in the distance. "And, there go the fields. Goodbye to the Vasquez Cartel!" he said smugly.

"Good bye, Diego. And goodbye Madonna," Annaliese whispered. Sadly she got up and started walking. One foot in front of the other, she thought.

Don't think about anything else. Her head was pounding with pain and her left eye was partially swollen. She felt something sticky on her left cheek and smoothed it away with her hand. When she looked down, her hand was covered with fresh blood. That couldn't be all Diego's blood, she thought. This has to be mine. Don't think about it, just keep walking. How far – she didn't know. But she'd walk miles without complaining to be free.

Suddenly, after walking for a long time, Kendrick paused and lifted his hand to halt. Lt Gardner stepped closer to him and they both looked ahead to a group of trees.

Annaliese looked around for something to sit on before she fell down but found nothing. Just as she was about to collapse, they started walking again. A low whistle sounded. Kendrick replied and several soldiers stepped out from behind the trees. Annaliese hung back. They all greeted each other. One spoke to Kendrick and looked back at her. She looked around and saw a place she could sit down and walked slowly to the area and almost fell down as she sat in the soft grass. Annaliese heard Kendrick tell the men, "All accounted for and no injuries. Good job, men."

No injuries, she thought. I guess I don't count. She looked up and saw that the men were drinking from canteens. Her mouth was so parched. What she wouldn't give for a mouthful of water. Just then, one of the soldiers started to approach her holding out his canteen.

"Stop!" Kendrick barked.

"This woman was not part of our deal with Vasquez! We have to take her with us, but she will receive no special treatment. We don't have supplies for her. I'll give her water when we reach the helicopter. Until then, no one speaks to her or gives her aid. I'll see to her needs." He looked at the men. They all avoided looking at Annaliese. "Move out, we've still got a ways to go."

Lt. Gardner shook his head and gave Annaliese one last sorry look before turning to follow Kendrick. Annaliese got up and stood still for a moment, gaining her balance, then joined in the line of soldiers. She was next to the last and hoped she could keep up.

16

Annaliese never said a word the entire march to the helicopter. Kendrick had to give her credit, she never complained, even though she looked like she was going to fall over any minute. When they reached the helicopter, the men quickly boarded and took a seat. Kendrick saw Gardner help her into the helicopter. She huddled in the web chair and closed her eyes. The men were tired. If he failed to bring Vasquez back at least they had destroyed millions of dollars of drugs. Whatever information he had had was hopefully going to be revealed by his woman. His Madonna, he thought with disgust. What a crock!

Annaliese dozed and awakened when the skids of the helicopter set down in the midst of a dust storm. The men swiftly rose and left the helicopter running toward an airplane farther down a dusty road. Again, Lt. Gardner paused and held out his hand to help her down. She was grateful and almost smiled at him, but just nodded instead. He continued to hold her arm and walked faster than she would have liked, but she doubted she would have made it to the plane without his help.

Once she was on board, the doors were shut and the men buckled into their webbed seats. Annaliese had crawled to the back of the plane as far as she could go. The webbed seat was big for her but felt comfortable. She hunkered down with Diego's backpack on her lap and her backpack she used as a pillow. The plane took off and sharply banked right, then straightened and seemed to go up at high angle.

Kendrick scanned the plane checking each of his men. It was always a good mission when he returned with all his men – but especially good, outstanding in fact, when he returned with all his men uninjured.

If this woman did have all the Intel he was charged to retrieve, it would be an exceptionally good mission. He looked for her and found her at the back of the plane, her knees drawn up to her chest and her face buried into the backpack she was holding. She appeared to be trying to shrink into the rigging. He watched her, waiting to see if perhaps she was going to be ill. Flight sickness was not unusual. Hopefully, the men sitting near her would catch her before she made a stinky mess on the floor.

Slowly, Annaliese raised her face and as though she felt him staring at her ---- she met his eyes with a steely glance and quickly looked away. She had removed her hat. Her silver white hair was no longer in a tight pony tail. Strings of hair came down around her face and neck. She had dirt smudges on her cheek and chin. Her hands were grimy, but she was still a stunner!

Kendrick wasn't partial to blondes, but she was the kind of woman he could look at for days. Her ice blue eyes were fascinating even though the look she gave him was cold and filled with dislike. She was beautiful. He understood what Vasquez had seen in her.

He didn't get the Madonna crap. Vasquez and the villagers worshipped her. It was strange that she was some kind of fake, but he thought she was beautiful. He had seen the picture in the church alcove and she did look like the lady with the halo – the Madonna Angel!

One of the men must have said something to her because she turned her head toward him and exposed the left side of her face. Kendrick drew in a sharp breath! He HAD hurt her! In the dark with her hat, he hadn't seen it. He had seen Vasquez touch her face with his bloody hand, but she had too much blood for just his hand print. Her eye was swollen almost shut. Shit! He had hurt her when he slammed her into the bathroom in anger with Vasquez. Her eyebrow and eye was turning purple staining her pale white face. A trickle of blood made its way down her cheek as he looked at her. Kendrick's stomach cringed with regret. Abusing women wasn't his style. No wonder Lt. Gardner had looked at him with a funny expression. He had acted rashly knowing he had just minutes to get help for Vasquez before the C4 started exploding. Vasquez had been such a valuable mission. More thugs could have blown up the bedroom door before he could get them all out and that had made him push too hard.

It occurred to him that he didn't really know who she was. Her name couldn't really be Madonna, could it? Even though she had been Diego Vasquez' whore--- woman, he shouldn't have hurt her.

Somehow, he had to back track with her and make her give up the information she had. It might be difficult now if she saw what he had done to her face. He had to act fast because once they landed she could get a good look at her face, then all bets were off she would cooperate. He'd have to figure out some way to convince her that she needed to give up whatever she knew or had hidden in those backpacks she was clutching with white-knuckled fingers.

Kendrick sighed and leaned back into his webbed seat. He should be able to relax now until they landed. But he couldn't doze off just yet. He needed to watch the woman. She must have the info in the backpacks. Unless it was somewhere in the states and she had to go there to retrieve it. If it was in the packs, he could take it by force, but he didn't want to do that --- yet. Something told him she wasn't just going to 'give it up' too easily. Either he would make a deal with her or his superior, General James Palmer would. He had been told the information Vasquez, now Madonna had, was incredible; a real coup for the Strategic Operations Unit.

The more he watched her, the more Kendrick thought she wasn't going to just roll over and cooperate. But, what she hadn't realized yet was that she was his prisoner. Those backpacks she was holding in a death grip, were going to be in his possession, and soon. She could give them up the easy way or the hard way. One way or the other, he would see the contents and take them into protective custody. What she had was the whole reason for this bloody mission! Maybe she had a criminal record. After all, she was down in Mexico pretending to be some saint. If she had a record, all bets were off. He had her! She would sing her guts out and beg mercy for a deal. It was interesting that she hadn't fallen to pieces when Vasquez had died. Pretty cold if you asked him. She had lived with the guy! What the hell was her story, he wondered.

Annaliese was exhausted and just barely holding herself together. She still hadn't gotten any water and her throat was on fire. Diego's backpack was all she had to hold on to and her fingers ached with fatigue. If she let go she knew she would lose it. Now Diego was dead and the soldier in charge thought she was a disgusting, money hungry whore. He hadn't wanted to bring her along because she wasn't part of the 'deal.' Kendrick was watching her, she could feel it. He kept looking at Diego's backpack and probably thought it contained the information he was looking for. Wouldn't he be surprised! She would wait and demand to see the man in charge when they landed.

Diego told her that the information on the microchip was worth five billion dollars. It also listed names of important people who were involved in the drug trade and the cartel. She hadn't thought before, but a lot of people would kill for this information. She had to trust the man in charge. She would make sure she wasn't alone when she told him. Safety in numbers, she thought.

When Diego had been dying he had whispered to keep both backpacks and that she was one rich woman. They weren't very heavy. What could he have put in them? Certainly the watch he'd had her take off his arm was worth a small fortune. Gold and diamonds shined in the half light of the plane. Well, whatever was in these backpacks was going to be part of her deal with the government agency who commanded this mission.

Diego owed her that and so did the government. She had almost died and still might if she wasn't careful. Her life was ruined. She could never go back to her simple existence now. So much time had passed that Derek probably had a new girlfriend. She hoped he did.

Mathias would want her back. They had rarely ever been separated. But her sweet brother would be overwhelmed with what had happened to her. She needed to see him but doubted she was ready to go home. Annaliese closed her eyes letting sleep overtake her. She felt nausea building up, again. If she only had a drink of water.

The plane jerked and banked to the left. It must be time to land, she thought. How long had she slept? Most of the men were still sleeping, but not, as she looked at him, was Kendrick. His eyes were on her. He would not be kind and understanding. Would he even believe she had been kidnapped? She shivered with dread. Maybe no one remembered the woman from southern California who had disappeared. She thought of saying a prayer, but quickly dismissed that. After all this time being Madonna, and no longer being Annaliese, God had forsaken her. All her prayers had never been heard.

The men had awakened and were talking in soft voices. Lt. Gardner leaned over and held out his canteen. "Here. You never did get your water," he smiled.

She grabbed it with both hands and drank greedily, water pouring down her chin. Lt. Gardner grabbed the canteen, "Whoa! You're gonna' make yourself sick!" Annaliese reluctantly gave up the water.

"Where are we?" she asked. Annaliese felt stiff. She touched her eye and it was all puffed out and halfway closed. She looked up and Kendrick was watching her again. Was that a flash of regret she saw in his eyes?

"We're landing at our base in Texas." The soldier next to her replied.

Well, Texas was a lot closer to California than Mexico had been. She hoped that someone would let her call her brother. What would she say to him, she wondered?

The plane made a soft landing. All the soldiers had risen and were exiting the plane. Annaliese took a deep breath and started to rise. A large hand appeared in front of her face, grabbing Diego's backpack. "I've got it." She looked up into the steely black eyes of Kendrick.

He half smiled, "Well then give me your hand."

Annaliese hesitated. Was he really going to help her? She slowly put her hand out. It was so grimy with dirt mixed with blood. Kendrick didn't hesitate. He grabbed her hand and hoisted her out of the webbed seat. The nausea erupted into a full blown pain in her stomach. By the look on his face, Kendrick knew it. He rapidly pulled her to the opening of the plane and down the steps to the ground.

.   While Annaliese was gagging he turned her away from the wind and the plane and held her so that she could vomit onto the ground.   Luckily, she held the backpack away from her mouth.   She dropped it and would have fallen if Kendrick had not held her around the waist.

"Jesus, Mary and Joseph!   Are you always throwing up?" he hollered above the plane's engines.

After a few moments, her stomach was empty.   She actually felt better! "Okay….are you okay now?"

"Yeah, I'm okay."   She leaned to pick up the backpacks but Kendrick had them in his grip.

"This way," he said and started walking toward a large building.

All of the soldiers were going a different direction and Annaliese was afraid to be alone with Kendrick.   This was the moment she had dreaded.   She needed someone – anyone to be a witness.

After they went through the doors, Annaliese saw lots of open cubicles with men and woman in uniform working on telephones at desks or in front of screens filled with data.   She felt a lot more at ease. A few steps into the building and people were starting to look up and take notice of her and Kendrick.   She was embarrassed to think how bad she looked.   "Is there a bathroom I can use?" she pleaded.

"Yeah, over here." Kendrick motioned his head to the side and Annaliese saw a door marked 'women' and quickly went inside.

Taking care of her immediate need, she entered the first stall and relieved herself. After exiting she looked up and saw her face. No wonder people were looking at her! "Oh, dear God," she moaned. She approached the solid wall of mirrors and slowly brought her hand up to touch her face. It was so swollen....and purple!

Annaliese turned on the hot water and grabbed a handful of paper towels. She would wash off the dirt and blood. That would help, but her hair was matted with blood on the side of her head as well. She pulled out the band holding her pony tail and finger-combed her hair as best as she could. There was knocking on the door, then it was pushed open. Kendrick came in!

"What are you doing in here?" she cried.

"Just checking on you. You weren't looking too good when you came in here. I just wanted to be sure you're okay." He looked at her face and almost said something else, but didn't and backed out the door.

Annaliese took several minutes to wash her face. She needed ice for her eye. It would be nice to have a cup of tea. Leaning on the sink, she felt a little faint. What in the world wrong with her? Rest, that's what she needed. A big soft bed and a big lock to be safe. Like that was going to happen any time soon, she sighed.

When she left the bathroom, Kendrick hurried forward to get her. The backpacks were nowhere in sight.

"I want both of my backpacks, right now!" She crossed her arms and narrowed her eyes in anger. "You have no right to take them. Besides, you cannot open them without the key which I have." She tapped her foot. "You have exactly one second before I start screaming. One, two,----- Kendrick grabbed her arm and jerked her down the hall and opened the last door. Annaliese was in the anti-room of a very nice office. This must be a person of importance, she thought, he or she, had two secretaries and really nice furniture. She'd been pulled in too fast to see the name on the door. She was dizzy, again, and nauseous. God! Would this never end?

The inner door to the office opened and a man with lots of medals on his coat came out. He looked shocked when he saw Annaliese. "Young woman, do you need medical attention?" Annaliese looked at the man and closed her eyes swaying. She reached out for support and everything went black.

17

When she awoke, Annaliese was on a gurney being wheeled into a hospital room. She was still dizzy and her stomach was threatening to go into dry heaves. She had nothing left inside. She decided not to talk and closed her eyes and let the sounds of the machines that she heard take over. Gently, the two men who had pushed the gurney lifted her onto a hospital bed.

When next she opened her eyes, a nurse was about to cut off her clothes. "I can take off my clothes. These are the only ones I have. Please don't cut them off," she whispered.

"Hi there! Glad to see you back. I'm Nurse Nancy Harper. I'm going to take care of you." She put the scissors down and leaned over Annaliese. "Can you sit up?"

"If you help me I can," she replied. Annaliese sat up, but swayed a little.

Nurse Harper put her arm around her, "Okay, let's do this together." A few tugs and pulls and her top half was gone. Nurse Harper quickly covered her nudity with a hospital gown. "Now you lay back down and we'll get these boots and pants off." She made quick order of those things and then placed a heated blanket over Annaliese. It was wonderful!

"We're going to draw blood, put an IV in your arm for some hydration, then we'll see what we're dealing with. Does your head hurt?" She sounded so nice.

"My head is pounding and my face feels awful!"

"Well, I will give you something after the doctor examines you and fixes up that cut on your eyebrow. Then you can rest. As soon as the blood tests come back, the doctor and I will come in and talk to you."

"Do you think I could have a cup of tea and maybe some toast then?" she begged.

"I don't see why not ----- after the doctor sees you, okay?" She smiled.

"Then, could I have a shower and wash my hair?" Annaliese felt so dirty.

"No. Later, I'll wash it with some dry stuff we use for people with head wounds. You'll be surprised with the results. But the shower we can do --- after the doctor sees you." Nurse Harper bustled around the room, folding up Annaliese' clothes and placing them and her boots in a small cupboard. "I'll be right back. You rest. As soon as we get you fixed up, some very important people want to talk to you."

Annaliese fell asleep waiting for the doctor to come and talk to her. Nurse Harper had drawn blood, cleaned her face and gave her some ice chips. The doctor came in, cleaned her face with stinging medication and placed two butterfly band aids instead of stitches on the cut over her eye. He placed a larger bandage over the area and told her he would be back later.

There was a knock on the door. Annaliese was dozing when Kendrick stuck his head in the room. "It's time to talk." Kendrick didn't know what to call her. "General James Palmer is here with me, as well as Lt. Colonel Curt Jansen. We need to talk to you now." He opened the door and the other two men came in. Kendrick brought in two chairs and the men all sat down.

The general started right in: "I hope you are feeling better," he said. "I'm sorry, I don't know how to address you." He sounded like he was trying to be nice to her. Kendrick sat behind the two men and was quiet.

Annaliese took a deep breath and began. "My name is Annaliese Marie Bergdahl." Her voice shook but she raised her head and proudly looked at the men. "I was kidnapped in June of last year from my home in southern California. I was drugged and put on a private plane and flown to a village named Villa Verdi by an order from Diego Garcia Vasquez, because he thought I looked like the Madonna in a painting in his church where he prayed ever since he was a little boy." She closed her eyes and breathed out.

"I tried to escape from the two men who kidnapped me and I was beaten and hospitalized for the first two weeks I was there." She paused and looked down. The men looked shocked by the expressions on their faces. Kendrick was frozen in place, his face a mask. Annaliese took another breath, then another, "When I was trying to escape from the man who was beating me, I ran to the church and crawled up on the altar where a nun, Sister Beatrice, held me and made the man stop. I guess the sun was shining through the church stained glass window and it made a type of halo on my head. The villagers came in to see what was going on and saw the halo and they all started making the sign of the cross, saying that I was the Madonna Angel of the painting that hangs in the church alcove. Even the priest and the nun believed I was the Madonna."

Annaliese stopped. She didn't want to cry but if she said another word, she would. The men stayed silent, waiting for her to continue. They shifted in their seats. Finally, Annaliese felt she could continue. "I was kept prisoner. If I didn't do what Diego ordered, he would threaten to hurt someone to make me obey. I was only allowed to wear white silk robes, white slippers and sandals. Diego took me to the church every week. The villagers would line up outside the church and file in asking me for blessings and benedictions," her voice cracked.

"My real name was never used – it was forbidden. I was told when to eat, what to eat, and I had no friends. One day, his drug partners showed up at the hacienda and wanted to share me. Diego told them he would not share, and they became angry that he was becoming too powerful and richer than they were. After that, Diego told me he thought they were plotting to kill him and take over. That's when he made a deal with the U.S. to give them information, and I knew I had a chance to escape. Then, he took me in to his bedroom and showed me the secret passage to leave the hacienda. Before we had the chance to escape, one or both of Diego's partners, invaded the hacienda and killed him." Annaliese looked up and paused.

The general sat up straighter, "I am so very sorry. I had no idea you were a part of this. I know that my team, who were sent in to extract Diego Vasquez, had no idea about you either." He looked over his shoulder at Kendrick who remained frozen and barely nodded his head.

"Would you please contact the police in California, verify my story, and tell them I have been found? And, I have a brother, Mathias Bergdahl, who must, by now, have given up on finding me, but I really need to see him. Could I use a telephone and speak to him?" she pleaded.

"Miss Bergdahl, after you give us the information we need, we will fly your brother here as soon as possible." His tone of voice and smile was like a father. "Before we begin with the information, I need to ask you one more thing." He leaned forward and touched her hand. "Were you injured in any way by Diego Vasquez?"

She knew what he was asking. Should she tell them? How could she look at them and tell them the truth? She was so embarrassed. Annaliese looked down and pulled her hand away from the general.

She cleared her throat and in a shaky voice said, "I was raped every night by Diego, for the last two months that I was kept in the hacienda." Without her realizing it, tears were rolling down her cheeks. The flood gates had opened and she couldn't talk. But she was oddly relieved. They knew everything about what had happened to her. She wouldn't tell it, except to her brother, ever again. Then, it would be buried forever and she would try to forget it ever happened.

The room was silent. The general looked at his officers with raised eyebrows. Kendrick thought Annaliese had just dropped the biggest bombshell of his life. And he had treated her with such contempt! How could he ever ask her to forgive him for his treatment of her? Now they expected her to continue and give information that would have huge repercussions. For one of the first times in his life, he was so ashamed!

General Palmer had heard a lot of bad things in his life, but this was on his list as one of the worst. This beautiful young woman had been held prisoner for almost seven months! She would need some counseling and time to heal. Palmer knew that a firestorm would erupt the moment he notified the police that she had been found. Her circumstances would only make it worse. Of course, the mission would have to be kept secret and certainly, how she had been treated – as much as possible. She was very beautiful. The press would have a field day as soon as they caught sight of her. It would be best for Miss Bergdahl if she could hide away somewhere until the firestorm blew over. The trouble was, she wasn't a soldier. He couldn't use his resources to help her.

Right now, his first priority was to get the information she may or may not know, about the drug cartel. If it was true that she knew where the information was, what she could reveal threatened her life. She would need protection. Palmer rubbed the back of his neck in frustration.

"Miss Bergdahl, what you have just told us goes no farther than this room. I will contact the police and your brother, but it is my belief that you should have counseling to help you heal from your ordeal with Diego Vasquez. If he wasn't already dead, I would be tempted to kill him myself." No one chuckled at his attempt at humor.

Kendrick got up and stalked to the window. Lt. Col. Jansen stood and walked closer to Annaliese' bed. "Young lady, you have been through a legion of hurt.

Obviously, you are strong and courageous or you wouldn't have survived. I'm sure that we will do everything in our power to help you return to your home after you have recovered." He looked at the general, waiting to see what he would do next. They had to have that information.

General Palmer motioned for Lt. Col. Jansen to take his seat. He moved his chair closer to Annaliese. "Miss Bergdahl, under normal circumstances I would try to give you more time. I dislike putting so much pressure on you, but I need to move forward and obtain any information you might have, or remember, about the drug cartel, Diego Vasquez, his partners, the operation itself, or any people you might have come in contact with during your stay at the hacienda. Can you help us with this information?" He waited for Annaliese to look up and respond.

Annaliese had been thinking about the backpacks while the general had been speaking. Now was the time to protect herself. Whatever was in the packs was hers. She needed to see the contents, alone, before she did any more talking or revealed her very own bombshell to these men. She didn't care what they did after they got the microchip but she needed to know what Diego had put in the backpacks.

"I want my backpacks returned to me. I want privacy to reveal their contents. I have no idea what is inside them, but Diego wanted me to have them." Annaliese looked at the general, then Kendrick.

General Palmer looked uncomfortable. "Yes, well, Major Kendrick handed over your backpacks as a matter of procedure. They are being examined as we speak." He leaned forward to look closer at Annaliese, "Is that where the information is contained?"

Annaliese pursed her lips, "No, General, that is not where the information is. I want those backpacks returned to me now, unharmed, or you will not get your information. And before we have our – talk – I want a written, legal letter saying the entire contents is mine --- period! I am sure you have legal counsel available, right? I will not cooperate with you any further until you give me the backpacks, time alone, and legal authority to keep them and their entire contents." She crossed her arms over her chest and waited.

The general made eye contact with Lt. Col. Jansen, his legal counsel, then after a brief silence, he nodded at Kendrick. Yes, he thought, she was tough. General Palmer stood up, "We are finished with you, for now, Miss Bergdahl," he said in a less friendly tone. "I will consult with Lt. Col. Janssen and Major Kendrick, and return to talk with you, shortly."

General Palmer and Lt. Col. Jansen left the room. Kendrick hesitated as if he wanted to say something more to Annaliese. She pointedly looked away. He sighed and walked out.

The young doctor she had seen before came into Annaliese' room with a clipboard of papers. He smiled at her, then pulled a chair over to sit close to Annaliese' bed. "The tests are back. You're dehydrated, so we will keep you plugged into some fluids for a few more hours. You're a little anemic so I'm going to give you some medication for that.

You have a mild concussion, and – you're pregnant, about six weeks I'd say. Unless you have already seen a doctor for your pregnancy, I can set you up with an ob-gyn for an examination because you'll probably need some vitamins." He waited for Annaliese to respond.

Annaliese stopped hearing the doctor. Her heart pounded more than her head. Pregnant! No! It can't be! Oh, my God! Her world just came to an end. She had a child with a man she loathed! Why didn't she remember that her birth control had worn off? Did Diego know what he was doing? Did he get her pregnant on purpose? He never used a condom – why didn't she think about that? Her periods had never been regular, even on the pill they were irregular! She didn't even think……!

Annaliese leaped out of the bed and ripped the tube from her arm. Blood started flowing, before the doctor could stop her. She saw the pitcher of water on the bed tray. She threw that.

Then, she started throwing anything she could get her hands on while screaming like a banshee. Tears were pouring down her face and she was completely out of control.

The young doctor dropped his clipboard and grabbed the screaming woman and tried to put her back on the bed. She was tall and strong and fought him hard. All he could do was hold onto her to keep her from hurting herself. The noise of the tray flying against the wall as she kicked it, had two nurses running in the room to see what the commotion was.

Between them, they finally got Annaliese in her bed. The doctor and one of the nurses held her down while the other nurse got a hypodermic needle ready with a sedative. When Annaliese saw the syringe, she went even more ballistic, screaming, "No, no, not again. Please not again!" she cried. Within seconds, she lay quiet, and was as white as the sheets the nurses put over her body, after they cleaned her arm and reattached the tube. The nurses picked up everything that Annaliese had thrown during her angry fit. The machine that monitored the bags of medication dripping into Annaliese, began a quiet clicking noise.

Kendrick was bringing Annaliese the two backpacks when he heard the commotion and ran into Annaliese' room. He watched, perplexed, and tried to figure out what had set her off. On the floor was the clipboard with paperwork attached. He picked it up and saw that the papers were test results. He didn't have the right to read this information, but that had never stopped him before when he wanted to know something. He quickly scanned the papers. Nothing looked bad until he saw the words, "positive" next to the word, "pregnancy."

He looked up at the bed in amazement! No wonder she had been throwing up. She was pregnant with Diego Vasquez' baby!

Annaliese was quiet now. Her eyes were closed and she was sleeping. The doctor saw Kendrick holding his clipboard and grabbed it out of his hand. "You have no right to see this!" he said angrily. "Who are you, anyway?"

"Yes, I do have the right. She is in my custody," Kendrick said with authority. He looked at Annaliese. "How long will she be out?"

The doctor hesitated. Kendrick continued, Doctor, General Palmer and I were just interrogating her and she was fine. You come in and all hell breaks loose!" He waited. "She is an important witness in a case we're involved with and I need to know when she will be able to talk!" he hollered into the doctor's face.

Reluctantly, the doctor responded, "She'll be out an hour or so. I'm going to speak to General Palmer. In the meantime, she is my patient and you need to get out." He pointed to the door and waited.

Kendrick stepped around him and sat down in a reclining chair next to Annaliese' bed and made himself comfortable. The doctor huffed out a breath, angrily pushed open the door and left. When he was gone, Kendrick got up and walked to Annaliese. He gently smoothed her hair away from her sweaty face. Lifting first one arm, then the other, he tucked them under the blanket. He watched her sleep for a moment. She was so beautiful even with the bandage on her face and the bruises. All because of him.

What kind of a monster had he become that he could harm someone this beautiful? He had to make it up to her.

Kendrick walked over to the wall by the door and picked up the phone and called General Palmer's office. He told the general about what had happened to Annaliese. General Palmer was a father to three daughters so, he understood Annaliese' reaction to the news that she was pregnant.

"This is a real mess for this poor woman. She has been through hell, and now this!" he sighed. "We still need that information. Let me know as soon as she's awake. I want you to be there when she is. She knows you, maybe it will help.

Kendrick sat back down in the chair. If the general only knew.... He would wait right here until she woke up. It was time for an apology. He would start with that, then go from there.

18

Major Jackson Kendrick was a fearless leader of his men: soldiers who went into dangerous situations thousands of miles from their base of operation. He was organized, meticulous in his preparation and passionate about the welfare of his men. Mission accomplished was his favorite saying. This mission he had just completed had left him drained. He had never encountered a civilian within one of his missions, especially one who was as complicated as Annaliese Bergdahl. She was on his conscience and he wanted to help her.

He went to see his old friend, Major Joe Carter, a psychiatrist. "Hey! The eight ball's back in the side pocket! How ya doin' man? You owe me a game of pool, fool!" They shook hands and half a hug and pounded each other on the back.

"Yeah, yeah. You can't stand it that I finally beat you at your own game." They both laughed.

Joe saw something in Kendrick's eyes, "Bad mission, huh?"

"No, not really. All my men got back, no injuries." Kendrick tried to ease his shoulders.

"I hear a 'but' in there. You want to tell me about it?" He stepped back into his office and indicated a chair.

"Come on in, put your butt in a chair and tell Uncle Joe all about it." He always made it easy to talk to him. He was a great "head guy." Kendrick had sent several soldiers to talk to Joe.

"Yeah, okay. As long as you've got a minute. I could make an appointment, though…."

"Hey, I'm here --- you're here….let's talk. Is this about you?" Joe sat back and waited.

"Not really. It's about someone I brought back. It's kind of a long story. I'd like you to see her if she will agree to see you."

"Sure, I'll see her. Why don't you tell me the story? I'll see what I can do to help."

Kendrick relaxed. Joe did that to him, even when they were playing pool and hanging out. He told Joe the whole story, including his part and how he had hurt her. It was good to get it all out. He knew that he had to get Annaliese to see Joe. He also knew that he cared about her.

Annaliese awoke sliding out of a dream; not sure where she was, wondering if she was with Diego. Slowly, she rolled over on her side. She had bars on her bed --- and there on the other side of the bars was Kendrick, asleep in a reclining chair next to her. Then everything came rushing back: with a sadness so deep, she ached with it – she was pregnant. Annaliese quietly studied the man. He wasn't dressed like a soldier now. His T-shirt was dark blue and looked like it had been ironed. The jeans he wore fit every bone and muscle and had a sharp crease down the middle of each leg.

He had sturdy hiking boots on and on the top of the right one, she could just barely see a small gun in a holster wrapped around under his pant leg. Her gaze slowly went back up his body until she reached his eyes. They were open, watching her study him. He didn't smile and neither did Annaliese. He seemed to be waiting for her to speak first. Well, that wasn't going to happen.

She turned over and laid on her back. Quietly, she said, "Go away." Annaliese closed her eyes. The damn tears came again and leaked out of her eyes. She tried not to make a sound, but her throat felt tight from holding the sobs she wanted to release. Kendrick got up and stood next to her bed.

"No, I have to talk to you. I'm not leaving and I am not going to wait any longer to apologize." He leaned on the bar and got close to her face. "I am not a man who abuses women. I don't know why I was so angry with you. I DON'T KNOW WHY! Do you hear me? I am sorrier than I will ever be able to tell you. You had been through hell and I only made it worse. I'm not asking for forgiveness. I just want you to know that I am so pissed off at myself and thoroughly disgusted that I mistreated you. And, I am sorry."

Annaliese never moved, never opened her eyes. She lay as still as a dead body with tears running down through her hair on to the pillow.

Kendrick started to say something else, but gave up. There was nothing else he could say. Sorry wasn't enough. Not for damn sure. He let go of the bar and stood waiting for another minute. She didn't move, but the muscles in her jaw were rigid, like she was biting something with all her strength. Kendrick backed away, watching her. "I brought the two backpacks. I'll leave them on this chair by your bed."

It was no use. She was not going to look at him. His apology hadn't made him feel any better, he thought, as he left her room and walked down the hallway. In fact, he felt a lot worse.

Annaliese relaxed her jaw and began to sob. She cried until she started hiccupping. Nurse Harper came to check on her and didn't say a word. Another syringe was used to inject the tube going into her arm. Annaliese didn't even know when she went to sleep. She just drifted away.

When she awoke, it was dark. Annaliese remembered where she was this time, and lay still listening to the sounds of the people moving around in the hall outside her closed door. She could hear voices murmuring, carts moving in and out of the rooms, and the beep-beep of monitors: the heartbeat of the hospital. Annaliese was ready to leave here. She was done being ill. It was time to find a place to stay and figure out what she was going to do. Not back home – not California, maybe never there again.

She had mixed feelings about seeing her brother, Mathias, too. She missed him terribly, but didn't want to tell him her story about the last seven months. Kendrick had told her he returned her backpacks. It was time to see what was in them. Maybe the contents would help her leave the hospital and go somewhere – anywhere, to regroup. She looked over at the chair next to her bed. There they were. It looked like they hadn't been opened, unless somehow they had picked the locks. Maybe they just X-rayed them – she didn't know.

She struggled to get up and not pull out the tube in her arm. The door opened and the duty nurse came in. "You're awake! How are you feeling?" she asked with a cheery voice.

Annaliese was tired of responding to health questions. Tired of everyone being in control of her. She laid back on her pillow and closed her eyes.

"Well, you look better. I'm going to bring in your dinner and a hot cup of tea. I'm told you like that." She hustled out and the door shushed closed.

Soon, she was back with a large tray. "Here we are," she said as she placed it on the over-the-bed tray and pushed it in front of Annaliese. "It's not bad for hospital food. I hope you like it." She looked at Annaliese, examining her face. "The swelling has gone down on your eye. It's still pretty colorful, though," she smiled.

Annaliese looked at the food on the tray. She wasn't hungry but knew she had to eat to keep her strength and now, for the baby. She touched her stomach and wondered why she was no longer nauseous.

As if anticipating that question, the nurse said, "We put some medication in your IV for the nausea. Is it working?" she asked.

Annaliese nodded, yes, and kept looking at her food. The nurse bustled back out humming a happy tune. The door opened again, and Annaliese didn't have to look up to know that Kendrick was back. She refused to look up and ignored him. He just stood there watching her.

"You're looking better," he said softly.

Annaliese still ignored him. She didn't want to talk to him yet. Maybe he would go away if she continued to ignore him. She waited.

Kendrick sat down on the recliner in the corner and got comfortable. Annaliese was ignoring him, but he wasn't going to let her drive him away. He couldn't get her off his mind. All day he had worried about her. She still had to give up the information they were waiting for, and tomorrow morning, the general was coming down on her like a bolt of thunder. He had spoken to Kendrick earlier in the afternoon and told him to be ready tomorrow morning at 9 o'clock sharp. General Palmer was through being patient with Annaliese. He had contacted the police and her brother. After tomorrow all hell would break loose with her story, and he wanted to be done with her by then.

Kendrick wanted to warn her and get her prepared for their conversation tomorrow. He didn't want to generate another crying jag or a fit of anger, but she had to "man up" like a soldier. She was still sitting there, waiting for him to leave.

"I'm not leaving, Annaliese. Go ahead and eat. I need to talk to you about tomorrow."

He had called her by her name. It sounded so good to hear him say it. In fact, it gave her a thrill to hear his baritone voice say, 'Annaliese.' She looked over at him. He had his arms crossed over his stomach and was resting his head back on the cushy headrest. Annaliese sighed and gave up her silence. "What about tomorrow?"

Kendrick smiled, "That didn't hurt, did it?"

She smothered her smile and refused to like him. "What time are they coming to get the information?"

"Nine o'clock in the morning sharp." He leaned forward and debated if he should tell her about the police notification and her brother being contacted by General Palmer, or let the general tell her. He decided to wait for the general. "Are you ready? Do you really have the information or know where it is?" he asked.

"Absolutely. I know exactly where the information is right now."

Kendrick smiled. She really did have it, thank God! "I didn't give the backpacks to anyone. I tried to get the locks open myself, and couldn't. I thought about cutting them open, but decided to leave them alone. Do you have a key?"

"That's why Diego told me to take his watch before he died." She said quietly.

Kendrick cringed. He remembered chastising her at the time. "Oh, I'm.....sorry about what I said." He got up and walked to her bed. "You'd better eat that before it gets too cold. You're gonna' need your strength for tomorrow." He hoped she would smile.

"Yeah, I guess." She picked up the fork and poked the food around. "I'm not too hungry. Do you want some?"

"Nah, I already ate. Is your stomach okay?"

Annaliese felt her cheeks go red. She didn't look at him. "They gave me some medication in the IV for the nausea." He knows, she thought.

"That's good. You'll feel a lot better now." He wondered if he should talk to her about what she revealed this morning. Maybe not. He wouldn't know what to say anyway. "If you promise to eat, I'll leave," he chuckled.

"Really?" At last she smiled.

Kendrick reached out and touched her shoulder. "I get the message. You want some alone time." He walked to the door and turned. "I'll see you tomorrow then, at 9. I hope you have a good night's sleep." Then he was gone.

19

The morning sun was shining brightly through the blinds of Annaliese' room when she awoke from the best night's sleep she had had in a long time. The nurse must have put something in her IV she mused as she stretched. Well, today was the day. She would be done with everything, as long as they agreed with her keeping the backpacks and whatever was in them.

Nurse Nancy Harper came in with her breakfast tray. "Good morning, Annaliese," she said, as she set the tray down. "Shall I remove the IV before you eat, or afterwards?" She smiled so sweetly.

Annaliese loved hearing her name. Something she would never take for granted again. She smiled back at Nurse Harper, "I think before, please." She held up her arm and waited while the needle was removed and a band aid was put over the injection sight.

"You look like you slept well. I'm glad, Annaliese. I washed your clothes for you if you would like to get dressed."

"Oh! Thank you very much. They are the only clothes I have. I......I don't know what to say. That was very nice of you." Annaliese smiled at Nurse Harper. She must know that the general was coming back to talk to her.

"No problem. You'll be ready for the visitors this morning. You can shower, you know. I can help with your hair. I brought you some dry hair wash and put it in the bathroom."

"You are so nice to help me. I'm sorry about yesterday. I'm not usually like that, you know, throwing things." She was embarrassed.

"I know. Don't worry about it. You've been through a lot. I don't know that I would do as well as you have." She got out Annaliese' clothes from a bag in the closet and placed them on the chair. "Here you go. If you need anything else, just press the button."

Annaliese ate her breakfast, showered and put the dry wash in her hair. She had removed the bandage before her shower. The swelling was down and the purple was still a deep color. Otherwise, she looked pretty good. Her stomach was still under control, but that could change now that she no longer had the IV in her arm.

At 8:45 she was standing in front of the window in her room, ready for the onslaught of the men. She almost smiled when she thought how they were going to react to her announcement of where the information was. But, they had better bring her the letter. She still hadn't looked inside the backpacks. She was almost afraid of what they would reveal. A knock on her door made her turn. First, General Palmer came in, followed by Lt. Col. Jansen then Kendrick, carrying a chair. Annaliese sat down on her bed and the men took chairs and sat down. They all had notebooks and pens ready to take down the information they thought she was about to tell them.

"Good morning, gentlemen," Annaliese said softly. "Do you have my letter?" She looked from face to face.

"Good morning, Miss Bergdahl. Lt. Col. Jansen will speak to that."

"Yes, good morning, Miss Bergdahl. Under these unusual circumstances, we have decided that because of the incredible possibilities of the information you are going to give us, we can use some latitude as to what can transpire between us. Have you looked inside the back packs yet?"

"No, I haven't yet. Do you have my letter guaranteeing that I keep the back packs and the contents?" She looked at General Palmer, not Lt. Col. Jansen.

General Palmer opened his notebook and took out an envelope. "This is your guarantee, Miss Bergdahl. The contents are yours. I hope that you can give a sufficient amount of information in exchange."

Annaliese bristled at his tone. "General Palmer, I believe you will have more information than your wildest dreams. I have all the information Diego collected -- ALL – I don't know what it is, nor do I care. Let me read the letter, first." Annaliese took the letter from the general, walked to the window and started reading. When she was done she looked outside and sighed, "Okay, this looks…. okay." She returned to the bed, but the far side away from the men.

"I have all of the information in one place. It's on a microchip." The men all leaned forward, waiting. "The microchip is implanted ----- in me." She almost laughed out loud seeing the expressions on their faces. They were utterly amazed!

"OH MY GOD!" General Palmer exclaimed. "When did he do this?" Lt. Col. Jansen and Kendrick were astonished! Kendrick pulled his fingers through his hair and shook his head.

"He had the microchip before he contacted you through Dr. Hermosa. Diego was afraid of needles and surgery. I allowed it to be implanted in me when I realized it was a way to escape from him. It's true I don't have any idea what's on the chip. He told me there was information worth five billion dollars on it, as well as names of people involved in the drug trade. That's all I know. And now, gentlemen, it will be yours. I suggest you arrange to have a surgeon remove it. I think at least one of you should be in the room with me. After all, you want to be as cautious as possible." Annaliese felt relieved.

"Major Kendrick, would you make arrangements immediately? Tell the surgeon I want to see him, it's an emergency." Kendrick left the room. "I thought I wouldn't be surprised about you anymore, but I was wrong! This is amazing!" Lt. Col. Jansen just shook his head.

Kendrick returned, "The surgeon will be here in ten minutes. I will volunteer to stay with Miss Bergdahl during the surgery." He looked at the general who nodded in agreement. Kendrick paced back and forth while they waited for the surgeon to arrive. General Palmer spoke quietly with Lt. Col. Jansen.

Annaliese picked up the hospital gown she had worn before she changed into her clothes, and walked into the bathroom and closed the door, pushing the lock. After she had changed, she opened the door and walked back to her bed. Kendrick's eyes followed her. Annaliese got into the bed and pulled the covers up and waited. The surgeon walked in, stopped and looked at each of the men, then smiled at Annaliese. Kendrick frowned. "Good morning, General Palmer."

"Come in, Dr. Donnelly," said General Palmer. "We need your expertise on a little matter," he motioned him over to Annaliese. "This is Miss Bergdahl, and Major Kendrick. I will let him tell you what needs to done. Major Kendrick will stay with Miss Bergdahl during the procedure. Lt. Col. Jansen and I will wait in my office. You will make this your priority this morning, Doctor." He and Jansen walked to the door. The general stopped and looked back at Annaliese.

"I would like to see you again before you are released, Miss Bergdahl." Annaliese nodded her head and waited. They left the room and Kendrick locked the door.

The doctor looked from him to Annaliese. "This looks serious," he said. "Exactly what kind of procedure am I going to perform?" He looked at Kendrick, then Annaliese, "I am presuming, on you, Miss Bergdahl?"

Kendrick spoke with authority, "Miss Bergdahl has a microchip implanted in her body. She will tell you where it is located. I need you to remove it and give it to me. You will do this alone. I can assist if you need help. There will be no one else in this room, but us. After the procedure is completed, you will forget you ever met Miss Bergdahl, or performed any procedure. Is that clear?"

He waited with his arms crossed. Dr. Donnelly looked at him and replied, "What procedure?" and smiled.

Turning back to Annaliese he leaned on the bed and smiled at her. Kendrick was annoyed with the doctor. He wished he would be more professional and stop flirting with Annaliese.

"Where is the microchip implanted, Miss Bergdahl?"

"In my hip. The doctor who put it there did it alone, too. He gave me a local anesthetic and then closed the area with two small dissolvable stitches. I'm hoping you can do the same?"

Dr. Donnelly smiled. "I don't think that will be a problem. Can you show me the location?"

Annaliese rolled to the side and started to pull her gown up to show the doctor, then hesitated. She looked at Kendrick who raised his eyebrows and waited. "Would you please turn your back?" she asked.

When Kendrick hesitated, the doctor said to him, "You can watch during the procedure. I will put a sterile drape over everything but what I am working on." He looked back at Annaliese, "That will shield your privacy. I will do what the other doctor did unless there is any problem once I get into where the microchip is located." Kendrick walked to the door and looked away. She showed the doctor where the site was, and he touched the area and nodded.

"Has it been there long" he questioned as he touched her hip and pressed.

"About a month, I guess."

"All right. I will get what I need and be right back."

Kendrick walked to the door, "I will go with you."

The doctor put out his hand, "After you." And they left the room.

Annaliese heaved a sigh of relief. She was close to being free once again. Why didn't she feel happy about that?

Kendrick and the doctor returned. The door was locked, and Annaliese was draped and prepared for the minor surgery. Kendrick stood   next to her on one side of the bed wearing a mask, the doctor was on the other side.

He had set up a sterile tray with medical tools and a syringe. Annaliese lay on her stomach and waited.

Ready?" he asked. He applied the syringe and Annaliese cringed. Kendrick patted her back without thinking. The doctor smiled underneath his mask.

The whole procedure took twenty minutes from beginning to end. The doctor pulled out the microchip and dropped it on the tray. He looked at Kendrick, "Open that sterile wipe and use it to clean the microchip, then it's all yours." He continued to work on Annaliese. "I put two stitches in your hip.

You should feel only a mild discomfort for a couple of days. You've obviously been through this before so you know the drill. Keep it dry and clean for about a week, then you'll never know it was there." He placed a small bandage over the site, removed the drape and pulled the sheet over Annaliese. He pulled off his mask, smiled at her and asked, "Can I get you anything?"

Kendrick stepped forward. "Thank you, Dr. Donnelly, but I can handle it from here." He pulled up the sterile drape on the table gathering up all the medical supplies and gave it to the doctor like a hobo's sack. The doctor looked at Kendrick, "I guess I'm done here." He left the room.

Annaliese rolled over on her back and looked at Kendrick. "I guess we're done here, too." She said softly. A tear escaped from her eye and Kendrick took his thumb and gently wiped it away."

"I spoke to a friend about you. I want you to talk to him before you leave."

"Why? I don't understand," she looked perplexed.

"His name's Joe Turner. You've had a lot to deal with, including me. There's a lot you're gonna' be faced with after you leave here. This guy can help you."

"I'll think about it." Annaliese fidgeted with the bed covers and avoided eye contact with Kendrick. "I would like to rest now, please. Besides, you need to get that microchip to General Palmer." She dismissed him----she needed to.

Annaliese didn't like that she enjoyed being with Kendrick. He was being nice to her now. She was noticing things about him, too: his light brown eyes were so expressive, and he was quite handsome in a rugged sort of way. She liked how he looked in jeans. His legs were long and muscular, and he made her feel almost petite. She had to look up to talk to him even though she was tall. She was attracted to him but she couldn't let it go anywhere. She was pregnant – she was going to be a mother. There was no room for romance in her life. It was time to open the backpacks. Time to plan her new life.

Annaliese carefully got out of bed and picked up the backpacks. She walked into the bathroom and locked the door. She rubbed her hand over Diego's watch that she had put on earlier this morning. Pulling the watch off, she turned it over and looked for a way to open it up. She saw a small indentation and used a bobby pin to separate the back cover from the main watch. When it came apart, a small key fell on to the bathroom counter. Annaliese picked it up and put the watch back together.

Before she put it back on her wrist she looked at the engraving on the face of the watch. It was a picture of the Madonna Angel from the church alcove painting. In her hand she held a diamond. Annaliese looked at it for a moment, then fastened the band. It was a heavy gold watch. Diego had worn it every day. Now she knew why. It was another saint-related reason. He was consumed with the Madonna.

His belief that the Madonna Angel was responsible for all the good things that had occurred in his life had been so much a part of him.

The lock easily opened and Annaliese pulled back the top. She peered into the bag and saw rolls of money, small manila envelopes, and soft felt bags.

The first things she removed was ten rolls of hundred dollar bills. The three felt bags were next. They felt bumpy and she had an idea what was inside: a handful of very sparkly diamonds. She didn't bother opening the other two because they felt the same as the first one. There were five envelopes. Each one had Spanish writing across the front. She opened the first one and saw it had a bank logo as letterhead. Since it was all in Spanish, she folded it back up and started to put it back in the envelope when she saw Diego's and her name: Annaliese Marie Bergdahl!

He HAD known her name all along! But what was it doing on this paper? The next envelope had another logo and looked like a contract, again, with her name next to Diego's. She would have to find someone she trusted to read these and then decide what she would do with them.

She put the bags and the envelopes back in the backpack. Before she put the rolls of bills back, she the band off of one and counted the money.

There was 100 bills in the roll! Annaliese compared the other rolls and they were exactly the same size! That meant there was $100,000 in Diego's backpack! She had no idea what the diamonds must be worth. An expert could tell her. But how would she find one of those? She had a find one of those? She had a lot to think about, she mused. At least she had money to live on while she put herself back together.

Next, she used the little key to open her backpack. It wasn't as big as Diego's but was filled with ten rolls of money and several different sized jewelry boxes. She would look at those another time.

The rolls of bills were the same size as the ones in Diego's backpack. That meant she now had $200,000! It was intimidating to have that much money in cash, but she couldn't very well walk into a bank and deposit them. She poured the contents of her backpack into Diego's. It would be better for traveling and she could get some clothes and put them in her backpack. Since she didn't look forward to going through security lines at the airport and having to explain the rolls of bills and all the other stuff, that left renting rather than buying a car for now. She could set off alarms there, too.

20

It was time to get ready to leave the hospital. She got dressed, again, in the only clothes she had. Annaliese wanted to thank Nurse Nancy Harper and the nursing staff for being so kind to her. Then, she would stop at General Palmer's office and speak to his secretary to see if Mathias was on his way here.

She was glad the hospital had given her a plastic bag with toiletries which included a brush. She brushed her hair and used a thick band to make a pony tail. She tucked her hat into her backpack and she was ready to go. One last look around and she opened the door. She felt like she was taking the first steps into her new life. She was, again, in survival mode.

Annaliese thanked the nurses, hugged Nurse Harper, and started slowly walking down the corridor where the general's office was located. Her side was tender and she felt every step. When she arrived, the two secretaries had big smiles for her. Immediately, one secretary pushed a button and notified General Palmer that she was here. His door was flung open and her brother rushed out and enveloped her in a bear hug and swung her off the floor. He was laughing and crying! Annaliese couldn't even talk. All her pain and suffering seemed to melt away. He smelled like her brother always did, and she didn't want him to let her go.

Annaliese hadn't realized that she was crying, too. Mathias pulled back and rubbed her cheeks with his shirt sleeve. "I can't believe it! I never gave up hope and now I know why. When General Palmer called me, I couldn't believe you had been found so far from home. Are you all right? Your face is all bruised and you're so pale, and you're limping!" He hugged her against his chest. "I'm going to take you home. Mary will be so glad to see you, too. She never gave up on finding you, Lissy. She never let me give up, either." Mathias kissed her cheek and laughed. "Oh, I have to tell you that Mary and I are in love. Can you believe it?" He choked, "I have so much to tell you. Come on, let's get a hotel room so we can talk."

Mathias started to pull her away when Kendrick stopped them, "No, I have to talk to you, first, Mathias. You can't leave before *we* talk, it's very important."

Annaliese panicked! What was he going to tell her brother? She looked at Kendrick with suspicion. "I will tell Mathias everything he needs to know! Not you!" She tried to pull Mathias away.

Mathias hugged her again, "Calm down, Lissy! We have plenty of time now. Let's hear what he has to say before we leave." He turned toward Kendrick still holding Annaliese. Kendrick motioned them into General Palmer's office and closed the door. The general was waiting for them and motioned for them to sit on the couch. He and Kendrick sat in front of them in chairs. Annaliese had a foreboding that chilled her bones. Both Kendrick and the general had solemn faces. General Palmer motioned for Kendrick to start.

"Annaliese, the press knows that you've been found. A picture of you was printed with an article about how you had been abducted, and hadn't been found for almost a year -- and it has gone national. Now, they're swarming the front of this hospital and want us to have a press conference. We don't want to do that and are considering our options. The second part of the problem is, the information on the microchip. We need to protect you, because when the press finds out that you were rescued from the home of a dead drug cartel member in Mexico, there will be a lot of inquiry about how we found out about you and got you out. We don't want anyone to know about the deal we made. Especially that you brought out information that is about to bring down some very important people and three more dangerous drug lords."

Kendrick paused and waited for Mathias to catch up. He looked very confused. General Palmer had not had a chance to fill him in on Annaliese' captivity. "I'm sorry, Mathias, but Annaliese could be in danger. I don't think it's possible for her to go home just yet." He looked at Annaliese. Her mouth was opened to object, but Kendrick saw that her mind was churning.

"Annaliese, until we know how things are going to go, you're in danger and you could endanger Mathias, too. I've discussed this with General Palmer and the Intelligence officer, and they agree that you need to disappear for a while." Annaliese groaned.

"Wait a minute," Mathias was angry. "You can't make her disappear! I won't let you!" He grabbed her hand. "I can tell she has been through hell, and I won't let you hide her away from me. What's going on here?"

Annaliese looked at her brother with regret, "He's right, Mathias. After I tell you everything you will agree, too. We can keep in touch by phone and face time, but I need to keep away from the press." She looked at General Palmer, "You can tell them I am ill and need time to recover. Maybe you can find me a place to hide out until its safe again?"

Kendrick was relieved. He didn't want to fight with her and force her to stay away from the public and the press. "It will take weeks for the task force to complete what needs to be done.

Mathias will have to go home without you for now, after you've had some time together. You have a lot to tell him." He felt a great need to protect her, "We have a place for you to stay while you're here on the base. Tomorrow we'll fly you back home, Mathias. All right?" He looked at Annaliese, then Mathias.

Mathias was first to reply, "I don't like it, but I will talk to Lissy and hear the whole story before I decide what is best for her."

"And ---- I will tell you the whole story before -- I ---decide where I want to go." She smiled at her brother to lessen the sting of her firmness to let him know that he wouldn't decide for her.

Kendrick watched the two of them together. They were a Scandinavian family portrait. Mathias was tall, with blonde hair and blue eyes. He could tell that Annaliese was his sister, but her coloring was even more dramatic; silver blonde hair, and ice blue eyes. Her beauty took his breath away. They continually touched as they talked. They seemed to have such a special bond. When Mathias smiled at his sister it was evident he adored her. Kendrick admired his tenacity in never giving up finding his sister. After all these months he had still believed she was alive.

Annaliese looked at Kendrick, "All right, take us to this place where you want me to stay. I hope it will be private so that I can talk to Mathias. Afterwards, I'll have to think about what I want to do and where I want to go." She looked at Kendrick and the general and waited.

"Good! It's settled then. Kendrick will tuck you away where you will be safe." He stepped forward and held his hand out to Mathias, "It was good to meet you. I'm glad we helped you find your sister. Good luck to you both." He shook Mathias hand, turned and started barking orders at the two secretaries about a new issue, dismissing them.

Kendrick smiled and shook his head. "Let's go. Do you have your things?" he asked Annaliese and Mathias.

Annaliese nodded, "Everything I have is right here," indicating the one backpack she had over her arm. Mathias had a duffel bag and he nodded that he was ready to go, too.

It was a short drive on the outskirts of the base to the housing unit where Annaliese and Mathias would be staying. Even though it was a desert area, the three streets of duplex housing had lots of plants, small trees and shrubs to make them quite appealing.

"This is where the soldiers of my unit and two others live. He pulled into the driveway of a duplex at the end of a cul-de-sac and they got out.

"It's so quiet here, are all the soldiers gone?"

"Right now they are in meetings. But they will be deploying within a couple of days, most of them anyway. The rest will spend the day training and preparing for their next mission. Come in." he opened the door into a living room.

The duplex was furnished with simple, yet attractive furniture. The colors were typical of a hotel room: beige and browns with accents of green and gold here and there in the upholstery. The kitchen was small but had everything one would need to cook and clean up. A small dinette set was near two large windows which looked out at the other duplexes. Nothing special, but good enough for Annaliese temporarily, she thought.

"I took the liberty of stocking the frig and cupboard with food," he pulled open the refrigerator and Annaliese saw all kinds of food and vegetables.

"Pretty sure of yourself, aren't you?" she asked in smug voice.

"Yeah, for the most part," Kendrick looked with a smug expression right back at Annaliese. "Well, I have things to do and you've got some catchin' up to do, so I'll leave you alone. I'll be here at nine o'clock tomorrow morning to pick you up, Mathias. We don't have far to go to your plane seein' as how it's right over there," he pointed at the window where they could see a plane taking off not far from the housing unit. They could hear the engines loudly preparing for flight.

"Thanks, Major Kendrick. I'll see you then."

Kendrick left and the house was silent. A large elephant was in the room. Mathias looked at Annaliese. For the first time, he was uncomfortable being with his sister. She wasn't the same Annaliese he had spent his life with. These last seven months had changed her. The always ready smile was gone. Her eyes were haunted, probably with bad memories he needed to hear, but was reluctant to know about. He cleared his throat, where to start? "Do you want to make some coffee or tea? We can talk at the table or sitting on the couch in the living room. Or, do you want to hold off for a while?

It's up to you, Lissy. I don't want to push you, but I really want to know about what happened, then we can decide what's next." Mathias waited.

"I think some coffee would be good. Go have a seat in the living room and I'll be right in." Annaliese searched in the cupboards for the coffee grounds and found two kinds: regular and a flavored blend. There was two kinds of tea, as well. She was surprised with how much care Kendrick had taken to shop for her and Mathias.

Annaliese watched the water turn into coffee as it filled the carafe. Why was this so difficult, she wondered? She knew Mathias better than anyone in the whole world. Telling her story had been difficult when it was to people she didn't know. It should be easier with her brother, but it was a million times more difficult. She was ashamed for him to hear everything she'd been through. He would be devastated when he learned she was pregnant. That information alone would open up a huge area that she didn't want to explore yet. Maybe that was why she was finding it so hard to tell him what happened.

She filled two cups, walked to the couch and set them down on coasters he had put on the coffee table. Annaliese chose to sit near him on a chair instead of next to him where he could touch her.

"I was feeling so sick when I got home from shopping for Derek's birthday that day," she said softly. "I had fixed a cup of tea and was going to sit on my patio and drink it. Then my whole life changed in a nanosecond." She couldn't look at Mathias.

Annaliese proceeded to tell Mathias everything she could remember that had happened, from the moment that she was abducted until she arrived at the army base. Everything, except the abuse and the fact that she was pregnant.

"Is that all?" he asked leaning forward. "Your face is pretty messed up."

After a brief pause, Annaliese finally looked up at Mathias, "No, there is more." She didn't want to talk about how she got the bruises on her face. "I'm pregnant with Diego Vasquez's baby."

Mathias looked horrified! Annaliese watched him get up and start pacing behind the couch. Then, his expression changed to complete red-faced anger. "That son of a bitch!" he spat. "I'll kill him!" he yelled.

"He *is* dead, Mathias."

Mathias stopped and rushed to the chair where Annaliese sat. He knelt down and threw his arms around her. "This changes everything. I'm not leaving you alone here with no one to take care of you." He stroked her hair like he was soothing a child. "I'll close the office. Mary can handle things, I'll......" Annaliese was shaking her head.

"No, you'll do none of those things." She pulled his arms away and held his hands. "I'm a big girl now. I can take care of myself. I have some money and I will stay here for a while and think. We'll keep in touch. But, you need to help me do some things I can't do here. You need to sell my condo. I can never go back there. Box up my things: clothes, pictures, dishes and stuff, and put them in a storage place." Mathias started shaking his head. "Please, Mathias, this is what I need you to do."

"You'll never come back home, then. I'll have lost you forever." He looked so dejected. He sighed and got up. "You haven't asked about Derek." He wondered why she hadn't mentioned his name.

"I know. I stopped thinking about Derek a long time ago. I guess I didn't love him as much as I thought. I should contact him. But, I don't even miss him at all." She smiled, shyly, at her brother.

"Well good, because that bastard was dating within a few weeks of your disappearance. Oh, he called to see if I had any information about you, but I found out he had a girlfriend within a few weeks of your abduction. Good riddance!"

"Well, that's a relief. I didn't want to call him anyway," she smiled.

He put his hands on his hips, "What are we going to do about the baby?"

"Mathias, there is no we," she whispered. "It's only me, and I'm darned if I know." Her face closed up and looked sad.

"I've got to know that you will be okay when I leave. Even though we'll keep in touch I won't be here, with you, to look out for you and take care of you. Can't you see how difficult this is for me? I've only just found you after almost a year!" Mathias was so frustrated.

"Yes, Mathias, I do understand. I would rather be closer to you, too. But I have to protect you and myself. Kendrick is right. The press isn't going to give us any peace. People of power who were involved with Diego are going to feel threatened by the destruction of the cartel. Please give this some time. I promise to stay here unless I find a better place. I will tell you everything as soon as I know it. Okay?" Annaliese pleaded with him.

Annaliese and Mathias spent the remainder of the day reminiscing and catching up on what had happened in his life while she had been gone. She was so pleased when he talked about Mary Carlyle, who was going to become her sister-in- law as soon as Annaliese could return to California for a wedding. The subject they did not about was her pregnancy. Annaliese would deal with that later. Mathias didn't know what else he could say.

They made dinner together and turned in for an early night. Annaliese was exhausted and could hardly keep her eyes open. During the night, Mathias spoke to Mary and told her everything. It was comforting to have her to talk to about his sister.

He checked on Annaliese several times and made sure she was sleeping. The morning came and he had breakfast ready for her when she awoke. Unfortunately, he heard her in the bathroom. When she came into the kitchen she looked a little green.

"You going to be able to have something to eat?" He looked at her with such concern in his eyes that she felt sorry for him.

Annaliese tried to smile, "Believe me, I'll be fine. I think I'll only have some toast, though. Thanks for making breakfast, you're so sweet."

"How am I NOT going to worry about you? This is going to drive me crazy! How long does this throwing up thing last?" he asked.

"I'm not even sure. I haven't seen an Ob-Gyn yet. That's another thing I have to do," she sighed and pulled her hair away from her face. Mathias saw the purple bruises more clearly and clenched his fists. "Annaliese, you're injured and sick. How am I supposed to leave you here like this?" Mathias rubbed his face and leaned against the counter. He framed her face with his hands and said with reverence, "You're all I've got, Lissy, and I adore you. You're the best sister a guy could have."

"Do me a big favor, Mathias. Give some of that love and adoration to Mary. Let her know every day how much you love her. Don't ever take for granted the love you share. I will come back into your lives and we will celebrate your wedding together, I promise. You have to let me go for a while." She hugged him and pulled away. "Now let's eat before Kendrick gets here.

They had just finished when there was a knock on the door. "That will be your ride." Annaliese said, getting up. "Do you mind getting the door? I'm going to ride to the airport with you and I'm not quite ready." She ran into her bedroom.

Mathias opened the door to Kendrick dressed in Army camouflage. "You going on another mission?" he asked.

"Yeah, just for two days, then I'll be back." Kendrick looked around Mathias. "Where's your sister?"

"She wants to go with us and is getting ready."

"She can't go, I'm leaving my car near the airport and I'm heading out as soon as I put you on a plane." He looked at Mathias, "How's she doing?"

Mathias looked down and rubbed his jaw, "I wish I really knew. She threw up this morning and would only eat a piece of toast. I can't believe I'm leaving her here all alone." He looked up at Kendrick and blew out his breath. "This really kills me, you know?"

"Yeah. Listen, I'm gonna' make you a promise. I will take full responsibility for her. I'll make sure she sees a doctor and stays safe. I have an idea for a place for her to stay, but it's not for certain yet. You'll know as soon as I do.

Mathias narrowed his eyes. "Why?"

"What do you mean why? Because she's been through hell and is single handedly bringing down a very dangerous drug cartel, that's why." He looked at Mathias with a frown.

"Do you have feelings for her?"

Kendrick didn't answer for a moment. He rolled his thoughts around in his mind. "She's an amazing person; very strong and resilient. I've never known a woman like her. She's so beautiful I can't believe it." He paused, "I have to keep her safe.

That's my job. Now, there's a baby to complicate things." He looked at Mathias, "But, yeah, I have feelings for your sister, Mathias." He watched Mathias and waited.

"I think you might be a good man. I'm going to trust you to keep my sister safe. When I get home I will limit my conversations with the press and I will say nothing about the drug cartel information. Only, that as a result of an investigation, my sister was found and returned to the U.S. and is now in a hospital recovering from injuries she suffered from the explosions in the hacienda where she was staying."

Mathias grabbed Kendrick's shirtfront. "I may not be as strong as you or trained to be a bad ass, but if I hear that you don't take good care of Annaliese, I'm gonna' kick your ass." He let go of Kendrick's shirt and picked up his duffel bag.

Annaliese was just coming into the room. "I'm ready to go." She looked at the two men, "Is everything all right?"

Kendrick had a smirk on his face, "Yeah, we were just getting a couple of things straight."

"Annaliese, you can't go to the airport with us." Her face fell. Mathias felt terrible. He hugged her and whispered, "This is better. We'll say goodbye now. I'll call as soon as I get home. I love you, Lissy. Everything will work out. You'll see. We'll make it work. Stay well and look forward to coming to my wedding." He walked out and waited for Kendrick.

Kendrick hesitated, "I'll check on you when I get back. I'll be gone a couple of days. If you need anything, see the general's secretary, she knows how to contact me." He walked out to the car and he and Mathias drove away.

Annaliese stood there, watching the car disappear. She felt empty. What was she going to do? Walking back into her side of the duplex, she decided she would take a nap. She wondered who lived on the other side. It looked empty. In fact, the whole neighborhood looked empty. At least it would be quiet. She lay down on the bed. Her stomach was queasy, but not as bad as before. Closing her eyes, she thought of her condo in California. She had been so proud when she bought it. The thought of living there again made her skin crawl. She could never be happy there again. Sleep took over.

When she awoke, Annaliese wandered around the duplex. She should eat, but didn't have an appetite. She thought of all the things she should be doing: making an appointment to see an Ob-Gyn, finding someone she could trust who could read Spanish, check the jewelry boxes Diego gave her, opening a bank account, and depositing a few thousand dollars, and buying a car. It all seemed so overwhelming. She hadn't opened the drapes so the living room was dark. Annaliese sat down on the couch and waited. She fell asleep, again.

21

Kendrick got home just after dark two days later. There were no lights on where Annaliese was staying. He listened at her door and heard nothing. Where could she have gone? He rang the doorbell and waited. Peeking through the blinds, he saw no lights on anywhere.

Now concerned, he loudly knocked on the door. When she didn't answer he went around to the back of the duplex and knocked on the back sliding door. Nothing. He was pissed! Where the hell had she gone? She had no car, no one here knew her. It wasn't safe for her to just wander around. Damn! He was tired and wanted to shower, get something to eat, and go to bed. Maybe she went for a walk, he wondered. Kendrick walked back to the front of the duplex and looked around. Most of the houses were dark, as many of the units were deployed. He had a key, so he let himself in to the living room. Maybe she took off. He'd know if the backpacks were missing.

He turned on a light and looked around. The living room was just as he had last seen it, and looking into the kitchen he saw only a cup and saucer on the counter, nothing else. Kendrick walked into the bedroom where she slept and was stunned to see her in her bed! Even in the darkened room he could see her silver blonde hair spread over her pillow.

She was lying on her side in a fetal position, not moving. Kendrick couldn't believe she hadn't heard the doorbell or his loud knocking. What was wrong with her?

Kendrick sat down next to her. He gently nudged her shoulder, "Annaliese, are you sick?"

She didn't move. "Go away. I heard you knock. If I wanted to see you I would have got up and answered the door." She refused to roll over and look at him.

"I just got home. Have you had dinner yet?" He waited and looked around the room. Nothing was out of place. "Have you been eating? What have you been doing since Mathias and I left?" She didn't move.

"Would you PLEASE, JUST, GO, AWAY!" she growled.

"I promised your brother that I would take care of you and keep you safe. So unless you're really sick, in which case I'm taking you to the hospital, get up right now. We're going to have some dinner."

He pulled the covers off Annaliese when he stood up. She rolled over and looked at him with daggers in her eyes. She was wearing sweatpants and a t-shirt. Kendrick switched on the bedroom light and turned to look at Annaliese. He was shocked to see dark circles under her eyes. She looked terrible!

"Come on, you're going to the hospital. You look awful!" he said.

"I'm fine, just tired. Go away! I don't need you! Please, just…" she started crying, laid back down and curled into a ball, sobbing.

Kendrick leaned down and picked her up. She protested and tried to fight him to let her go. "I'm not going anywhere with you!

Just put me down and let me rest. I'll be fine!" She continued to struggle.

Kendrick walked with her into the kitchen and put her down on a chair at the counter. Trapped between him and the chair he leaned forward into Annaliese' face, "Let's get one thing straight. I gave your brother my word that I would take care of you and I'm going to -- PERIOD! If that means watching you twenty-four seven, I will. Now, I'm fixing us some dinner and you're gonna' eat it, God damn it!" he hollered.

He gave her credit. She didn't cower or look frightened. But she looked defeated, which was worse. Kendrick had been thinking about Annaliese while he had been on his two-day mission. Her present mental condition confirmed that he needed to get her some help and then take her away. Tomorrow he would take her to see his friend, Joe. Meanwhile, she would eat.

Annaliese sulked and picked at the dinner Kendrick made. He ignored her behavior and let her sulk. Neither of them spoke. After he was done, Kendrick removed their plates and loaded them in the dishwasher. He fixed Annaliese a cup of tea and one for himself. He sat down next to her and without looking at her said, "Tomorrow I'm taking you to see a friend of mine. You'll like him. Some of the missions my men and I have been on in the past have been pretty stressful and they have seen some pretty bad things.

He's talked to them and without exception, he's helped them get their heads back on straight.

Annaliese didn't say anything, just sat next to him with her hands in her lap. At lease she wasn't crying anymore.

"I'm going back to bed now. I'll see your friend. Then, I'm leaving."

Kendrick left the duplex and came back ten minutes later with a small bag. He was entering the second bedroom when Annaliese heard him and marched out ready to do battle.

"What are you doing in here?"

"Getting ready to go to bed." He put his bag down and pulled the blankets back. Sitting down he started to remove his boots.

"You're not sleeping here! I'm perfectly fine to stay here without you. Where do you live, by the way?" She stood with her hands on her hips

"Close by." Kendrick stood up and loosened his belt, undoing the button on his pants. He looked at Annaliese and challenged her, "I'm gonna' remove my remove my pants and get into bed. So if you're squeamish about seeing me in my boxers, you'd better go to bed." He looked at her, hardly waiting and started to unzip his pants.

Annaliese was outraged! He didn't trust her to stay alone! What had Mathias said to him? She stomped back into her bedroom, closed the door, locked it, and got into bed. She hated to admit it, but his being in the house with her was a comfort.

Kendrick knocked on her bedroom door at 7 o'clock in the morning, "Annaliese, it's time to get up so we can have some breakfast before I take you to see Joe. Are you up?" he knocked again.

Groggy and grumpy, Annaliese groaned, "Yes, I'm awake. Go away! I'm not hungry. If you make me eat I'm only going to throw it up! I'll get dressed, but I don't want to smell any food." She went in to the bathroom and promptly threw up. Ugh, how much longer would this last? Just the *thought* of food in the morning made her gag.

Kendrick heard her and rested his forehead against the door. He felt sorry for her. He would comfort her if he could. She'd probably bite his head off. He went into the kitchen and made a cup of herbal tea for Annaliese and took it back to her bedroom. He knocked, "Open up. I made you a cup of herbal tea."

Annaliese opened the door a crack. She was still in the sweatpants and t-shirt. She had brushed her hair and she looked a little better but still pale. Kendrick handed her the cup of tea and she gave him a little smile. "Thank you. I'll get my clothes on and we can leave." She closed the door.

Kendrick smiled. She wasn't going to fight him, this morning anyway. When Annaliese came out he realized she was dressed in the same uniform she'd been wearing for days. When she saw him staring at her she got embarrassed. "Other than the sweatpants and t-shirt that Mathias gave me, these are the only clothes I have. Do you think that after I see your friend I could go to a store and get some new clothes?"

"Absolutely! I'll take you to the PX. It's the store on base where military personnel do their shopping. They have clothes there – nothing special, but you should be able to find some stuff.
I'll have to do the purchasing since you're not in the military."

"Oh, I have money. I can pay cash. I'll pay you as soon as we're done shopping."

"Whatever. You feeling okay now? You're not gonna' throw up in my car are ya?" he smiled.

"I ought to just for payback," she said and pushed by him opening the front door and walking to the car.

They didn't speak on the way to the hospital. When they arrived, Annaliese looked at Kendrick with a question, "His office is here?"

"Yeah, don't worry. He's real low key." He got out and rushed to open her door. "You okay?"

"Will you quit asking me already? I'm fine, just pregnant." She pushed past him and walked to the hospital doors.

"You're tough. I like that." Kendrick winked at her. "He's on the third floor. Want to walk up or take the elevator."

"You're kidding, right?"

"Well, if you're nauseated, the elevator might make it worse." He waited. "Elevator. I want to be able to breathe when I talk to your friend." Annaliese walked into the open elevator and pushed the button for the third floor. She liked verbally sparring with Kendrick, it was kind of fun.

When they got to Psychiatrist, Major Joseph Turner's office, he was waiting for them. "I'm pleased to see you, Miss Bergdahl. Please come on in. Kendrick – get lost." He closed the door in Kendrick's face and laughed. "I've known him for ten years. Great guy.

"Have a seat wherever you choose, Miss Bergdahl." He indicated the couch and two chairs. She chose to sit on a chair, not too close to Joe.

"How do we do this?" she asked as soon as she sat down.

"Well, you talk, I listen. Then we figure out a way for you to cope and feel better.

"Please call me Annaliese."

"Then, please call me Joe," he said as he took his jacket off and hung it on a coat rack, then loosened his tie.

"Perhaps we should start with your story. Kendrick has told me only a little about you. I must admit, I was intrigued. But why don't you start from the beginning. I'm going to have some coffee, would you like something to drink, Annaliese?"

"Yes, some water would be good. I never get tired of hearing my name." She smiled at him. He was nice and she found she was ready to share her story again. She couldn't let Diego win. She had decided on the elevator ride up that she was going to stop feeling so bad and regroup.

Once he was settled, fixed his tablet on his lap and sipped his coffee, he indicated that she could start. Annaliese started talking. As before, she told about when she first saw Diego until she arrived here. Then, she told him about the microchip, although she worried about the secrecy and asked him about that. He gave his word he would not reveal anything they discussed. She even told him about the contents of the backpack waiting for his negative opinion of her keeping ill-gotten gains, as she thought of them. The last thing she spoke of was the most difficult. When she spoke of her pregnancy he stopped making notes and looked closely at Annaliese. He hadn't made any comment until this point.

"How do you feel about being pregnant?" Annaliese looked forlorn.

"How far along are you?"

She shrugged her shoulders, "I'm about six weeks."

"Have you thought about having this baby?" They stared at each other for a moment.

"I have tried NOT to think about it. But I really must decide soon. That's mainly why I agreed to see you. I've been feeling quite sorry for myself. This baby is from a man I hated. How can I love it? I mean will I hate the baby, too? And if I terminate the pregnancy, will I hate myself? I was hoping you could help me decide," she pleaded.

"That's not how it works, Annaliese. My job is to help you come to terms with your crisis. For you, that's your pregnancy. Then, I help you make your own decision and be at peace with it. You also have some other demons to exorcise. The fact that you felt yourself disappearing was very stressful. How did it feel being a saint?" He smiled and she smiled back.

She frowned, "I've given up religion as a result of my abduction." Annaliese drew in a big breath, "I prayed to be saved, or helped, many, many times --- all for nothing. Then, all these villagers worshiped me and think I'm a living deity, including a priest and a nun for God's sake! I didn't hear my name for seven months. I wore white silk robes." In a quiet voice she said, "No one helped me. Not even God."

Dr. Turner talked to Annaliese some more about her captivity. He was soothing, she thought. It was easier to talk about it with him. He even made her smile a couple of times. He made her think about what had happened. Not to be ashamed for anything she had done. He agreed that she shouldn't go back to California for a while. The hour he gave her flew by, but eventually, they came back around to the pregnancy.

"Have you thought about what it would be like to keep the baby?" he inquired.

Annaliese looked surprised. "No --- well, just a little." She put her hand on her stomach. "That's why I'm worried. What kind of a mother would I be if I hated my own child because of who their father was?"

"What if you love the child when it's born and you don't care how it came to be?"

Annaliese looked at Joe with wonder. "Do you really think that could happen? What if it doesn't? What then?"

"There is adoption. You would give the baby up right away and someone else would love it and raise it. Maybe you should think about that option." Joe leaned forward, "Whatever you do, don't make a hasty decision. You don't have a lot of time if you decide to terminate your pregnancy. But, you have to make peace with yourself first. We can talk again, if you'd like."

He got up and stretched. He looked at Annaliese. She returned his stare, then looked down clutching her hands. "There's something else, isn't there?"

"Yes. It's probably nothing, but it's bothering my conscience and it makes me angry."

"Do you want to talk about it, or let it simmer for a while?" Joe sat back down in the chair.

"No, as long as I'm getting things out I might as well tell you this, too." Annaliese paused, "When Diego was dying, I told him that I forgave him. I lied to him. I don't think I could ever forgive him." She looked so guilty. "He was dying! I just said it! I don't know why."

"Have you ever seen a man die before, Annaliese?" Joe asked. She shook her head but didn't look up. He leaned forward, "It's not an easy thing to see. You may have hated Diego Vasquez, but when you saw him dying, you wanted to comfort him. You're a good woman, Annaliese. You did it for him, not yourself. There's no need to beat yourself up." Joe got up and walked over to Annaliese and put his hand on her shoulder.

Annaliese got up and took his hand. "Thank you, Joe. This has helped me. I've got a lot of things to work out. I'm going to make a decision about the baby very soon."

"Don't assign yourself a time limit. Just think about it and let it come." He walked her to the door.

"You have a friend here, you know?" He nodded his head toward the door.

Incredulously she asked, "You don't mean Kendrick? What makes you think he's my friend?"

"He came to see me right after he returned from his mission and brought you back. He asked me to see you and help you out." He looked at Annaliese. "You don't know much about him, do you?"

"No. He hated me when we first met. It's been okay since he heard my story. He told my brother that he would take care of me and keep me safe."

"He cares about you, Annaliese. He's a good guy, give him a chance to redeem himself. I know how he treated you. We talked about it. He has some serious regret. Let him tell you about the place he wants to take you to be safe. Kendrick's perfect for your white knight.

Joe walked over to his desk and picked up a business card, "Here's my card. You can call me anytime. My time is free of charge." He put his hand on Annaliese' shoulder, "That microchip is priceless, Annaliese. General Palmer owes you a

debt of gratitude. You've brought about the demise of some dangerous people and seriously dangerous drugs. That's a good thing," he smiled.

Annaliese shrugged her shoulders. "I'm getting paid by keeping what belonged to Diego. So I'm not that great."

"Don't degrade yourself. Aside from the backpacks you are a brave woman. What you decide to do with everything in those packs is up to you. You could do some real good. Don't decide anything until you see where Kendrick wants to take you." Joe opened the door and Kendrick quickly got up from the chair he was sitting in. He looked at Joe, then Annaliese.

"How'd it go? She ready to go with me?" Kendrick was talking to Joe.

"I'm right here, Kendrick. I'm fine, thank you." Annaliese turned to Joe and put out her hand. Joe smiled and put his arms around her.

"I'd rather give you a hug. I think you need a few dozen of them." He released her and stepped back. "I want your promise now, in front of Kendrick. "You'll go with him, you will eat and take good care of yourself. I will keep in touch with him and check on you, unless you want to call me once a week?"

Annaliese was surprised, "You'd do that? Talk to me once a week no matter where I go?"

"We're friends now, Annaliese. Friends keep in touch." He looked at Kendrick, "Take good care of our girl." Joe went back in to his office and they were alone.

Annaliese looked at Kendrick who seemed to be waiting for her to say something. "Okay, what's this place you want to take me to?"

"Why don't we go back to your place and talk about it over some lunch?" Kendrick held his arm out toward the elevator.

22

Instead of going straight back to the duplex, Kendrick took Annaliese for a drive around the base. She enjoyed the drive, especially since he didn't demand that she talk. Nor did he ask any questions about her time with Joe. Leaning back in her seat, she let her mind go blank while looking out the window. There wasn't much to see. The base was fairly small, but very attractive with desert landscaping. Rocks were a part of each building's plants and shrubs and they were colorful in red, gold and yellow tones.

"Is this a secret base? I mean do people know about this place and what you do here?"

Kendrick smiled, "Of course people know the base is here – it's an Army base, with planes taking off and landing. But our missions are almost all secret. That's why we all live on the base. The hospital is accessible to the public because they also treat civilians in the area. But it's impossible to go onto the base without clearance. That's why the press was able to hang out waiting to see you. They are gone now, by the way. No press conference was scheduled. You're still there, recovering from your injuries."

They went around a nice park with a little pond filled with ducks. Several children were playing in an area with swings and a climbing square. Annaliese looked at Kendrick, "I didn't see any children where I'm staying. Where do they all live?"

"There is a separate area of small homes and duplexes for the married men." Kendrick drove around another corner and pointed, "Over there is a school for kindergarten through junior high school. The kids move into town for high school. There's a bus that picks them up at the gates to the base. We even have a church. It's non-denominational if you want to attend."

"No, thanks." Annaliese didn't say anything else. Not in this lifetime, she thought.

"Okay, enough touring. I'm hungry. Seen enough?"

"Yes, I'm done. Thanks. It's a nice place." Annaliese was ready to leave the base. She wanted to find a home, even temporarily, where she could be comfortable and feel at peace. It had been so long since she had read a book, watched TV or baked cookies. She was a good cook and missed being in a kitchen preparing meals for Mathias and her friends.

Kendrick broke into her thoughts, "What's got your wheels turning?" he chuckled. "You're lost in thee. Where did you go?"

"I was just thinking how long it had been since I had read a book or watched TV or...." she sighed. "It's not important, I was just daydreaming." She was getting too sad thinking about what she had lost. Joe had told her she would mourn the loss of time. She would go through different fazes in order to deal with the last seven months – almost like losing a loved one.

"Yeah, I know. You're strong, though. Don't forget that." He turned into the driveway on the opposite side from where she was staying.

"Wait! You're on the wrong side!"

Kendrick parked the car and looked at Annaliese. "I live here." He took the keys out of the ignition and got out. Annaliese smiled. He was such a control freak! She was practically under his thumb! It shouldn't make her smile.

"Well, you don't have far to go to get home. What do you want for dinner? You bought all the food so you ought to know." Annaliese waited for him to unlock the door. She didn't even have a key.

"Come on, Annaliese. Let's go cook together." Kendrick clapped his hands together and rubbed them back and forth.

They decided on steaks on the grill, potatoes and salad. Together, they prepared the meal, working side by side. Kendrick used the inside grill and even made his own barbeque sauce.

Annaliese enjoyed the time with Kendrick. When the lunch was ready, she ate with relish. They talked a little about what foods they liked and restaurants that they had been to in different cities. Kendrick helped clear the table and loaded the dishwasher as Annaliese rinsed the dishes. When everything was done, Kendrick poured a cup of coffee and another cup of tea for Annaliese. They took their cups into the living room and got comfortable on the couch, sitting almost side by side.

"My aunt and uncle live on a ranch in Montana. It's a working cattle ranch, but in addition to that there is a sanctuary for abandoned and mistreated animals. I'm half-owner and I live there when I'm not being a soldier. It's in a place where you can get lost for a while. You can help out if you want or just rest and relax. My Aunt Linda was a psychologist and my Uncle Ray was a stockbroker in New York City. They lived in a big penthouse and made big bucks.

"Before my dad passed away, he contacted them and asked them to consider taking over with me and keep the place going. Originally, they had equally inherited the ranch, but my uncle wanted to work and live in New York. He met his wife there, so he never came back except to visit. By the time my dad was dying, they had tired of the big city and decided they were ready to give up the money and the penthouse. We had a foreman and several good cowboys so it was easy for them to come back and take over.

With their backgrounds and contacts for fundraising, the sanctuary has really grown. Animals come in from all over the U.S." Annaliese could tell he loved the ranch.

"It's a beautiful place. I think you'd be happy there." Kendrick waited for Annaliese to consider what he told her.

She was thinking that she might enjoy being in the country, surrounded by animals It sounded like heaven. "Do your Aunt and Uncle know about me?" she asked, hoping they didn't know everything.

"Yes, I called them and they'd love to have you for as long as you want to stay." Kendrick looked relieved, it might not be so hard to convince her after all.

"I will take leave. I've got about six weeks before I need to come back. We'll fly up as soon as I get the nod from my superior officer. Okay?" He looked hopeful.

"It shouldn't take but a day or two to get clearance. In the meantime, we can shop for some clothes for you to wear. You must be tired of your uniform and the sweats, huh?" he smiled.

"Yes. I haven't worn normal clothes in a very long time." She smiled at him. He looked so different now. She thought he was so tough and scary before. Joe might be right. Maybe he was a nice guy.

"Okay," Kendrick got up and walked to the kitchen. He washed his cup and put it away in the cupboard. "We'll shop tomorrow. Get a good night's sleep." He walked to the door. "You're safe here. Your bedroom wall is the same as mine. If you get scared, just knock on the wall and I'll be here in a flash." He winked at Annaliese and went out the front door, pausing to set the lock.

"I can answer the door, you know," she chided him.

Kendrick grinned and handed Annaliese the paper bag. "Ummm, this smells good!" she said, smiling up at Kendrick.

"They're from a great little bakery in the PX. I thought we'd spoil ourselves this morning with some doughnuts."

He plunked himself down on a chair at the table and leaned back looking at Annaliese. He reached over, opened the sack took out a fat, sugary doughnut and took a huge bite.

Annaliese laughed at him and did the same thing. Her lip gloss made the sugar stick to her lips. Kendrick looked at her and thought about kissing the sugar away. He'd really scare her if he kissed her, he thought. She looked so happy and relaxed for the first time since he met her.

Even in her black uniform with no makeup, her beauty overwhelmed him. He was content to stare at her while she ate. Her silver blonde hair and icy blue eyes were like nothing he had ever seen before. She was graceful when she walked and moved around the kitchen, fixing her tea and putting napkins on the table. He was fascinated and very attracted to her.

Annaliese wiped her hands on her napkin and smacked her lips. "Thank you so much! I haven't had a doughnut in so long! It was delicious." She smiled again and Kendrick tucked his hands under his legs to keep from touching her. "I'll wash up and be ready to go in a jiffy." She bounced away from the table with energy he hadn't seen before. Suddenly, it dawned on him -- she hadn't been sick this morning!

"Hey!" he hollered. "How's your stomach? You ate that doughnut down so fast, I hope you won't be sick." Kendrick laughed, "Maybe we better take a plastic bag with us so you don't throw up in my car." He waited to hear her reply.

Annaliese came back into the kitchen, "I'll have you know I did not get sick this morning and I feel just fine," she said smugly.

"Wow! Maybe you turned a corner and you're over the stomach thing." He waited for her at the door. She was still smiling as she walked toward him.

"I can only hope. But, I feel pretty good and ready to shop till I drop!" She walked out the open door giggling. Kendrick thought it was a wonderful sound.

The shopping trip was a new thing for Kendrick. He had bought gifts for girlfriends before, but he had never shopped for an entire wardrobe. When they got to the lingerie department, he left Annaliese and went to the snack bar for a soda. He had really wanted to stay with her and help her pick out some frilly underwear, but she had shooed him away. He had seen a couple things he would like to see her wear.

They finished up the shopping trip with lunch. Annaliese was in a good mood and excited with her purchases. She had overpaid him in cash, not allowing him to help her out except to bring her to the PX. That was okay. She needed to feel independent.

On the short drive back to the duplex, Kendrick noticed that Annaliese looked tired. He hoped she hadn't done too much. He didn't want anything to happen to her. He carried five bags of purchases inside the duplex. She fussed that he was babying her, but her sparkle was gone. After a trip to the bathroom, she looked like a soft breeze would knock her over.

"Okay. I have some things I need to do. I'll come over later and we can go out for dinner or I'll fix us something." He watched Annaliese yawn. "Does that work for you?"

Annaliese shyly smiled. "That will be fine. I think I'll put my feet up for a while."

Kendrick walked to the door, "I had a good time. I'll see you later." He looked at her.....God! She's so beautiful! He wished he could stay, but he wouldn't push. It was too soon to want more from her. He felt guilty.

Two hours later, Kendrick couldn't wait anymore. His leave was approved and the plans for flying to Montana were complete. He wanted to be with Annaliese. He knocked, but she didn't answer it. He waited, then put in his key and opened the door. The house was quiet. Kendrick walked down the hall and pushed open her bedroom door. Annaliese was curled around the shopping bags, sound asleep. Her silver hair was spread out around her head. He wanted to lie down behind her and pull her against him.

Kendrick sat down on the edge of the bed and watched her sleep. Her lips were slightly pursed and she lightly huffed when she breathed in and out. He wanted to lean over and kiss her lips, but he chickened out and touched her cheek instead.

Slowly, her gorgeous eyes opened and she looked at Kendrick. He was surprised to see so much sadness. "Did you have a nice nap?" he asked.

Annaliese sat up and looked around. She looked so lost. Kendrick knew something had changed. "You want to tell me what's wrong? You came back from shopping smiling and now you're looking like your dog just died." He smiled at her.

Annaliese frowned, "I feel so lost. The life I had is gone, and I'm faced with a new responsibility so big I can't even think about it." Annaliese stood and picked up one of the bags. She pulled out her purchases and started taking off tags and folding them for packing. "I don't know if I want to go with you, but I have nowhere else to go." She sniffed and looked at Kendrick, "I don't even know you and I certainly don't know your aunt and uncle. I'm going someplace I've never been before. What if I hate it there? What if they don't like me? I could bring so much trouble there if the press and the people involved with Diego find me!" She balled up the empty sack and threw it across the room.

"Hey! I thought we had this all settled. My aunt and uncle live several miles out of town on a ranch. They are the kindest people you ever want to meet. I told them about you and they WANT you to come to the ranch. End of story – you're going! Now you finish packing. We're leaving tomorrow morning – early!" Kendrick walked out and Annaliese heard the front door slam shut.

A few seconds later she heard the door open again. Kendrick came back in to the living room. "Annaliese!" He stopped when he saw her, "The ranch is beautiful, with lots of animals, a big lake, good food and nice people. There will be no pressure for you to do anything. You'll have lots of time to rest – I can guarantee your privacy and safety there." Annaliese still looked sad.

"Come on Annaliese, I know you don't have a lot of reason to, but will you trust me? Give this a try. If it doesn't work out, then we can do something else. I'll find you another place equally private and safe."

Annaliese looked at Kendrick in amazement. She started laughing, then almost hysterical, she sobbed, "I'm a freak! I'm going to a rescue sanctuary for abused and abandoned animals. How appropriate!" She was laughing so hard she could hardly get her breath.

Kendrick hurried to her and grabbed her. He tried shaking her, but she still kept laughing. He put his arms around her and held on, whispering soothing words and rubbing her back. Gradually, the laughing slowed and stopped. She sniffed, "I need a hankie. You got one?" Annaliese pushed away and walked to the bedroom. Kendrick followed her, concerned with her behavior. He wondered if he should call Joe and have him talk to her again.

Annaliese got a Kleenex and wiped her eyes and nose. "The show's over for the night. You can leave now," she said sarcastically and turned her back on Kendrick.

"Whoa, whoa, whoa, sweetheart. It doesn't work like that." Kendrick turned her around. "I'm sticking to you like glue. You're not a goddamn freak! You're a beautiful woman who's had a shit load of trouble and has done a damn good job of handling it! I'm not gonna' let you climb into a tub of regret and stay there! You got that?" he hollered. "I'm part of the reason you're feeling so bad. I'm gonna' make it right for you. You're gonna' love the ranch. Give yourself some time, please?"

"I'm now one of the rescue animals. I'm a hopeless case you're trying to help. I'm broken, Kendrick! How do you think that makes me feel?" At least she was mad now. That was better than the hysterical laughter, he thought. "Stop. Enough pity for one night. Just like a soldier who's lost an arm or a leg, you're gonna' get past these feelings and find a new life filled with happiness." Kendrick waited until she looked at him.

"Here's what you're gonna' do: shower, pack, eat dinner, and sleep. I'll be back in one hour with sandwiches and soup. Tomorrow, be ready to go at 8 o'clock. We'll have some light breakfast before we leave." Kendrick looked sternly at Annaliese. "Those are orders." He left her duplex, hoping he was doing the right thing.

23

Major Jackson Kendrick took control of the Cessna 210, turbo-charged airplane. After they were airborne, he retracted the landing gear, banked to the left and after eight hours and one stop for fuel, flew Annaliese to a landing strip in the middle of the most beautiful prairie she had ever seen. It was such a smooth flight that she slept like a baby for the last four hours, curled up hugging Diego's backpack.

Several times, Kendrick wanted to wake her up to keep him company and see the countryside and cities below the airplane, but he knew she needed to rest. Before they left the base, he had called Joe and talked to him about Annaliese' breakdown. Joe told him that she was 'downloading' her months of captivity, and this wouldn't be the last time she experienced an episode. As far as her constant fatigue, that was due to both the pregnancy and the trauma. With a great deal of patience and support she would recover, not overnight ---it could take months. More important than that, she had not yet come to grips about the baby she carried. She needed more counseling. Joe told Kendrick his Aunt Linda could subtly help her, since she had been a psychologist before retiring to Montana.

Kendrick told Joe that he was becoming more attached and attracted to Annaliese. Joe told him to tread lightly and not to overwhelm her. His support was very important, but not so much that she felt, once again, that she was under a man's control. Joe told Kendrick to put him on speed dial for any problems, and to get her to an Ob-Gyn as soon as possible.

They landed on the ranch's private air strip just after dinner time. A jeep pulled up shortly after they landed. A tall handsome man with a big cowboy hat and sheepskin jacket jumped out of the jeep and trotted over to the plane. As soon as Kendrick hopped down, he enveloped him in a huge hug and they both laughed. Kendrick turned to Annaliese and helped her down and into the arms of the cowboy. She was grateful that Kendrick had made her purchase a heavy coat, scarf and gloves for the temperature was very cold. She could see her breath like heavy smoke.

"Annaliese this is Uncle Raymond," Kendrick laughed.

Annaliese recovered from her surprised hug and smiled at Uncle Ray. "And what do I call you besides cowboy?" she smiled.

"How about Ray?" He gazed at her, "You're every bit the beauty, just like Jackson described you." He reached out and took Annaliese' hand, "We're very pleased to have you here, young lady. We want you to just relax and enjoy your stay for as long as you can put up with us. Feel free to enjoy the ranch and all the amenities – just make yourself at home."

Ray looked at Kendrick, "Let's load up the jeep with your luggage and get you both to the warm house. Linda and Grace, have some great cookin' for you to enjoy!"

Annaliese enjoyed listening to Kendrick and Ray catch up on ranch business while they drove to the 'main house,' as they called it. She watched the enormous Montana sky slowly turn from blue to a deep pink and purple as the setting sun ordered a myriad of color in the last gasp of light. She could hear the lowing of the cattle as they huddled together and prepared to bed down for the night. Breathing in, she smelled the clean, crisp air with a hint of pine---it was lovely!

Annaliese' knew she was going to really enjoy staying at the ranch after the delicious dinner made by Linda and their cook, Grace. The two women were warm and welcoming to her and invited Annaliese to cook or bake whenever she wanted to help out in the kitchen. They had talked about recipes, and she told them about the Scandinavian foods and desserts she learned to make from her mother and grandmother. They were eager to have her cook and share her recipes.

After dinner, Kendrick pulled Annaliese away from the women and gave her a quick tour of the house. The ranch house had been built in the 1930's, but had been updated three times. Three stories and a basement was packed with beautiful antique furniture that shined with the oiled brightness of loving hands.

A wide planked veranda surrounded the entire house. Large rocking chairs with thick pillows were strategically placed for the ranch views, inviting family and guests to linger outside. No matter which place you looked, the views were breathtaking: from the snow-laden pastures, the distant snow-topped mountains to the tree lined ice bound lake. It was beautiful and Annaliese felt a sense of peace descend over her and…. total exhaustion!

Annaliese dragged herself behind Kendrick to the bedroom she would be using during her stay. She was too tired to pay much attention to her surroundings, just enough to say goodnight to Kendrick, slip into her nightgown and lay her head on the pillow. In the morning she would explore the ranch on her own. She loved animals and wanted to spend time in the sanctuary. Maybe they could use a volunteer to help clean and feed them. It's funny, she thought as she went to sleep, I think I might be happy here.

The morning dawned with bright sunshine through the lace curtains in Annaliese' bedroom. She yawned and stretched enjoying the plush mattress and thick quilts. She felt something lying on top of her foot. She looked down and saw the ugliest cat she'd ever seen. It was a brown and white tabby with one white paw. One of its ears was sliced down the middle and the other was missing the top half. When the cat looked up at her and yawned, she saw it had only one eye and was missing some teeth.

The cat stretched out its paw, looked at Annaliese, then snuggled back down in the covers. She smiled, "Well good morning, my friend." This poor thing must be one of the rescues. It was a good thing she liked cats. She cautiously reached out and touched the cat's head. It stretched again and began to purr. Annaliese rubbed his head and stroked his plump body. The purring grew louder and made her laugh.

Someone had made a fire in the fireplace while she was sleeping. Probably Kendrick looking out for her as she slept. She could feel the warm glow of the burning logs and snuggled down into the soft bed and dozed. When she awoke later, the fire was still burning with logs that looked newly placed on the iron stand. The cat was gone, her robe now on the end of the bed and her slippers nearby on the floor.

She didn't remember putting them there before falling into bed. Another Kendrick favor, she'd bet. The thought made her smile.

Dressed warmly and ready for the day, Annaliese went down to the kitchen. The wonderful smell of baking cinnamon bread drew her to the kitchen and made her stomach growl.

I'm not nauseated, she thought with a thrill! When she stepped in to the room, two smiling faces greeted her, "Good morning! I hope you slept well," Linda said as she gave Annaliese a hug. Grace took her hand and gave her a cup of tea, "What a nice addition to our kitchen you are Annaliese." The two older women made her feel as though she was family, as though mother and aunt had greeted her. She could get used to this feeling.

"Yes, I slept very well, thank you. I had the strangest bed partner," she laughed.

The women exchanged curious looks, then looked at Annaliese. "How strange?" Grace asked.

"It was the most beat up cat I have ever seen!"

Grace laughed, "Its old Custer. Did he have one eye and sliced up ears?"

"Yes, poor thing. He purred when I petted him, and I went back to sleep. He was gone when I got up this morning."

"Well he moves around wherever he wants to go. He focuses in on one person or animal at a time. It seems like he knows when he's a comfort and when it's okay to move on. We found him beside the road a few years back. A car had hit him and left him for dead.

We saw him move when we drove past and stopped and brought him to the Sanctuary. We almost had to put him down, but he rallied and healed up. We named him Custer because we figured this was his last stand." The women laughed.

The kitchen door opened with a whoosh of cold air. Kendrick walked in bundled up in winter gear carrying a clear plastic dish filled with…. Oh, my, gosh! Strawberries! He presented them to Annaliese with a flourish. "Good morning, Annaliese! Here's a treat for your breakfast. Fresh strawberries from our greenhouse just for you." He looked pleased with himself.

"How did you know I love strawberries? Thank you! I'll share them." Annaliese was touched by his thoughtfulness. She didn't know if she should assume he had been the one to make her fire, add the log and put out her robe and slippers, but she was pretty sure he was. All of a sudden, she felt shy. She would ask him later, when they were alone.

"Nah, they're all yours, Lissy. You just enjoy them. There's more in the greenhouse. I'll show you around after you eat. I'll finish up outside and be back to get you. Enjoy!" Kendrick opened the door and left the room. His aunt and Grace watched him go, "That boy is such a sweetheart."

Annaliese watched him leave and wondered if they had any idea of his other side. But he sure was different now, since he knew her story. She was beginning to like him --- a lot. But that was wrong. She couldn't afford to become attached to any man. Not now.

Annaliese sighed and finished her breakfast. After clearing her dishes and thanking the women, she hurried up the stairs to her room.

Her new coat was perfect for the cold Montana morning. The thick collar had buttons so she could remove the hood she needed today. She added a colorful blue plaid scarf around her neck before she zipped up her coat and pulled on thick, fleece- lined gloves. Kendrick had picked out her boots. The calf-high boots had thick rubber soles and a water proof coating on the leather. She felt like she was warm enough for the North Pole. Trudging down the stairs, she was careful not to trip and fall in her stiff new boots. By the time she reached the kitchen, Kendrick had returned and was drinking a cup of coffee waiting for her.

When he saw her, Kendrick held his breath. Even all bundled up, she took his breath away. He put his coffee cup in the sink and walked over to Annaliese. He needed to touch her. Reaching forward he touched her cheek with the back of his fingers and smiled at her. Embarrassed, he quickly took her hood and pulled it over her beautiful hair. "Let's go." The kitchen was too quiet. Both his aunt and Grace were watching them. As Kendrick guided Annaliese outside, Linda and Grace exchanged looks and smiled. Nothing was said.

They were walking toward the sign that said Animal Sanctuary when the wind blew Annaliese into Kendrick. He caught her around the waist and steadied her with a chuckle, "We call this wind a 'chinook' around here. It can either heat us up in the summer or cool us down in the winter. Right now I'd say we're in for some pretty cold temps. I'll have to take the tractor out with a wagon full of hay for the cattle and horses in case everything freezes and they can't get to their feed. You can come along if you'd like."

"Oh! I think I'd like that. I've never ridden on a tractor before."

"You won't have to worry about being cold, the tractor has heating and air conditioning." Kendrick opened the gate and pulled her into the first barn, out of the wind, "We'll take along some hot coffee and sandwiches. You'll have a great tour of the ranch land this way."

Annaliese got a brief tour of the Sanctuary, but knew it was a place she would return to many times. The volunteers working there were warm and welcoming to her and encouraged her to come back any time. The one place she had difficulty leaving was when Kendrick took her into the nursery. Annaliese was infatuated with the babies. She slowly walked along the rows containing different newborns, exclaiming and murmuring endearments to each one as she passed. He explained to her that newborn calves, goats and sheep from the ranch were lovingly cared for in the Sanctuary, as well as those animals they received from the public.

Stalls and cages of all sizes were filled with an amazing collection of animals. Annaliese was surprised that there wasn't a lot of animal noise considering how many there were. When she encountered babies with bandages and tubes her face filled with pain and she murmured soft words and looked like she wanted to cry.

Kendrick let her take her time here. His mind was churning with ideas. This could be a place that Annaliese could begin to heal. Helping those unable to care for themselves and were innocent victims might serve a serious and healthy purpose. Kendrick watched Annaliese and waited for her with quiet patience. He didn't want to hurry her in any way.

She was relaxed and enjoying herself, interacting with the two volunteers.

Denise and Jonathan Ross were the first to volunteer to help the Sanctuary animals. Both he and Ray trusted them implicitly to know when to save, treat and release, and when to end the life of the young ones who came to this section. They were a married couple who didn't know each other when they showed up one day and offered to help in their spare time.

As a result of being together after only a few months, they fell in love and married. A bungalow was built for them and in exchange for their volunteer services, they lived rent and utility free.

Denise went back to school and received a degree as a Paraveterinary Technician and trained Jonathan to help her. They were able to treat the animals on their own when the full time veterinarian was busy in other areas of the Sanctuary. They made a great team and the ranch was proud to have them as workers and friends. In addition to them, a revolving crew of twelve volunteers made the Sanctuary a successful place for rescued animals.

Finally, Annaliese looked around searching for Kendrick. When she saw him the smile she gave him lit up his insides. Yes, he thought. I've found the perfect place for her: I found the hook to keep her here at the ranch. He returned her smile and held out his hand for her to hold. After a brief hesitation, she took it. They walked back out into the wind and he showed her the rest of the Sanctuary. At the end she turned to Kendrick, "I want to work here each day. Okay with you?"

Annaliese looked up at Kendrick and waited. "I know I'm not trained, but Denise told me to report to her and she would train me to help out."

"I think that would be great! I watched you and I think you're a natural caregiver. I'm very glad you want to help out."

Kendrick wanted to hug her. She was standing next to him holding his hand. He was tempted to pull her in to him, but scared. The decision was taken from him when he heard his name being called.

"Hey, Jackson! You're gonna run out of daylight if you don't get on that tractor and deliver the hay to the troops out on the range." Uncle Ray bellowed.

"We're on our way, Ray." Kendrick tugged on Annaliese' hand and started walking out of the Sanctuary and down to another even bigger barn.

"This is our vehicle barn. We have several so that we can cover the ranch in an emergency." He chose a really large tractor and slung his backpack with their coffee and lunch, up in the interior and turned to Annaliese.

"Okay, climb aboard and I'll hook up the wagon. The ranch hands loaded it up so all we have to do is hook it up and take off."

Annaliese felt she was sitting on top of the world. The tractor had large windows so she could see a 360 degree view. Kendrick fired up the heater and soon they were very comfortable. The large engine would have made talking impossible but for the air tight cabin. Kendrick kept a running commentary and description of the areas, what they did there, and information about the animals. The bright red tractor stood out in the white winter land they drove through.

When they seemed to be in the middle of nowhere, Kendrick stopped and jumped down, grabbing a large pitch fork, and shoveled out a big portion of hay. Soon, Annaliese saw the cattle moving toward the food. One started, then two, then a group and more came walking up and started eating. Annaliese laughed when several of the white faces looked up at her with globs of hay hanging out of their mouths as they chewed.

Kendrick jumped back in the tractor and off they went to another place a mile or so away. Two hours later, as they were heading back to the ranch house, they came upon an abandoned stone house with a big bubbling fountain in front. He sat for a moment and stared at the house. "This is the original homestead from the 1800's. My great-great grandparents built it and my relatives lived here until our present home was built. The fountain is fed by an artesian spring. It comes up twenty-four hours a day every day, even during the deepest, coldest winter. We draw on it all over the ranch; best water in the world!"

He turned and looked at Annaliese. "Isn't that amazing?"

It was clear that Kendrick loved the entire ranch for its beauty and because it represented his family's roots. The house was still surrounded by trees and an old rock Wall.

She looked forward to seeing this place when the snow melted. Then, she realized that would mean a few months.....would she still be here – maybe so.

24

The next morning, Annaliese awoke early, dressed quickly and hurried down the stairs. The kitchen already had breakfast smells emanating from the oven. A pot of tea was already steeping, and Grace turned from the stove to smile a morning welcome at her. "Well, aren't you bright eyed and bushy tailed?"

Annaliese smiled back. She felt good and looked forward to going out to the Sanctuary. "So that you don't have to wait on me, would you mind showing me where the cups are and the silverware? And don't forget, I could help you prepare meals, if you'd like."

"Well, aren't you thoughtful? I would love to have your help when you're available. But, don't you worry about when you're outside and helping out there. Usually, Linda and I run the kitchen just fine. We're still interested in sharing some of your recipes, don't forget." Grace was opening drawers and cupboards, showing Annaliese where everything was kept. "We want you to make yourself at home here, for as long as you stay."

Annaliese poured a cup of tea while Grace pulled out a breakfast casserole from the oven.

Several pieces had already been cut away, so she knew she was the last to eat. "That looks very good, Grace. Have you eaten already?" She cut a small square and placed on a plate.

"Is that all you're going to eat? That's not enough to feed a bird, young lady, and you're eating for two." She was matter of fact and not looking at Annaliese when she said it, bustling around the kitchen.

Annaliese paused, her stomach clenched. She didn't know that Kendrick had told them she was pregnant. How embarrassing, she thought, what must they think? She stared down at her plate, not eating, wondering what she should say. Grace felt the silence and looked at Annaliese then realized her faux pas.

Grace walked over to Annaliese' back and patted her. "I'm real sorry, honey. I wasn't supposed to let you know I knew about the baby. Jackson is gonna kill me. I want you to know we are 100% in support of you. We love babies of any kind here. Anything we can do to help you we will do it. Yes, we all know that you were kidnapped, held for seven months and are pregnant. We don't know, and don't need to know, any of the details. He only told us so that we can help you heal. You're a smart, beautiful young woman who's been through hell. Kendrick brought you here because it's the perfect place for you to get back on your feet. Please don't feel bad. You've got nothing to be embarrassed or ashamed about. Forgive me for blabbing. You're here to heal and make some decisions about your life. I'll do anything for you. Please don't be upset." Grace leaned forward and hugged Annaliese.

Annaliese sat quietly. She didn't know what to say. When Grace hugged her, a tear crept down her cheek. They all knew, she thought. But they have all been so nice to her – they really didn't care about her circumstances and wanted her here. She had to deal with her circumstances and stand proud with any decision she made. This was a good place.

"Don't worry, Grace," Annaliese put her hand over Graces, "I won't tell Kendrick. It's okay. I have to be brave and stop letting this get me down. I feel safe here." She squeezed Grace's hand before she let it go.

After finishing her breakfast, Annaliese donned her coat, scarf, gloves and boots and waded out to the sanctuary. It had snowed during the night and was even colder today. When she reached the barn it was full of activity. Kendrick was helping Jonathan and Denise with a baby goat that had wounds around its neck where a chain had left deep cuts. His voice was low and soothing as he encouraged the goat to let them treat the wounds. Annaliese held still and watched them work as a team. Kendrick was a big man with strong hands, yet he gently held the little goat and soothed it with words. It was a beautiful sight.

Kendrick knew Annaliese had come into the barn, but couldn't look up. She didn't say a word, just waited. He finally looked up at her, their eyes locked. He smiled, she returned his smile, and they both felt a pull between them. Denise and Jonathan finished bandaging the baby goat and after washing his hands, Kendrick walked to Annaliese. "Hi. Did you sleep well?" His voice sent a warm chill down her arms.

"Yes. I had breakfast and couldn't wait to come out here. It's cold this morning, but the barn is heated and it's feels good in here." Annaliese walked over to the baby goat. "Will it be okay?" She reached out and the goat shied away from her hand.

"He's head shy we think from being smacked around and chained. It will take a while for him to trust anyone." Denise shook her head. She put him in a small pen and closed the door. "We'll work with him, he's young and eventually we'll have him eating out of our hands. Then he can be adopted." She smiled at Annaliese.

"Isn't it difficult to give them away? When you take care of them don't you become attached?" She leaned over the fence and touched the goat's head. This time it didn't back away when she scratched its head. She was thinking about the baby she carried. Could she give birth to a child and give it away?

Denise took Annaliese under her wing and started teaching her the sanctuary routines. At first Annaliese wasn't sure she could help treat the wounds, but she was stronger than she thought. When Denise plunged her in to help with a wounded dog, before she knew it, she was cleaning and bandaging the dog and moved on to re-bandage other rescued animals with Denise. At the end of the day, Annaliese looked around, pride filling her heart as she saw the animals filling the little cages and pens. She had made a difference. It was a wonderful feeling.

The volunteers stopped for lunch and ate sandwiches that Grace had sent out for them. It was a friendly group and Annaliese was relaxed with them.

It was fun listening to their stories and heartwarming to know that these people gave so much of their time for free. After lunch the staff took out the animals who needed exercise and attention. Annaliese took one of the dogs who had been burned on its back. Denise told her that the poor thing would never grow back all of its hair, but already because of its wonderful disposition, a single woman in town wanted to adopt him. Annaliese enjoyed playing with the dog and reluctantly returned him to his cage. The afternoon passed quickly and she said goodbye to the Sanctuary crew telling them she would be back the next day.

When she entered the kitchen, Kendrick turned to look at her. He saw her eyes shining with accomplishment. Denise had taken him aside earlier and told him how helpful Annaliese had been today. She thought she would be an asset to the sanctuary. Kendrick proudly smiled at Annaliese.

"How was your day? You look tired. I hope it wasn't too much for you." He helped her take off her coat and hung it up on the coat rack. When he knelt down to help her with her boots, she tried to push him away. "I can do that, really. But, thank you, Kendrick." Annaliese bent over and loosened the ties.

"Hey, let me help. You look tired." Kendrick refused to get up and made her let him help with her boots.

With a sigh, Annaliese gave up, "I feel tired, but it's a good tired. I really enjoyed helping Denise. In just a few hours I learned so much. I know why people want to volunteer here in the sanctuary," her smile grew wider.

"I can't wait for tomorrow." She walked over to Grace who was cooking on the stove, "Can I help you with dinner?"

"No ma'am, you just wash up and sit yourself down at the table. I've got it all handled." Grace pushed her toward the bathroom. She smiled at Kendrick. After Annaliese closed the bathroom door, Kendrick said, "She needs an appointment with a doctor for her pregnancy. Can you help her do that tomorrow? I don't want to push her, but you could," he whispered.

"Don't you worry, I got a recommendation for a doctor in town and I'll get her to make an appointment tomorrow." Grace shooed Kendrick away, "Now go wash up and let Ray and Linda know we're ready to eat."

"Okay, I'm going." Kendrick ran up the stairs whistling.

Dinner was a happy affair. The food was plentiful and as good as always. Grace was a wonderful cook. Ray and Linda talked about the herds of cattle and horses and how well they were doing with the cold and snow. The trips Kendrick had made taking out the hay was working well. They all talked about the weather and decided the latest reports meant that spring was coming. Then talk changed to Kendrick and how much leave he had left.

Annaliese looked surprised. "Are you leaving soon?" She looked at Kendrick and held her fork full of food near from her mouth.

"I have a couple of weeks left. Lots of time," he smiled at everyone.

"Well, I've sure enjoyed having you be here for more than just a few days. It takes a lot of pressure off me and Steven, and lets us concentrate on the spring roundup and marketing the herd. And, I like sharing the ranch and having you around during meal time, too. Any time you want to trade full time soldiering for ranching I'd be a very happy man to have you around." Ray looked at Kendrick waiting for his response. He and Linda loved Kendrick like the son they never had, and worried about Kendrick every time he left and returned to his base.

"I know you guys worry about me and I'm sorry about that. You know I take great care when I'm on a mission, but it's true that things can happen. I'm getting older and it may be time I thought about retiring. I've been doing some thinking. Maybe it's time I make a big change in my life." He looked down at his plate, concern written on his face.

Linda reached out and squeezed his hand. We don't mean to put pressure on you, Jackson, but you know how we worry."

"I know and I hate that you do. I've been a soldier for a long time. It's been my way of life, except for a few weeks each year, but I've been thinking about changing that." He looked at Annaliese as he talked. Ray and Linda exchanged looks and Grace smiled.

Annaliese looked at Kendrick. There was something big being said here. He was talking to her indirectly. She didn't know what to say.

Grace looked at them and decided to help out, "I hope you all left room for dessert. I made a sour cream cake and there's fresh raspberries from the green house and fresh whipped cream to put on top."

She pushed her chair back and started gathering up dishes. "Annaliese, you want to get the raspberries from the back porch for me?"

Annaliese broke her stare with Kendrick and pushed back from the table. Her head was spinning. What did he mean? She had no idea he was thinking about her like that. Walking to the back porch Annaliese was wondering what she should say to him. She felt a tingle of excitement and didn't know why.

Grace served dessert to a quiet table. Very little conversation was exchanged and Annaliese avoided eye contact with Kendrick. As soon as she was finished she excused herself and went into the library. It was her favorite room in the house. One wall had a floor to ceiling bookcase with a ladder that was attached to the shelves and could slide the entire length of the wall. She enjoyed using it to look at the many books. The chairs were deep leather and so comfortable, she struggled not to fall asleep as she read. The red patterned carpet was thick and made footsteps almost silent. Every night a fire was set and glowed brightly with a heavenly smell.

This night, Kendrick joined her and sat in the chair next to her. "I thought I'd join you, if you don't mind." He settled in and opened a thick book. "This is a comfortable room, isn't it?"

Annaliese watched him settle in and smiled, "Yes, it's one of my favorite rooms. I'm starting to really like it here."

"I'm glad, Lissy. This is a really great place to be. Ray and Linda make a really nice home for everyone who comes here. I've always had a deep sense of peace when I come. It's important for me, doing what I do the rest of the time, you know, a constant place I can go to in my mind or in person."

"Yes, I know what you mean. I want to thank you, Kendrick, for bringing me here. Wait - I don't think I want to call you Kendrick anymore. Linda called you Jackson. Do you like being called Kendrick or Jackson? I'd really like to know."

"You can call me whatever name you want, Lissy. I didn't ask if it was okay to call you what your brother calls you, but you don't seem to mind."

Annaliese laughed, "My brother has called me Lissy since we were little kids. It's a special name for me and I don't mind if you use it, if you'd like." She looked at Kendrick, "I think I'll start calling you Jackson. It's not as formal."

"Whatever you'd like." Kendrick looked down and started reading. He looked good sitting there with his plaid wool shirt sleeves rolled up his to his elbows. His face was clean-shaven and looked soft in the lamp light. Annaliese studied his face: he was rugged looking with high cheek bones. She thought he was a very masculine man with strong arms and muscled legs.

He kept his dark blond hair cut short and the shaved area around the bottom was sharply tapered. It had grown out a little since they had been in Montana. He would look even better with longer hair, she thought.

But, soldiers kept their hair very short like this, she knew. His skin was bronzed from the sun. She could see a few little scars on his arms and hands. His eyes had little crow's feet where he squinted from his exposure from long hours working outside in all kinds of weather. She liked that he had long dark lashes and brown eyes. Kendrick suddenly looked at her.

"You're staring," he smiled.

Annaliese was embarrassed. "I'm sorry. I was just thinking." She hadn't meant to say that. He was going to ask what she was thinking about. She waited, but he didn't say anything else. He went back to reading and then so did she.

The large grandfather clock in the corner of the library chimed nine times. Annaliese stretched and put her book on the table between the two leather chairs. "Well, I'd better get to sleep. I'll start early tomorrow in the sanctuary. Denise is training me and I don't want to be late."

Kendrick put his book down also. "I guess it's time to head up for the night." He walked over to the fireplace and banked the fire down and secured the screen. Annaliese waited for him at the doorway and watched him as he turned off the lights.

They walked up the stairs together. At the top, she turned to him, "Good night, Jackson." Her smile was big and her eyes were bright.

"Good night and sleep well, *Lissy*," he said with an equally big smile.

25

Kendrick awoke feeling refreshed and eager for the day to begin. He wondered how Annaliese was feeling. He pictured her getting ready and what she looked like in the early morning. Was she starting to show her pregnancy? She would be a beautiful pregnant woman. It's funny, he thought, he'd never thought about a woman being attractive and pregnant before. He thought about her off and on all day when he was out working on the ranch. Meals and quiet times together in the library were highlights of his day. He'd never been quite so taken with a woman before. She fascinated him with her beauty and spirit. Laying in his bed with his arms crossed behind his head he continued to think about Annaliese. She was getting stronger every day.

The sanctuary and staff had definitely helped. She had told him she was happy here. He hoped so because he wanted her to stay here.....forever. He'd fallen in love with her. It had hit him like a sledgehammer last night in the library. She'd been looking at him, studying his face. She was attracted to him, he knew. Today, he would start getting closer to her and see where this attraction for each other could go. He would be careful not to push too much. She'd had enough of that from Diego.

Ray and Linda had been surprised with his announcement of resigning his commission and remaining on the ranch full time. It had been a long time coming, but he knew he was ready for a wife and family. He'd found the woman he wanted to be with and have children. The only problem was, if she was willing to give him a chance. He had to be patient. He wasn't very good at being patient. Kendrick ran his hands through his hair and looked at himself in the bathroom mirror. Yeah, you, he said to the face he saw looking back at him, you've got to take it slow. If he grabbed her and kissed her like he'd wanted to do last night in the library, she'd run or panic --- or both. Slow and steady. Show her she's more than just a beautiful woman. She was it for him ---now he had to convince her that he wanted her in his life and the baby, too. That child would be his just as if he'd put it in her womb and not Diego. Wouldn't his old friend, Joe Turner, be surprised? She was it for him ---- now he had to convince her that he wanted her in his life and the baby, too. That child would be his just as if he'd put it in her womb and not Diego. Wouldn't his old friend, Joe Turner, be surprised!

When Kendrick walked down stairs for breakfast, Annaliese was in the library talking to someone on her cell phone. He wanted to eavesdrop and find out who and what she was talking about, but he went in to the kitchen.

"Good morning, Jackson," Grace greeted him. "You look bright eyed and bushy tailed this morning."

"Yup. Feeling good, Grace. Heard you're about to be a grandmother again. That's good news, huh?" he smiled.

"I am so happy their having another little one. I love being a grandma so much I hope they have a dozen more!" she laughed.

"This makes three but I can't see too many more young'uns from them. Steven was saying their house is gonna be full as it is."

He started piling pancakes on his plate. "Maybe since I'm gonna be around a little more pretty soon, I can help him add on another room."

"You know Jackson, you can be a pretty nice guy when you put your mind to it," Grace teased.

Kendrick just smiled and poured syrup on his plate then licked his fingers like a kid.

Annaliese came in to the kitchen smiling. "I just talked to my brother. He and Mary have set the wedding for the first Saturday in April. I'm going to be her maid of honor." Her smile faded and she looked pensive. "I'm not looking forward to going back. Everyone will want to ask so many questions." She looked up at Grace who had walked to her side, "It's going to be so different there. Mathias sold my condo and he wants me to stay with him. He wants to keep the wedding small and is telling only close friends about it because he's afraid the newspapers will get word and disturb the wedding ceremony. I told him he might be right and that I could sneak back after they're married but he insisted that I was going to be in the wedding. I'm so torn ---- I want to be there, but I don't want to be in the spotlight having to answer questions. Plus, I don't want people to know I'm pregnant. I'll be so ashamed!" She looked so forlorn Grace put her arms around Annaliese.

"Listen honey, you've got nothing to be ashamed of! None of this was any of your fault. Besides, you still look thin and we'll go shopping and find some clothes that will hide your little baby bump, don't you worry." Grace pulled Annaliese to the table and put her in a chair. "Now you sit right down and eat some breakfast. Jackson, pour Annaliese some tea."

Kendrick sat still listening to Annaliese. He'd wanted to comfort her but Grace had beat him to it. "You want some company for the wedding? I should be back from the Base by then. Your brother and I were becoming friends before he went back to California. I don't think he'd mind if I came along and kept the press away while he's busy with the What do you think?" Kendrick waited for her answer.

"Well, I don't really want to go there alone. If you think you'd like to go, I think that would be okay," she said hesitantly.

Kendrick let out a sigh. He hadn't wanted to insist he go with her, but he was going to go no matter what. She needed him to be at her side. Returning to California was going to be very emotional for her and he wanted to be there.

"Okay. I'll make reservations for us when you tell me the dates we need to leave and then return." Kendrick poured her tea, then juice, and placed bacon and fruit on her plate. Annaliese looked up at him and frowned.

"What? You need sustenance," he tweaked her nose to take the frown away. He knew he was being pushy but he wanted her to eat a good breakfast.

"Bossy!" she chuckled. She didn't mind that he was being bossy because he cared about her.

They finished breakfast while discussing plans for their travel to California. Annaliese won the decision to purchase the plane tickets. After another conversation with her brother, Mathias, it was decided both she and Kendrick would stay at his and Mary's new house.

Mathias had been relieved and pleased that he would accompany his sister. Mary had the last part of the telephone conversation and discussed what Annaliese would wear for her role as maid of honor. They agreed on the dress Mary had sent a picture of it to Annaliese' cell phone. She would purchase the dress and shoes for Annaliese.

Luckily, the lovely blue georgette dress would disguise her pregnancy. Mary had a private conversation with Annaliese and both ended the conversation in tears.

"Now that everything is settled, let's take a walk." Kendrick was holding Annaliese' coat and scarf for her.

Both bundled up for the still cool temperatures, Kendrick and Annaliese walked down the lane dividing the ranch from the sanctuary. The split rail fence seemed to go on forever with cattle and horses grazing amid the snow and grass. Small stacks of hay dotted the land. Annaliese smiled at the winter-wooly horses and cattle. Steam actually hovered around some of the animals who were huddled close together. Kendrick walked close by Annaliese' side, not quite touching her. They chatted about their upcoming trip to California and what they should take with them to wear as well as her work in the sanctuary. Kendrick reminded her that she should see a doctor before they left for their trip.

He was concerned about her flying since she was pregnant. She laughed when she told him he was fussing for no reason. Lots of women flew during this time. As the road became less used, deep ruts in the snowy mud caused Annaliese to stumble. Kendrick immediately took her hand and for the rest of their walk he never let go. It seemed very natural to hold hands, she thought.

An uphill grade ended at the old ranch house Kendrick had shown her when they drove the tractor delivering hay. When Annaliese saw that the fountain was still bubbling, she took off her glove and put her hand into the ice cold water. "Ohhhh! It's so cold! Is it safe to drink this water?"

Kendrick scooped his hands into the water and took a big noisy slurp. "Of course! Don't you remember -- it's our well water for the entire ranch. Mmm, it's deliciously cold! Try it."

Annaliese leaned over and scooped the water into her mouth. "It's so cold my tongue is numb," she laughed.

They sat down side by side on the rough stone wall of the fountain and enjoyed the surrounding beauty of the trees and shrubs grown wild.

"I need to ask your advice about something," she said without looking at him. Kendrick dreaded what she was about to ask. He hoped it didn't concern her pregnancy.

"Go ahead...."

"Well, there was a lot of paperwork in Diego's backpack. It's all written in Spanish, but my name is on every paper. They look like legal papers but I haven't the slightest idea what they are. Since you speak Spanish, will you look them over and let me know what they say?" Annaliese looked at Kendrick. "Diego told me that those backpacks would make me a very wealthy woman. I need to know what those papers represent so that I can make decisions about what to do with them. He also told me that he had dealings with people in Grand Cayman. I know that a lot of off shore banking takes place there." She put her hand on his arm, "Will you help me?"

"Annaliese, Diego was a very wealthy drug dealer --- you realize his money was ill gotten gains, don't you?"

"Ahhh, yes, of course. Diego also had a winery and cotton fields, too. He invested his money from that as well as from the drugs." She looked, pleadingly at Kendrick, "Everything in those backpacks is mine. The government gave it to me for the information I brought them. Now, I'm having his baby. I'm not giving it up. I'll make the decisions about whether to keep it, use it or dump it. I want to know exactly what those documents say." Annaliese got up and started walking back to the house. She turned, "If you won't help me, I'll have to find someone who will." She turned back and started walking down the road.

Kendrick trotted after her, "Now, Lissy, I haven't said I wouldn't help you. Of course I'll read them with you sitting by my side in the library. Tonight, if you want." He grabbed her hand and smiled down at her. "Don't get your fur up. You didn't give me a chance to finish what I wanted to say."

Annaliese sighed, "I'm sorry. I guess I feel sensitive about this stuff. I do feel a little guilty, but I'm serious about maybe keeping whatever those papers say I have."

"Okay, let's take a look tonight. I have a lawyer friend, Tom Gepson, in Florida, who will probably be a big help. We can talk to him after I read the documents." He swung her hand back and forth a couple of times and smiled at her. "Feel better now?"

Annaliese smiled, "Yes, I do, as a matter of fact." They continued down the road in comfortable silence. Tonight was going to be interesting, that's for sure, she thought.

When they reached the house, they split up. Annaliese went to the Sanctuary and Kendrick went out to the barn. There were saddles and bridles that needed to be repaired. They called it *down time,* when the weather was so cold, when he and the ranch hands had time to make catch-up repairs to the equipment used all year long.

Dinner time came as the sky darkened early. A storm was approaching again. The ranch hands had made sure the feed was plentiful for the herds and all other areas were battened down in case the wind became too fierce. Tomorrow morning, they would spread out and break the ice in the water troughs so the herds would be able to get a drink. It would be a cold job and not one any of the hands enjoyed, especially if it was still storming. But it was necessary for their survival.

Grace had prepared a thick stew that smelled heavenly. A large pie was cooling on the cupboard near a bowl of whipped cream and a stack of small plates. A mound of fresh butter was sitting on the table with a large basket of thick sliced bread. A huge soup tureen was full of stew topped with large fluffy dumplings. It was a perfect winter meal and Grace had outdone herself. Everyone complimented Grace before even taking their first bite, it smelled that good.

Dinner was enjoyed by everyone as they discussed the coming storm and news around the ranch. Ray and Kendrick talked about the routes the ranch hands would explore after the storm, making sure the cattle and horses had fared well and rescuing any in distress. This was a common job during the winter on all ranches. Old stories were told about mishaps and amazing rescues. Annaliese was enthralled with these stories which made her admire these brave men and women. Survival was always the utmost concern for the herds as well as the ranchers who were out among them almost daily through even the most dangerous conditions.

After Annaliese was through helping clear the table and putting the dishes and left over food away, she found Kendrick waiting for her in the library. She had brought both backpacks down from her room and cleared away a table top to have a place to empty the contents.

Kendrick watched as Annaliese made a pile of documents, then a mound of bags which she had not told him about, on the table. He got up from the chair he'd been sitting in and stepped up to the table. "What's in these bags?"

"I'd rather wait to show you the contents of the bags until we see what these documents are." She pushed them to the side and handed Kendrick the top page of documents. "I will need your help with these as well."

Kendrick took the first document and returned to his chair. Annaliese waited quietly while he studied the document. He had a tablet and pen next to him on the small table between the two chairs they sat in each evening. After he finished reading the document, he got up and exchanged it for another on the stack. He repeated this note taking after reading each document.

Finally, he re-stacked the documents and turned to Annaliese, "Well, Diego was right. I think you just might be one hell of a rich woman. These documents are bank statements and real estate documents that are probably worth a major fortune."

On one of the papers, Diego wrote down all the account numbers and pass words for access to the money and property. You must have signed some papers when you were living at the hacienda because the bank and property statements have you as a signatory and owner. You and Diego have joint bank accounts and are joint property tenants, which means that with Diego Vasquez' death, all this automatically goes to you, according to a document signed and witnessed by an attorney in Grand Cayman. His contact information is listed here as well, so that you can get in touch with him."

"Hmmm, I do remember signing some papers. Diego made me and wouldn't tell me what they were." Annaliese paced the floor, "Can you talk to your lawyer friend in Florida so he can contact the attorney for me? Tell him I can pay for his services. I need to find out all about the accounts and the property and how I go about handling all of this." She was deep in thought, "I wonder if I should go down to Florida and see your friend in person?" Looking up at Kendrick she said, "Maybe I will have to go to Grand Cayman to settle all of this. I don't want to, but I will if I have to. What do you think?"

"I think I will call my friend in the morning and you can be in on the call. He can contact this attorney in Grand Cayman and let you know what's next."

Kendrick was secretly happy that Annaliese was trusting him with all this. There was no way she was going to do any traveling without him. The only catch was, he had to return to duty soon and put in his paperwork to resign his commission and retire. She would have to wait to travel until he could go with her. His friend would make all the contacts and then they would see where they would go from there. He hoped she would wait for him and not go without him along to protect her.

"Okay. That's a good place to start. If you have a fax machine I can send copies of these documents to him. But, I think I should sign some kind of paperwork so that I'm legally protected before we give him all the information, don't you think?"

"Yes, I do. You can trust my friend. We served together in the Army and I would trust him with my life.....I did, in fact." He smiled at Annaliese and walked over to the table with the documents and bags. "Now, what's in these?" he asked as he picked one up and bounced it in his hand.

Annaliese took the bag out of his hand, opened it and poured out the bright stones on the table top.

"Oh, my God!" he exclaimed. "I don't believe this!" Kendrick touched the stones, moving them around. "How many are there?" He looked at Annaliese in shock.

"I haven't counted them, but there are several bags. I'm pretty sure they are real diamonds, and the rest are rubies, sapphires and emeralds. I have no idea what to do with these."

She looked at Kendrick and shrugged. "I have to believe that they are all real. Where Diego got them we'll never know." As she put the gems back in the bags she said, "Do you know of a reputable jeweler, too?"

"Holy hell! I've never seen anything like this! I guess I'll ask Tom, when we talk to him tomorrow. In the meantime, I think you should lock these backpacks up for safe keeping. We have a safe where we keep guns and paperwork for the ranch. If you trust me, you can put them in there. It's fireproof, too. " He waited for her to decide.

Annaliese hesitated. "I guess that would be alright." She needed to trust Kendrick. This was too big a burden to handle by herself and Mathias was too far away to help her. "It's a little overwhelming," she sighed.

"That's an understatement if I ever heard one!" Kendrick stood looking at the treasure trove and rubbed his face. "I think you've just opened a huge fortune cookie, baby. You should probably ask Tom for the name of a good money manager, cuz you're gonna have to figure out where to put the money from all this stuff." He looked at her, "I have no idea about taxes and all the other legal things involved. This could get really crazy, Lissy, but I trust Tom to take good care of you. He'll give you good advice, but for heaven's sake --- don't go off on your own! I have some things to do when I return to the Base in two weeks. I'll be gone several days, but I'll come back and help you. You'll know more tomorrow after we talk to Tom." Kendrick put his hands on her shoulders, "Would you promise me that you will please wait for me to go with you if you travel to Florida or Grand Cayman?" One hand lifted her chin and held her, "Don't make me worry about you, okay?"

Annaliese returned his stare, "All right. I promise to wait for you. We can't travel anywhere until after we go to California to my brother's wedding. I cannot miss Mathias and Mary's big day. We'll see what your friend, Tom, has to say."

They remained still, looking at each other. Slowly, Kendrick lowered his head and put his lips on hers, gentle at first. Annaliese lifted her arms and put her hands around his

his neck. That's all it took. Kendrick put his arms around her and pulled her against him and the kiss went wild. They couldn't get close enough, pulling on each other, and the kiss went on until Annaliese had to push away to catch her breath.

They were both breathing hard, staring at each other. "Oh my," she whispered.

"Yeah. That was pretty amazing," Kendrick whispered back. He started to pull her against him again, but she pushed back.

"I think I'd better go up to my room," she said as she backed away.

"Wait a minute. We need to put these backpacks in the safe, unless you trust me to do it for you?" He waited.

Her lips were swollen and very pink. Kendrick swallowed hard and forced himself to get back into control. He really wanted to hold and kiss her again, but he'd scare her if he grabbed her, which is what he wanted to do. He needed to get away from her and quick.

Grabbing the two backpacks, he stuffed the documents and bags of gems into the biggest one and started walking out of the library.

"Where are you going?" she asked then started to follow him down the hall.

"Go to bed, I'm taking these to the office to lock them up in the safe." He kept walking and didn't look at her. "You can get them out with me in the morning. Now, good night."

Annaliese stopped and watched him go down the hall and turn into the office. She was afraid to follow him. It was too tempting to be alone with him. Her heart was pounding and she still felt their kiss. And, if she followed him into the office, there was no telling what they would end up doing. She went up the stairs chiding herself.

She was a pregnant woman for goodness sake! What the hell had she been thinking? But she admitted to herself that she wanted him to kiss her again. Damn! What a mess!

Annaliese entered her room and almost slammed the door. Leaning back against the closed door she let out a breath and touched her lips.

Wow! He was a good kisser! Better than Derek had ever been, that's for sure. She hoped she could sleep tonight without dreaming about that kiss. Hopefully, their kiss hadn't changed things between her and Jackson.

It was just a fluke and wouldn't happen again. She would make sure of that. Annaliese put on her nightgown, pounded her pillows and got into bed. Jackson Kendrick's face was before her eyes when she closed them. Instead of upsetting her, she felt warm and tingly. She went to sleep remembering the feel of his arms around her.

26

In the morning, Annaliese awoke with her mind churning. She lay there thinking about what she could do with a huge fortune and it suddenly came to her – she knew exactly what she would tell the attorney in Florida. Her face lit up with a smile and she stretched her legs out. There was that lump at the end of her bed, again. Custer raised his head and looked at Annaliese. The cat stretched out one long front leg and then he rolled into a ball and went back to sleep. She stretched again and smiled...she felt so good! There were so many plans to make that she was going to get up and make a list of all she had to do for next week and the wedding.

She hurriedly got ready for the day and then sat down to make lists of all she wanted to talk to the attorney about. Then she planned out a schedule for the following week. She had to make a doctor's appointment – she dreaded that, but Grace would go with her. Going on the internet would take care of shopping for a wedding gift for Mathias and Mary. The only problem was that she didn't have a credit card. She needed to talk to Mathias about her bank account in California. She hadn't even thought about her credit cards and checking account.

Luckily she and Mathias were signatories on each other's accounts. Mathias must have taken care of her accounts and paid off all of her bills.

There would be money from the sale of her condo to spend on her brother and Mary. She would use it to buy them the honeymoon of their dreams.

Knowing Mathias, he had probably made plans for a modest trip lasting only a few days. Well, now he and Mary would celebrate in style! She felt happier than she had in months!

Kendrick awoke in a haze. He hadn't slept well at all and was grumpy as hell. He'd come on too strong with Annaliese. He couldn't help himself. She was so damn beautiful and he had wanted to kiss her for a while. Well, he'd kissed her all right! Trying to sleep after that had left him hot and hard, and now frustrated. He'd have to take a long cold shower before he went down for breakfast. Damn! What a way to start the day.

Annaliese and Kendrick arrived at the kitchen at the same time. He waited for her to say something first, trying to gage her mood. She avoided eye contact and tried to act like nothing had happened last night. Well, okay. He could play that game, too.

"Good morning, Jackson. We can get the backpack after breakfast and then call your friend if you have time." She went to the far side of the table to sit down.

"Yeah, that'd be fine. The time difference is three hours so we'll try to talk to him before his lunch time. I figure we can put the phone on speaker so we can both hear him at the same time." Kendrick sat down near the other end of the table.

Grace watched them dancing around each other and could barely suppress a smile. Who did they think they were kidding? It was as plain as the nose on her face that they were crazy about each other.

Everyone knew it but them, and she couldn't be happier for these two she thought. Who'd a thought that Jackson could fall so hard after the life he's led and the women he's met? He was the perfect hero to save this beautiful girl. He wouldn't quibble over whose baby she was carrying. He had a heart as big as Montana and constantly proved it with all the nice things he did for the Sanctuary and the people around town. It had been his idea to develop the sanctuary in the first place. Even as a little kid, Ray talked about Jackson bringing one animal after the other back to the ranch house that he found out on the range or on the road to town. He'd cry like a baby and have funerals for each and every one that didn't make it. Yes, Grace thought, he'd make a great husband and father.

Ray and Linda joined them and the table was soon filled with food and conversation.

Annaliese was relieved that she could let them talk around her. With so much on her mind, just looking at Jackson made her heart pound. She forced herself to eat and tried not to squirm in her seat with anticipation of their phone call to Jackson's friend. Annaliese felt like today just might change her whole world, again.

Grace gave her the name of the doctor to call for an appointment. Annaliese promised to call as soon as possible and let Grace know when they would go together for her first appointment. She hugged Grace for being so kind and understanding. That would be another life changing event with some serious decisions she would have to make. Kendrick saw a huge frown on her face when she met him in the office.

"Everything all right?" he asked. "You look a little upset." He hoped it had nothing to do with his behavior last night.

"I'm just a little overwhelmed with all I have to do and the decisions I have to make. I'm also nervous about what I'm going to find out when we talk to your attorney friend, Tom." She looked so vulnerable. Kendrick wanted to put his arms around her and give her some comfort --- make her feel safe. But he couldn't do that yet.

"Well, here's your backpack. Let's get started on the phone call to Tom." Kendrick pulled a second chair over to the desk and sat down, motioning Annaliese to sit next to him.

"Pull out the documents while I get Tom on the phone." He dialed the number and took out a notebook and pencil, handing them to Annaliese. He mouthed, "For notes and things he'll tell us we need to do." Kendrick reached and took Annaliese hand and squeezed it then he placed it on the table and patted it before taking his hand away. He smiled encouragement at her hoping to make her feel more at ease.

Kendrick got through to Tom in his office and greeted him in Spanish. They spoke for several minutes, laughing and what she thought must be reminiscing. Finally, Kendrick spoke in English and introduced Annaliese to Tom, telling him she didn't speak Spanish and described the reason for his call.

He greeted her warmly and said he would be glad to help her as she was the friend of someone who had saved his life. Kendrick shook his head and told his friend to "shut up" about the past.

Tom told Kendrick to read the titles of each document and give him a brief description of what each one entailed. She could tell by his questions that Tom was intrigued by the documents she owned.

When he was finished with the last document, there was a brief silence from Tom. Then, "Okay, got a pen and paper? Here's what I need you to do, and this is what I'm going to do on this end." The next half hour was filled with orders to her from Tom and a list of what he would be doing in Grand Cayman. He told her he would keep track of his expenses and bill Annaliese when it was all over. Before they ended their conversation, Annaliese told Tom she would have additional information for him on their next conversation. He would have a clearer picture to the extent of all the documents represented.

Kendrick looked at her with surprise and wondered what she meant by her statement. He wanted to know, but didn't want to intrude. He had to trust that she knew what she was doing.

Kendrick and Tom spoke again in Spanish before ending their conversation. Kendrick laughed at something he said and then ended the conversation.

"He's a great guy. You'll like him when you finally meet him in person. He comes from a huge Cuban family and they live all around Miami. His mother and grandmother cook the best Cuban food in the world and everyone's invited to their table. They keep trying to marry him off to a nice Cuban girl. He tells the best stories about how they're always bringing girls home or to his office for him to meet. Kendrick laughed.

Now that the telephone conversation was over, Annaliese was relieved. This had been easier than she thought. Now she had to wait to hear the exact bank figures and what property Diego had purchased and where it was located. She had made a decision about what she was going to do about the fortune and was anxious to move forward. There would be some surprised people when she was done. It gave her a reason to look forward to the future with excitement and not dread.

Next, Annaliese needed to see Grace. She had the telephone number for the OB-Gyn. After dialing the doctor's office, Annaliese had an appointment for later in the day because of another patient's cancellation. Her stomach was rolling with anxiety. This was an appointment that would, literally, change her life forever. She had only a few hours to make her final decision about the baby she carried.

Right now, she needed to be alone. Grabbing her coat and scarf she hurried out the back door before anyone could stop her to ask questions. Grace watched her through the kitchen window and looked at the time. She would give her an hour, then at the time. She would give her an hour, then she would go in search of her. Perhaps she should tell Linda that Annaliese might need a friend right now. Grace decided that she would talk to her in the car as they drove into town later. Lost in thought she didn't hear Kendrick come into the kitchen and stand next to her looking out the window.

"Where's she going?" he said concern etched on his face. "She seem okay to you?"

"I think she needs a little space. She has an appointment with the doctor later this afternoon and I think she's trying to make a difficult decision." She turned to look at Kendrick, "I think you should let her take a walk. In an hour if she's not back, either me or Linda will go in search of her." Grace sighed and wiped her hands with the dish towel and sniffed, "That poor girl."

Kendrick stood at the window for several minutes trying to decide if he should go after her or let her be, like Grace said. He wondered if he should tell her that they could have a future together. Their future.... No, it was too soon. He had to wait. Maybe after the wedding in California. Why wasn't life ever easy? Kendrick wanted to go with her to the doctor today. He wanted her to need him, not Grace. He was in love, maybe truly for the first time, and he hadn't even slept with her. She had no idea how much he wanted her. He only hoped that he could make her see how good they could be together. He wanted a family and she was 'ready-made' which he thought was a good thing.

Annaliese stopped walking and looked around. She had reached the old homestead and the fountain she loved. What was it about this place – this ranch, that she loved it in so short a time? She was a California girl....had...been a California girl. This 'living out in the country' thing was so peaceful, not to mention beautiful. She never knew how much she loved animals. There was something so comforting about holding them and petting their fur. The look they gave you was so innocent and sometimes just plain adoration, even the ones who had been mistreated. Was this what it felt like, being a mother and holding your children? She had never thought about it before....had never wanted kids yet.

She looked around, again, knowing for certain that she wanted to stay here. She hoped that Mathias would understand her decision never to go back to California to live. She didn't miss her old job now that she had the Sanctuary. She was going to talk to Ray and Kendrick about taking over the books and running the Sanctuary. Linda told her she didn't enjoy that part of the Sanctuary, anyway. Roots.   That's what she wanted here: permanent roots to raise her child.

Yes, she had decided not to give up the baby for adoption. She had been terrified to carry a child that had been made without her permission from a man she hated. But last night she had felt her stomach and there was a large bump there – growing.

She wanted it – this child – her child. The hell with Diego! She had unlimited money and she would buy some property and build a home close to the ranch and the Sanctuary. Another big plus was that she had friends here; people she could trust. Annaliese had big plans. She was waiting for a phone call from Tom about her fortune, and then she would put her plans in motion. She felt the power in her decision about how she would manage her money.

Annaliese looked at her watch. It was time to go back to the ranch and help Grace with lunch. She wanted to talk to everyone during lunch about her idea to be the accountant and manager for the sanctuary. The thought was exciting because of her other decisions regarding her money. But it was too soon to tell them about that.

The weather was changing. Her coat was too warm and she was perspiring. Spring would be so beautiful and now was so full of promise. Annaliese looked up at the bright sky with big puffy clouds, put out her arms and smiled. Life would be good again.

Grace watched out the kitchen window every chance she got while preparing lunch. Any moment she would alert Linda that she needed to drive out and find Annaliese. She could see Kendrick outside pacing. He was worried, too, but had agreed with Grace that he shouldn't go after her. Just as she was getting ready to phone Linda, she saw Annaliese in the distance, walking back. A huge sigh of relief came out as a large blow of air from Grace. Thank God! She cared about that girl and wanted her to find happiness again. Kendrick and Annaliese would be a good match. She was going to tell her today to give him a chance. Well, she thought, I can relax and get on with lunch.

Kendrick ducked out of sight. He didn't want Annaliese to know that he had been waiting around for her. Hovering and snooping on her behalf would only alienate her. She had been a prisoner for seven months. Now she needed to feel independent, again.

Boy! Trying to establish a relationship with Annaliese wasn't going to be easy. He wanted to get things squared between them soon. She was a breathtaking beautiful woman and everyone who saw her knew it. In no time at all, any single man within a hundred miles would be coming around. He couldn't allow that to happen.

Annaliese entered the back door to the mud room, humming a tune. She was smiling when Grace peeked her head out, "Good. You're back. Did you have a nice walk clearing your head out?"

"Yes, Mother Duck. I did have a nice walk. Can I help with lunch?" She came in to the kitchen and grabbed an apron, tying the strings while she walked. "I'm ready for my doctor's appointment.

You don't have to go with me now, that is, unless you really want to?" She busied herself setting the table.

Grace reached out and grabbed Annaliese' hand, holding her in place. "Annaliese. You've been here only a few short weeks, but I care about you like a daughter. I'm not going to let you go to town by yourself to see the doctor. I know you can do this by yourself, but I'd feel very good if you'd let me go with you and share this time. This is your first time and today you will be bombarded with lots of 'to do's' and 'don't do's' as well as information that you might be overwhelmed with, and I don't want you to be alone. Okay?"

Annaliese didn't say a word. She put her arms around Grace and held her in a tight hug. "You're the best Mother Duck I know. I would love for you to come with me," she said in tears. She released Grace and they both took out Kleenex's to wipe their eyes and noses.

"Well, now that that's settled, let's get the lunch out before the others get here." She smiled and patted Annaliese' shoulder.

27

Annaliese was very grateful for Grace's company as she waited her turn in the doctor's office. The wall facing their seats was filled with various happy pictures of mothers who were holding new born babies. Many pictures were of three people: mother, baby and daddy. The heading over the display was "Happy First Birthday!" She couldn't imagine her picture up there. She noticed that the babies were bound up in either pink or blue blankets. Boy or girl….she hadn't even thought of it being one or the other! What did she want? She thought for a moment while studying the pictures. Could she love someone who reminded her of Diego? Would she be cruel to a child who was a constant reminder? What kind of a mother would she be? Her own mother had been wonderful; kind, loving and patient. Maybe it would be better if she had a girl. It was too late to worry about the sex of the baby now. She would be a good mother or she would give the baby away if she couldn't be as good a mother as her own had been to her and Mathias.

Her name was called. Grace patted her shoulder and smiled at her. "I'll be right here waiting. I'll come in if you need me. Okay?"

"Thank you, but I'll be fine. I'm glad you're here." She got up and followed the nurse into a small room. The nurse gave her a list of what she had to do before she saw the doctor. Because of all the paperwork she had filled out when they arrived, the nurse held a folder with several papers inside.

After disrobing and putting on a pink hospital gown with puppies and kittens on it, Annaliese was ready. Next was a urine sample and blood was drawn for additional tests. The doctor came in and continued with the friendly assault. When it came time for the pelvic exam, Annaliese broke out in a cold sweat and her heart started pounding.

She felt light headed and the doctor took note, "Annaliese, are you all right? This is no different than your annual pelvic exam would be. Before I do an ultrasound I want to exam you."

Annaliese had not wanted to tell the doctor of how she got pregnant, but there was no escaping that now. She told the doctor of her recent history, apologizing for taking more of the doctor's time. He was a very nice older man and he immediately pulled up a chair and made her feel that she was important to him.

He told her that in order to help her have a healthy pregnancy and baby, he needed to treat all of her; mentally and physically. As she told her story he sat quietly and simply held her hand and gave her tissues for her tears. When she finished, he told her she was a very lucky woman having ended up at the ranch with Kendrick's family and Grace. She agreed with him on so many levels.

The doctor took his time afterward and slowly put her through the process of her examination. When it was time for the ultrasound, he asked Annaliese if she wanted to know what the sex of the baby was. She didn't answer right away. He was patient with her and told her it wasn't important. People never used to know until the baby was born. The most important thing, he told her, was the health of the fetus. Suddenly, while he was talking and pushing the wand over her stomach she heard a whooshing noise.

"What's that noise?" she asked and turned her head to look at the doctor.

He smiled at her, "That's your baby's heart pumping."

The room was quiet for a moment except the whooshing sound of the baby's heart. Annaliese was astounded! "Why is it so fast?"

"It's a normal rhythm for a baby. Don't worry. It's a healthy baby, too. Look! See, there's the head, that's the body, arms, legs, and there's the heart beating away. It's a real miracle, isn't it? I never get tired of looking at this picture and hearing the heart beat."

He looked at Annaliese. Want to know what it is?" He smiled, waiting.

"

"No! I don't want to know yet, maybe not until it's born." She was taking the coward's way out. She couldn't take the chance that she would hate the poor thing before it was even born.

"I'm just glad that it's healthy." She would be glad when this was over.

When he was all through, Annaliese got dressed and met him in his office. Sitting behind his desk he looked at her. "I'm going to give you a prescription for vitamins and a healthy diet, as well as a list of things to avoid. Get lots of rest, nothing too strenuous or any kind of dangerous activity like mountain climbing or anything, and you should be fine." He chuckled.

"I would like you to talk to Linda at the ranch. She's counseled some patients for me for various concerns. You might want to talk to her about your anxiety. I think I know one thing you're concerned about and it is a valid concern, Annaliese. You didn't choose to have this baby and you probably are a little afraid that you might not love it. Is that about right?"

Annaliese was ashamed. "Yes, I'm afraid I will hate it and not be a good mother," she said.

"Have you thought about giving the baby up at birth? There's a lot of folks who would love to have a baby and can't have one of their own." The doctor leaned forward, "It's not a sin to give up a child, especially one that was conceived like yours."

"Yes, I know. I'm not sure I could give it up after holding it. I'll be able to know by then, I think."

On the way home she was quiet. Grace sat silently driving the car, giving Annaliese time to decide what she wanted to tell her. Once she started talking to Grace she couldn't stop. All of her fears came out and she told Grace what she had told the doctor: that she wouldn't keep a baby she couldn't love. She sounded horrid! But she had to be honest; with herself and with the baby.

Grace said she understood and then told Annaliese her story. The rest of the drive to the ranch was about Grace: "I met my husband, Carl, when I was nineteen years old. I had boyfriends, but I had never met anyone like him before. He was so sure of himself and good looking that I was crazy about him from the start. My parents didn't like him a bit. They though he was cocky and rude, and they didn't want me to have anything to do with him. So after a couple weeks of dating, I ran away with him in the dead of night. Never even said goodbye. So, I thought we'd stop by a justice of the peace and get married, but he just kept on driving until we got to a little hick town a couple of hundred miles down the road. He had an old rat-trap room in a hotel and that's where I had my first sex. There was no romance involved, just rough and quick. By then, I knew I had made the biggest mistake of my life. But I had no money – I'd given it all to him.....no car, and no friends.

We lived like that for a few months and I got a job waitressing in a real greasy spoon restaurant. One morning I woke up and was so sick I couldn't go to work, knew I didn't have the flu, but I didn't want to admit I was pregnant, so I sucked it up and went into work late. I hid my pregnancy for almost four months, when one night Carl felt my stomach and told me I was getting fat and I better be careful. I told him I was pregnant and he threw a real scary fit. Luckily he didn't hit me, then. The next day he drove to the courthouse and we got married. He said he wasn't going to have anyone say he had a bunch of little bastards running around without his name. It was real romantic," she said sadly with a smirk.

"It was not long after that he would come home at odd times, drunk and throw things around and break things. I wanted to leave him and go back home, but when I called my parents and told them about the pregnancy and how Carl was treating me, they said I had made my bed and now I could just lay in it." Grace's voice was hard and brittle.

"Oh, Grace, I'm so sorry. That must have been so sad and scary for you." Annaliese put her hand on Grace's arm.

"Yeah, it was pretty bad, but it got worse." She swallowed hard, "I was pretty far along with Steven when he hit me for the first time."

Annaliese gasped! "Dear God! He hit you when you were pregnant! I can't believe he could do that to you."

"Me neither. But I made a vow that he wouldn't ever do it again. I started hiding part of my earnings from the restaurant and looking around for a place to stay. I was going to leave Carl as soon as I possibly could. Then fate stuck her nose in and Carl was hit by a car on his drunken walk home from the local bar one night.

I waited for him and after two days, I went to the police and found he was in the hospital as a result of a hit and run. After I found him, he lasted a week then died. I couldn't even cry. I was so glad that I was finally free of him. I loaded up the car and moved to a nicer hotel. The woman who cooked for the restaurant where I worked turned out to be my good friend. Alice taught me how to cook and I got a job in a nicer restaurant, cooking and making more money. I put away as much money as I could and then moved in with Alice to get ready to have my baby."

"I was a mess. I didn't want Steven. I knew if he was a boy he'd look like Carl and I'd hate him." She looked over at Annaliese and smiled. "You don't think I know what you've been worried about? I've been there, honey."

"But I went into labor one night, and after about thirteen of the most painful hours I've ever known, I gave birth to this beautiful, pink baby boy.

And suddenly, it didn't matter who he looked like. He was MY beautiful baby boy. Mine! I knew he would be who I helped him to be. And he is: kind, patient, loving and the best husband and father. He was a wonderful gift I never for a moment regretted keeping."

"When my friend Alice died from cancer when Steven was nine years old, I was lost again. She and I had been closer than my own mother and I. Once again, I was alone. I answered an ad for a housekeeper and --- here I am. And when I need a little male company, there's an old cowboy whose wife died, that I can spend time with." Grace laughed and laughed at Annaliese surprised face.

"So life is good and full of surprises. Take it from me, honey. You're gonna love that baby no matter what it is. I've seen you with those animals in the sanctuary and you're gonna be a great momma, too." She paused, then looked at Annaliese with a serious expression. "I'm gonna stick my nose in where it probably doesn't belong." Grace took a big breath and let it out, "I think you should know that   Jackson Kendrick is in love with you and you would be a fool not to love him back. He's a good man and he can take good care of you and raise your child as his own." She nodded her head to Annaliese' shocked expression.

"I don't know what to say. He's attracted to me, I know that, but he's not in love with me. How can he be?" she asked with wonder.

"Yes, he is. I've known that man for a long time and I know he's crazy in love with you, but is too afraid to scare you. He's gonna wait for a sign from you that's it okay before he's gonna do anything. So it's up to you. You've got to let him know that you love him, too, because you do, don't you?" Grace waited as Annaliese looked at her with her mouth open.

"I'm not sure. I'll have to think about it."

The rest of the drive home was silent. Annaliese had a lot to think about. She avoided Kendrick and went straight to her room. Kendrick was puzzled and asked Grace if everything had gone okay with Annaliese' doctor's appointment. She wasn't sure how much to tell him, so she just said that the Annaliese and the baby were fine. Kendrick stood at the bottom of the stairs wanting to go up and talk to Annaliese, but he didn't. He scratched his head and left the house, grousing about stubborn women.

Annaliese didn't come down for dinner. Grace took a plate up to her room and sat with her while she ate. Nothing more was said about Kendrick. They talked about baby things and what Annaliese would soon be needing. They would shop together and pick out neutral colors for clothing. She told Grace that she planned on buying some land close by and building a home for her and the baby. Grace didn't tell her she thought that wouldn't be necessary because she knew Kendrick would never let her leave the ranch.

The next few days, Annaliese ate her meals after everyone had left for the day. Then, she went to the sanctuary and worked until dark and ate a plate of food that Grace left for her in the oven. Ray, Linda and Kendrick made a pact to give her some space for a few days while she came to grips with what was bothering her. Linda was waiting until she thought Annaliese needed her advice. She would eventually come to her for a talk if she needed it.

In the meantime, all arrangements were made for the trip to California. Mathias had sent Annaliese' checkbook and credit cards to her, and she used them to purchase everything she needed for the trip. Kendrick had returned to his Army base and was due back two days before they left. Annaliese had purchased luggage and was packing when she heard a commotion downstairs. She heard Kendrick's voice and was surprised that he was back early. Without thinking, she hurried to the stairs and collided with Kendrick as he ran up to her.

"Ooof! You're back early!" she laughed.

"Mission accomplished. I'm almost officially out of the Army," he laughed. "Do I look different to you?"

"Well, let me see," she looked him over. "No, I don't think so." Then shyly she said, "I missed you."

Kendrick couldn't wait any longer. He grabbed her and kissed her as if his life depended on it. Annaliese kissed him back and they sighed and held onto each other.

"Annaliese. I want to tell you how I feel about you." He held her tightly and waited for her reply. "I love you. I love you so much I don't believe it myself." Kendrick stepped back and took her hand and pulled her back into her bedroom and closed the door.

"I was going to wait and not overwhelm you, but being away from you this past week only made it more clearly to me that I want to be with you all the time. I want you to stay – with me – at the ranch." Kendrick held on to Annaliese' shoulders and looked in her eyes. "I'm asking you to marry me, Lissy." Kendrick waited as the shocked expression widened her eyes.

"But you can't want to marry me! With everything you know about me…..and I'm pregnant, Jackson!" She pushed him back and walked to the window wrapping her arms around her stomach. Kendrick waited, afraid of what she was going to tell him. "I am really attracted to you, I want you to know that. I want to stay and live here, but….I was going to buy some land and build a house nearby…" She turned and looked at Kendrick, "You've just turned my world upside down! I need to think. I never thought that you'd…. I wanted to talk to you and Ray about the sanctuary and this is just so……"

Annaliese bit her lip and frowned "…amazing!" She start pacing back and forth in front of the window hugging herself.

She stopped pacing and looked at him in wonder! "Can I think about this for a while and then give you my decision?" He thought she looked so vulnerable and sweet. She was it for him. It didn't matter she was full of doubt. He would make life good and secure for her and their children.

"This isn't a business agreement, Lissy. I'm asking to be your husband and the father of your children." He slowly walked toward her, "I want it all, sweetheart. The good, the bad and the ugly.

Whatever life brings us we will handle it together." Kendrick reached and gently pulled her against his chest. "We'll build a whole new world for us here on the ranch. I know you love the ranch and the sanctuary already and it's only going to get better." He pulled her chin up and looked into her eyes, "Do you believe me?"

Annaliese still had a stunned look of wonder on her beautiful face. The afternoon sun was shining on her silver blonde hair and she looked like an angel. He would never tell her that or refer to her as his angel. But she was. "I tell you what – let's talk more tonight after dinner. Just let this all settle in for a while. No decisions have to be made right now. We have nothing but time, Lissy. I'd love to tell your brother, but it's all right if you can't make a decision before the wedding. I'm gonna be a patient man….." he chuckled, "even if it kills me." They stood looking at each other and smiled like goofy teenagers.

At dinner, everyone chatted and caught up on Kendrick's trip and what had happened at the ranch while he was gone. Kendrick acted like he and Annaliese hadn't had the life changing conversation earlier and she tried to act normal while sneaking looks at him. Once he looked directly at her and gave her a wink and she blushed.

Grace was enjoying every minute of seeing them together. When there was a lull in the conversation, Annaliese cleared her throat and spoke up. "I hope this is an okay time to ask you all a favor." She had everyone's attention.

Kendrick had a slight frown on his face. "I was wondering if it would be okay for me to take over the accounting and daily running of the Sanctuary."

She waited. When no one responded she rushed, "I wouldn't want a salary or anything. I just thought since that sort of thing was what I used to do, and I am fairly good at it…and I know Linda and I talked and she's not crazy about having to do the books and stuff…." Annaliese looked around at the faces.

All at once everyone started talking and smiling, and Ray reached over and patted her hand on the table. "We'd like nothing better, Annaliese. You have no idea how much we would love it for two important reasons: one, you will make my wife very happy and two, that means you will stay here with us."

Linda got up and came to Annaliese' chair and hugged her, smiling. "I am so happy to give you this job. We could give you a salary if you need it. But certainly room and board are included if nothing else. Thank you so much, my dear friend."

"I couldn't be happier knowing we're going to keep Lissy right here on the ranch." He made a loud *thunk* when he lowered his chair back to the floor, "Now how about some of that dessert I saw you put in the refrigerator, Grace?" He never took his eyes from Annaliese' and watched her cheeks turn pink.

The rest of the meal passed with the conversation all about the Sanctuary and the new director. Annaliese had more to tell them, but until she spoke to Tom in Florida, she would wait for that surprising news. Right now, she felt happy and secure as part of this wonderful group of people. The ranch and Sanctuary was such a dream ending after the bad months before had been a nightmare for her.

When it was time for everyone to separate for the night, Kendrick suggested that Annaliese looked tired and they could continue their conversation the next day. He walked her to her room, but came inside with her and closed the door. It was dark, with just the outside lights shining. Kendrick gathered Annaliese against him and held her. For such a strong man, he was very gentle. She inhaled his male scent with just a hint of woodsy smelling soap. It occurred to her that she wasn't afraid to be alone with him. She wasn't even afraid of him holding her and, hopefully, kissing her again. Which he did and melted her heart. Afraid to admit she might love him, she didn't want to say anything to him. She just wanted to enjoy the feeling of his arms and lips.

Kendrick pulled away and smoothed his hands over her hair and down the sides of her face, stopping at her jaw. He rubbed her lips with his thumbs and then kissed her softly one last time before letting her go. Stepping back he put his hands in his back pockets as though he had to or he would grab her. He watched her for a brief moment. "You are the most beautiful woman I've ever known. I love you, Lissy. I swear that I will never hurt you, or take advantage of you, or mistreat you in any way, for as long as we live. You have my word." Kendrick turned and opened the door, never looking back.

He closed the door and leaned against it, sighing in frustration. One more second of kissing her and he would have shamed himself. There was no way he would sleep well tonight.

28

The next few days passed in a whirlwind of activity for Annaliese. She had taken over the office in the Sanctuary and in a matter of hours had completely rearranged everything including the furniture, and was already immersed in the accounting information on the computer. The computer would be one of the first things she replaced, she thought. She had begun making notes of how she would change the running of the Sanctuary, what she would replace and what she would add. It was an exciting time for Annaliese because she loved to organize things, and the Sanctuary had been begging to be re-organized. What she had planned for the future would enlarge the facility and make it more efficient and state of the art.

Kendrick stuck his head in her office at least once before lunch and once after to make sure she wasn't 'over-doing it.' He didn't interfere with what she was doing but was quick to help if it involved moving anything including books on the shelves. Linda had lingered long enough to know that Annaliese was in her own heaven, then hugged her and left her alone to do as she wished. Ray had stopped by and left a small vase of flowers on her desk, and Grace had brought a tin of cookies and a glass of milk for her to snack on. How could she not love these people? Even Jonathan and Denise stopped in to congratulate her and remind her that the baby goat was looking for her and missed her loving and treats. He was almost ready to be turned out in the pasture with the other goats and sheep. Denise thought Annaliese should do the honors of releasing him when she returned from California.

Ray and Linda drove them to the municipal airport for the two hour flight to southern California. When they landed, Mathias and Mary were waiting for them, excitement radiating from their faces. Mathias hugged Annaliese and didn't let her go until Mary pulled his arm away and then she hugged her and cried until Kendrick called a halt saying they'd better let her go to the bathroom before she had an accident. As soon as she walked away, Mathias looked at Kendrick, "She looks real happy. I can't tell you what a difference I see in her even before I've had a chance to talk to her. I know you must have something to do with that, and I want you to know I'm forever in your debt for all you've done for her." Mathias cleared his throat and clung to Mary.

"She's got a lot to tell you. But I want you to know up front, I'm trying to talk her into marrying me. I love her more than I ever thought I could love anyone. She's an amazing woman." He looked at Mathias, "I hope you don't have a problem with that." He waited for a challenge.

"I thought you probably had feelings for her when you were still in Texas. All I ask is that you treat her like the special woman she is." Mathias stuck out his hand, "Welcome to the family."

Kendrick took Mathias' hand, "Thanks, Mathias, but she hasn't said yes, yet."

A smiling Mathias watched his sister approach, "You're here with her and I've talked on the phone listening to her go on about how wonderful the ranch and Sanctuary are and how wonderful you are." He turned to Kendrick. "I don't think it's going to be a problem."

During the ride to Mathias' condo, Annaliese silently watched out the car window at the passing cement and asphalt scenery. The crowded freeway made it easy to see the changes that had taken place during her absence. She found herself making constant comparisons between southern California and Montana, and found California not even close to the beauty of Montana.

As they drove closer to Mathias' condo, Annaliese felt more uncomfortable. Linda had talked to her about the possibility that memories could come flooding back. Kendrick was watching her without being obvious. He felt her unease and decided that he would subtly comfort her by holding her hand. He reached over and took her hand in his, gently squeezing it to get her attention. When she glanced over at him he gave her a wink and smile of encouragement. She gratefully returned his smile and leaned toward him putting her shoulder against his.

Immediately, she felt calmer and squeezed his hand in return. He was an instant comfort to her, she realized. If she stayed close to Jackson, it would be easier to return to her old haunts. She needed to drive by her condo – not to go inside, but to just see it one last time. Closure, Linda had said, but it was her choice whether she wanted to do it or not. Maybe right now would be a good time to get it done and over with.

"Mathias, could we drive by my condo?" she asked.

Everyone in the car froze. "Lissy, are you sure you want to do that?" He looked at her in the rearview mirror, concern etched in his eyes. Mary turned to look back at Annaliese, about to say something, but hesitated.

"I need to do this and now, with all of you -- seems to be the right time. If we get close and I can't do it, then I'll tell you. Okay?" She looked at Jackson for assurance.

Kendrick leaned toward her and whispered, "You're sure?" He squeezed her hand.

Annaliese just nodded her head.

Soon, Mathias was entering the gate code and the gates were sliding open. Slowly, he drove through the gate toward her street. "Do you want to drive around a little before we go by your place?" He slowed down and stopped the car.

"No, let's make this a 'quickie' trip down memory lane." Annaliese took a deep breath, "I need to do this, Mathias. Linda, Jackson's aunt who's a psychologist, said it would be a good thing if I could do it, and I need to see my place one last time."

Kendrick put his arm around her and pulled her tight against him. Annaliese looked up at him and sighed, "Thank you." She tensed up as they approached the front of her condo. Kendrick took her hand and held her steady.

Mathias stopped the car, "Do you want to get out? We can all get out with you." He put the car in park and turned around to Annaliese.

"No, this is good enough." She stared at the condo, "It looks like I remember it." Annaliese looked at Kendrick. "This was a place I really loved.

Now it seems so small and plain." She sighed, "It was easier than I thought. It might be difficult if I went inside, but this is okay." She smiled at her brother, then Mary, then a brighter smile for Kendrick. "It's okay!" She looked at the condo one last time, "I'm glad I came her one last time. We can go now," she said softly. As they pulled away, she glanced over one last time and whispered, "Goodbye."

Kendrick squeezed her shoulder, leaned over and kissed her temple, "You're my brave, strong, beautiful girl."

The rest of the ride was filled with talk of the wedding. Mary took over the conversation and bubbled with details about what they had planned. It was difficult not to get excited for Mathias and Mary. They were happy and in love. Annaliese was now ready to enjoy her brother's big event. She looked at Kendrick, put her hand on his thigh and squeezed. His eyes widened with surprise and he wagged his eyebrows up and down. She giggled and he leaned over and kissed her lips. He made her feel like she was ready to have fun. What they hadn't discussed yet was whether or not the newspapers had heard about the wedding and Annaliese' return to celebrate with her brother.

"Do you think we have to worry about newspaper people bothering us?" Annaliese asked Mathias.

"We asked only our closest friends and relatives to attend the ceremony and reception, and to keep the location a secret. They all agreed and understood our need for privacy. Besides, I haven't seen any press around for a while now, so I'm hoping they've forgotten all about you, Lissy. But, we did hire a couple of security people who will be on guard, so you have nothing to worry about. And, I think the fellow sitting next to you wouldn't let them get within a hundred yards of you." Mathias exchanged a look with Kendrick in the rear view mirror and saw a very grim smile.

Annaliese shrugged. She refused to let anything take away the happiness of her brother's special day. The worst for her was over. She had conquered her fear of returning to the place where Diego had found her and changed her life. She was moving forward now, putting her old life behind her. It was not a surprise to her that she longed to return to Montana.   Annaliese and Kendrick were staying with Mathias in his condo. Mary had given up her apartment and had moved into their new house which wasn't far. He had leased his condo, so most of the furniture and all of the dishes had been removed. He had left just enough things that they could stay there comfortably for the three days of celebration. They would eat all of their meals in local restaurants. Tonight was going to be Annaliese' treat. She had made reservations for them to eat at a well-known restaurant that had been one of her favorites. They had a private room so she wasn't worried about people watching them.

Mathias gave Annaliese and Kendrick a tour of their new house when he dropped Mary off to change for dinner. She was thrilled for them and enjoyed watching her brother proudly show her all the things Mary had done to make it their special home. Watching them together made Annaliese so happy to see how much they were in love and ready to begin their new life. They would stay close even though miles apart. She couldn't wait for them to visit the ranch and sanctuary. It probably wouldn't be long that they would bring nieces and nephews to visit her.

After a brief rest, they changed their clothes, picked up Mary and drove to the Cliff's Restaurant for dinner.   High on a bluff overlooking the Pacific Ocean, the restaurant was famous for the view as well as the seafood cuisine. The inside was all glass, driftwood and various silver fish hanging from invisible lines. Annaliese looked forward to enjoying to surprising Mathias and Mary with her gift. She had contacted the travel service she and her brother had always used for personal and business trips. Mathias' and Mary's reservations had been changed to a luxurious honeymoon on a private island in the Caribbean she knew they would enjoy.

Annaliese was following Mathias and Mary to their private room when suddenly she heard a loud gasp and the sound of glasses and dishes falling. "Oh my God! It's Annaliese!" She turned, and there stood an astonished Derek, his napkin hanging from his waist and wine dripping down his shirt front.

"It is you! I can't believe it!" He rushed toward her and Kendrick quickly blocked him from grabbing her arms. The people in the restaurant were silent and watching the disturbance with curiosity.

"Where's the private room we're using?" he asked the waiter who had been escorting them. The waiter pointed and Kendrick grabbed Derek, "Go, take us there now!" He started forward then ordered Mathias, "Help your sister and let's get in there, now!" Pulling Derek along with them they reached the room and closed the door. The restaurant was now buzzing with conversation and Kendrick knew someone might remember the story of the beautiful kidnapped girl.

Derek was babbling and Kendrick shoved him into a chair. Annaliese stepped forward and put her hand on his shoulder. "I'm sorry I didn't tell you I had been rescued, but Mathias told me you had already found a new girlfriend. I thought you had forgotten about me."

"Holy shit, Annaliese! Okay, I have a new girlfriend, but you could have at least warned me before I thought I'd seen a ghost and scared the crap out of me! You could have at least given me some warning," he whined. "How could you do this to me?"

Mathias spoke to the waiter and told him that everything was all right and they would be ordering dinner soon. In the meantime they needed a bottle of wine and glasses. He left and they all sat down.

Annaliese sat next to Derek and calmly talked to him, trying to explain how she had been rescued and he sputtered and interrupted until Kendrick sat down on his other side and placed his hand on Derek's shoulder and got his attention.

"Listen to me. You stopped caring about her long before she was rescued. She's back, she's fine and you've moved on. End of story!"

"But everyone needs to know! I need to tell all of our friends that you're back!" he exclaimed.

Before Kendrick could reply, Annaliese said firmly, "No, Derek. You will NOT tell our friends I am back. I am only here for Mathias' and Mary's wedding, then I will return to where I live now. I don't want or need anyone prying into my life. You've moved on and so have I."

She looked at Derek and waited for him to reply. He wiped his face with the napkin he had tucked into his waistband and huffed out, "Well you certainly don't think I'm going to keep this all a secret! Why should I? Your friends have worried about you and even helped look for you when you first disappeared. This is big news that you were found and are back."

Before she could reply, Kendrick grabbed Derek shirt, "Listen, Derek," he growled. "Here's how it's going to be. You're going to say goodbye to Annaliese and return to your dinner out there and keep your mouth shut! She doesn't want people to bombard her with questions. Do you understand?"

Derek tried to make Kendrick release his shirt, "Hey, who the hell are you? You can't tell me what to do!" He tried to shake Kendrick off.

"I'm protecting Annaliese and you are not going to make a big deal out of her being here. Now I'm telling you to say goodbye and leave. We are going to have a quiet dinner now and you're going to keep your mouth shut." Kendrick released Derek with a shove.

Derek stood up and so did Kendrick. They stood eye to eye, "Well, I don't give a crap what you want. Now back off!" Before Kendrick could lunge at Derek, Annaliese got between them.

"Derek, you and I were together a long time. I'm asking you to let my presence here be a secret. You have no idea what I have been through. It would serve no purpose for you to tell everyone I am here unless you want publicity – which I don't! Tell our friends I have been rescued, I'm recovering from my kidnapping and I have a new life far away. Please do this for me because we once loved each other. Please," she begged. Annaliese took his hand and held it between her two hands and waited.

Derek smiled at Annaliese. "You're still beautiful Annaliese. I never could believe you belonged to me. I guess if you still cared for me you would have contacted me to let me know you were back. I'm a little pissed that you didn't, you know."

He released a big breath, "All right. I'll let our friends know you're okay and want to be left alone. They won't understand, but I'll tell them." He glared at Kendrick. "Your secret will be safe with me." He turned to leave, then turned back and took her hand, "Have a good life, Annaliese." He leaned over and kissed her cheek, then opened the door and left the room.

They all sighed with relief. Kendrick pulled out Annaliese' chair and had her sit down. Mathias and Mary looked at Annaliese with concern in their eyes as they, too, sat down.

Annaliese blinked back tears, "I'm all right you guys. I'm glad I saw him. He's right, I should have let him know. I just didn't think about it when Mathias told me he had a new girlfriend. I thought he wouldn't really care."

Mathias was relieved. He'd worried that Annaliese would want Derek back. It was plain that he was in her past now. Kendrick had nothing to worry about.

"Well, that's enough excitement for one night!" They all laughed. The waiter returned with wine and glasses for all except Annaliese. After a while, they ordered dinner and the evening celebration began. Mary cried when Annaliese revealed her honeymoon surprise for them. Mathias hugged Mary and grinned, "You splurged more than I did, Lissy! We were going to have a little romantic weekend and now you've given us the big time romantic trip. I love you little sister."

Annaliese enjoyed the dinner but was glad when the evening was over. They returned to Mathias' condo and prepared for bed. Tomorrow would be a long day finishing up last minute wedding details. Kendrick would join Mathias tomorrow night for his groomsmen party and she would be with Mary's friends. She hoped she could get a good night's sleep. Too bad she hadn't given Jackson a good night kiss. Wait! She could still do that!

In her robe and slippers, Annaliese opened her door and listened. Everything was quiet, Mathias in his room, Jackson in his. She softly knocked on Jackson's door. In one swift move the door opened and she was pulled into his arms. "You beat me to this, Lissy," he whispered as he kissed her neck, then jaw, then her lips with a blazing kiss. "I couldn't let you go to bed without kissing you good night. What I really want is for you to stay with me, but not for our first time. That will be somewhere special." Kendrick kissed her again, "What are you thinking, Lissy, tell me, please?"

"I want you, too, Jackson. But I'm so afraid you'll be disappointed with me."

Kendrick held her tighter and chuckled. "Lissy, you could never disappoint me. You're the most amazing woman I've ever met." He pulled her over to the bed, "Sit down. I want to talk to you." After he sat down next to her he took her hand and kissed it. "I was afraid tonight when you saw Derek. You'll never know how much it meant to hear you tell him you were no longer in love with him. I worried about that. He could have come into our life and you might have chosen him over me. I've never wanted to slug someone as much as I wanted to just let him have it. But he did the right thing, wished you well and walked away." Kendrick put his other hand on Annaliese' cheek and pulled her to face him.

"He could never love you more than I do. And, there's no way he knows you better than me. I've seen you go through some difficult times, some I made, and you were the bravest woman I know. I've seen your goodness and your heart, Lissy, and I'm in awe of you."

Kendrick got up from the bed and kneeled down in front of Annaliese. "Annaliese Marie Bergdahl, will you give me the honor of becoming my wife?" He waited, "I wasn't going to do this now, and I don't have a ring. I thought we could pick one out together." He watched as Annaliese wiped the tears streaming down her face. Could she be about to refuse him?

Annaliese leaned forward and put her arms around him. "Jackson Kendrick, I would be honored to be your wife. But, we have to talk about something very important first."

Before she could say more, Kendrick put his finger on her lips and stopped her. "Lissy, if it's about the baby," he place his hand on her stomach, "from this point forward, THIS is my child. He or she will know only me, and I will love this child as if they had been mine from the very start. Okay?"

"Oh, Jackson," she cried. "I love you so much!" He stood up and pulled her with him, kissing her and loving her with his hands. Kendrick pulled her nightgown over her head and let it fall on the carpet.

Kneeling in front of her, he put his cheek against her stomach and hugged her. Then he turned his face and kissed her where the baby lay inside her. When he stood, Annaliese unbuttoned his shirt and pushed it off his shoulders. She kissed his tattoos and scars one by one, while Kendrick groaned. Then, she started to unbuckle his belt but Kendrick pushed her hands aside and quickly had them opened and pushed down his legs. They stood almost touching, staring at each other. "Tell me it's not too much, too soon, Lissy, and I'll stop right now."

Annaliese smiled at Kendrick, amazed that this big strong man was giving her control. "I'm nervous but I don't want you to stop, Jackson. I'm going to stay with you all night so we don't have to rush."

"Oh, Lissy darling. I'm going to take lots of time loving you." He pulled the covers back and they lay down together holding each other close. They were soon touching each other memorizing every tender, sensitive inch of their bodies. Kendrick was true to his word. They took their time off and on all night.

In the morning, Lissy awoke to find Kendrick watching her. "Good morning, Lissy. Are you all right?"

Annaliese grinned and stretched. "I'm better than all right. I feel wonderful." She wrapped her arms around him and snuggled.

Kendrick held her then put his hand on her stomach. "How's our baby doing?"

She put her hand on top of his and kissed his neck. "We're both fine and not quite ready to get up yet." She pushed against him, "And I think you're not quite ready, either."

"Oh, Lissy, you're so right!"

Much later, Mathias rapped on Kendrick's door. "Are you guys ever coming out? A guy could starve out here!" He laughed and rattled the door knob. "You've got twenty minutes before I come in there and pour water on you two."

Annaliese was shocked! How did he know she was here? She looked at Kendrick, then started giggling. "I'm going to be so embarrassed! What must he think?"

Kendrick untangled himself from Annaliese and kissed her soundly making a smacking noise, "That I'm m the luckiest man alive, Lissy!" He pulled the covers back and swatted her behind. "Up, woman! Your fiancée is starving!"

Annaliese pulled her nightgown on and walked to the door. She looked hesitant when she turned back to look at Kendrick. "I....I'm a very lucky woman, Jackson." Before she could open the door, Kendrick had her in a fierce hug, kissing her with so much passion her toes curled.

"We're gonna have a good life, Lissy. Don't ever be afraid to tell me whatever you want. It's the only way we can continue to grow together. I love you, darling. I'm gonna tell you every day so you won't forget it." He kissed her again, then opened the door for her. "See you in about fifteen minutes."

Mathias was in the living room waiting for them. When he saw Annaliese he didn't say anything, just smiled. "Thought you'd sneak into your room, didn't you?" He laughed and shook his head.

Annaliese could feel how red her cheeks must be. She put her head down and kept going into her room. "Nosy brother!" she slammed her door shut.

The morning of the wedding was a picture perfect southern California day. Mathias was very handsome dressed in a tuxedo. Annaliese felt a sense of loss wishing her parents could be here to see their son marry in the church where both she and Mathias had been baptized. The only family they had left were their aunts and uncles as their parents had only one sibling each. Since they had never lived close to each other, they didn't know them well. But they both happy that they would be in attendance today.

When Kendrick walked out of his bedroom he took Annaliese' breath away. He was the most gorgeous man she had ever seen! His dark gray suit was perfectly tailored, showing off his muscled body. The tie and hankie he wore was a perfect match to Annaliese' blue dress. They made a beautiful couple and would turn the eyes of anyone who saw them together.

A limo took them to the church where Annaliese joined Mary and the bridesmaids. Mary's wedding dress had been worn by her mother and grandmother. The beautiful gown had been altered for the bride allowing for subtle changes. Mary had chosen to add 'something old' by sewing a neckline of pearls from a broken necklace that had belonged to her grandmother. She was a beautiful bride and Annaliese couldn't wait for her brother to see her. A small arch of delicate flowers and baby's breath was placed on Annaliese and the bridesmaids' heads. They carried a small version of Mary's large bouquet of blue, pink and yellow spring flowers with blue ribbons hanging down. Mary hugged Annaliese, thanking her for the honeymoon present and for being with her on this special day and that she was grateful for her best friend becoming her sister.

When the doors opened and the wedding processional began, all Kendrick saw was Annaliese in the background. He could hear the intake of breaths as one by one, the congregation saw her, too.

She was breathtaking as she smiled and walked down the aisle. Her silver blonde hair was pulled back in an elaborate chignon and on top of her head, the flowers made her look like a porcelain statue of a goddess. She seemed to attract the rays of the sun as she walked with such grace down the church aisle.

Kendrick wanted to go to her and drink in her beauty, but he made himself sit down for the ceremony to begin. He barely heard the minister speaking, he was so taken by her beauty. He clenched his fist as he watched the best man take her arm to escort her out of the church. Excusing himself he hurried out to join her. She waited for him on the steps as though she couldn't wait to be with him as well. After a long kiss, she went back into the church for pictures. It would be a long night before he had her to himself again.

The reception was held in a nearby hotel that looked like an old California mission. The arched doorways and pillars were painted with flowers and scenes from the 1800's. The floors were made of large terra cotta tiles that looked they had been there since Father Junipero Serra, a famous California priest, had walked with his Indian parishioners.

Palm trees lined the court yard and huge hibiscus plants brightened the area in pink, orange and yellow. The tables were covered with white table cloths, and copper lanterns in the center of each table, were already shining soft candle light.

Blue napkins were wrapped with flowers that matched the bridesmaids' flowers. A small white box with blue ribbons sat in the middle of each plate.

To ward off the cool spring evening, tall gas heaters radiated heat. A group of musicians played music from show tunes and people started dancing in the middle of the courtyard.

As soon as she was shown where they would be seated, Kendrick bowed, "May I have this dance milady?"

Annaliese held out her hand and he brought it to his lips for a kiss while he gazed into her eyes. Then he led her out to the dance floor and put both arms around her. She placed her arms around his neck and they barely moved to the music. She had never felt more happy and secure in her life. Kendrick kept his lips against her temple and kissed her periodically.

"I'm ready to go home now," Annaliese whispered.

"I wish we could fly back to Montana tonight," he whispered back.

"That's what I meant by going home," she said.

Kendrick turned his head and kissed her lips. "You make me so happy. I have always loved the ranch and wanted it to be where I lived and had a family when I left the army. I'm so thankful you love it too, Lissy." He kissed her again, "You're perfect! How soon can we be married?"

"I've been thinking about that. Let's have a ceremony at the ranch. We can start planning it as soon as we get back. We have to wait until Mathias and Mary can come, but maybe in a month?" She smiled and kissed Kendrick.

He smiled back, "That long, huh?"

They danced and ate and enjoyed the reception but left as soon as they said goodbye to Mathias and Mary. When they reached Mathias' condo, Kendrick ordered a car to take them to the airport early the next morning. They both wished they were leaving then.

29

Ray and Linda met their flight and saw the pair glowing with happiness and knew it wouldn't be long before a wedding would happen for them. The topic turned from Mathias' wedding to Kendrick announcing they wanted to marry at the ranch in one month. When Grace heard, she shrieked with joy. By the next morning, plans were in full swing!

Kendrick's phone rang and Tom Gepson asked to talk to him and Annaliese. "It's necessary for you to come to my office here in Miami. Can you do that, Annaliese? I have all the information for you, but you will need to sign papers with a notary. I've got to tell you, you've got some serious decisions to make about a hell of a lot of property and money. I won't go into detail over the phone. It's better for you to come here at your earliest convenience."

Annaliese covered the phone and asked Kendrick, "Can you take the time to go with me?"

Kendrick took the phone, "We can come any time you say, Tom. Give me a hotel to make reservations and we'll be there next week. Is that soon enough?" He spoke to Tom for another few minutes, made some notes then hung up. "You up for another plane trip?"

"I am if you go with me." She looked tired.

Kendrick kissed her and took her hand, leading her up the stairs to his room. Once inside she noticed her personal things were laying on his dresser. He saw her looking and opened the doors to the walk-in closet where all her clothes were hanging.

"What do you think?" he smiled.

Annaliese walked over to him and hugged him, "I think it's just fine, Jackson."

At dinner, Ray and Linda surprised them by announcing that they were expanding a bungalow near the ranch house and were going to move in there and give Jackson and Annaliese the house. Kendrick and Annaliese were shocked!

"I would never kick you out of here! This big old house has plenty of room for us all!" he exclaimed.

"Jackson, we're hoping you and Annaliese fill this house up with children. We will always be close by, but we don't need all this room. We can still have meals together, but Ray and I can have meals together in our home as well. Of course, Grace will still be here running the place." She looked up at a smiling Grace.

"We discussed this already and have drawn up plans with an architect. We'll get it done before summers over and be out before the baby comes in September," Ray said proudly.

"Well, I'll be. I never expected this." Kendrick scratched his head and looked at Annaliese. "You're sure?"

Both Ray and Linda nodded their heads and smiled.

"There's a lot of furniture in all these rooms that we can share, and a lot up in the attic. We'll need to get whatever you want out to the barn and polish it up. We'll also share the quilts and dishes and any-thing else you guys will need. I guess after you move all your stuff out of the master bedroom, I can my things in there." He looked at Annaliese, "You can choose some new colors for paint and drapes, quilts, and pillows for the bed."

He got up and walked over to his aunt and uncle, "Thank you for this generous gift Uncle Ray and Aunt Linda. I'm just bowled over. It's good that you won't be too far away. That's a beautiful place you're gonna have."

Annaliese hugged them both, "I can't thank you enough for everything you've done for me."

That night as they snuggled under the covers together, Annaliese a sudden pressure on her feet and looked down to see Custer curling up to sleep on the bed with them.

"Hey, Custer. How ya doin old buddie?" He ignored her and cleaned his paws.

Kendrick sat up and looked at the cat, "Is this a nightly duty? Does he sleep with you every night?"

"He's slept with me every night since I've been here. He thinks I'm special, I guess." She lay back down and put her head on Kendrick's chest. "It's been a long time since I've said this, but…. life is so good, Jackson. I haven't thanked God or prayed to him for months, but I think he's been watching over me. I thanked him for bringing me to you, and I prayed that the baby is healthy."

Kendrick swallowed and kissed her forehead. "Yes, Lissy my love. We're so damn lucky to have found each other! I want this baby to be healthy just as much as you do. I don't care what it is. I'm gonna love it no matter what."

The following week, Annaliese and Kendrick flew to Miami, to see Tom Gepson. They checked in to a beautiful hotel right on the beach. After an afternoon swimming and laying in the sun, they enjoyed a raucous dinner with Tom Gepson's family.

Kendrick was overly happy after drinking rum with Tom's brothers and cousins. Annaliese was in love with Tom's grandmother who was dictating recipes so that she could write them down for use in Montana. Tom refused to discuss any business, but did tell Kendrick that he had the name of a money manager that Annaliese would need after their talk the next day.

After a breakfast at the hotel, Annaliese and Kendrick arrived at Tom's office ready to hear about Diego's fortune which Annaliese was about to own. After greeting each other,

Tom told them that there was so much involved with the banking and property that they would probably work until lunch. He motioned to his desk where a stack of papers and books took possession of more than half of the desk top.

"I will call in a notary as soon as we have a chance to read over each of these reports. Let's begin with the bank accounts, then go on to the real estate and businesses. Ready?"

Kendrick and Annaliese nodded they were ready. For the next four hours, reports were read, notes were taken and a notary came to make the official transfer of each of the accounts and deeds.

By the time they were done, they were all exhausted and ready for lunch. The amount of wealth was incredible! Kendrick couldn't comprehend how Annaliese was going to cope with the enormous responsibility, work for the Sanctuary, and have a baby. He didn't want to say anything until he knew how she felt, so he bit his tongue and just listened and watched as she signed, and signed, and signed her name to the papers. The notary had left and Tom was gathering up the papers. He had a new shiny leather brief case where he placed half of the papers inside.

After closing and locking the case he smiled and handed it to Annaliese. Kendrick could see her perplexed expression as she took the brief case. Tom handed her the key, "These are for your records, Annaliese. We'll keep in touch, but I'm giving you the name of a person I trust with my own family to advise and counsel you on your money and property. He will help you with taxes and any questions you could possibly ask. Here's his card. I suggest you contact him at your earliest convenience. He's located here in Miami. I told him you might be calling him, and he does have some time available for you."

While they were at lunch together, Annaliese called the office of Michael Estrada and made an appointment for the next day. They enjoyed a Cuban lunch which ended in plantains for dessert. Annaliese had acquired a new favorite food since she had arrived in Florida. She was going to be as big as a horse before this baby was born.

That evening, Kendrick took Annaliese to a club for dinner. They enjoyed more Cuban food and plantains, then were treated to the music of Cuba with a full band and dancers. The colorful costumes and headdresses had Annaliese fascinated and clapping with delight.

By ten o'clock, she was exhausted and Kendrick took her back to their hotel. She had had a big day. As she prepared for bed she was very quiet. Kendrick waited for her to share her thoughts. When they were settled on their pillows and in each other's arms, Annaliese told him what her plans were. At their appointment she would direct her new money manager to distribute her money and property in several ways. Kendrick knew she had put a lot of thought in her decision. It was well planned and extremely generous. He felt a swelling of love for this incredible woman.

Annaliese had decided to create a foundation for the Sanctuary. She knew how much property the Sanctuary had, and she had plans to add new barns and stables to house the injured animals.

There would be new equipment, two full time paid veterinarians, more staff, an ambulance, truck and trailer for only the Sanctuary to use. Ten charities would receive yearly checks in the amount of millions of dollars. She would make a major impact on these organizations to help people. The property she owned would gradually be sold off and that money would go into the Sanctuary foundation and the ten charities she had chosen.

Money also would be invested in the ranch: improvements to the bunk houses, new equipment, tractors, and another large barn for the nursery of healthy animals. Kendrick was overwhelmed listening to Annaliese talk about how she would improve the place he loved so much.

In addition, a college fund would be set up for their children and those of all the people who worked at the ranch and Sanctuary. The small town near the ranch where they shopped and went to the doctor, would benefit as well. Platteville would get a new fire truck, paramedic van, the hospital would get new equipment and a new wing, a new roof on the library, the schools would receive money for improvements, the high school would have a scholarship program, and a senior center would be built. She had thought of everything and everyone. Amazing!

Diego's money would be used for the good of the people. She had created a dynasty for their children. Her legacy would extend to their grandchildren and beyond. Kendrick felt tears well up in his eyes as he listened to her talk. She was the Madonna Angel, but he would never tell her. Diego had been right.

Epilogue

Four years later....

The shiny red wagon was heavy to pull, but the little boy turned and tugged gently using all his concentration not to disturb his precious cargo. The dusty trail was bumpy with small rocks and even though he was strong for his age, the going was difficult. Walking backwards and slowly pulling the wagon, he was determined to make it all the way to his destination without spilling his cargo.

He was almost there now. Almost to the fountain near the ruins of the old Montana homestead. It was his favorite place to play. Finally, with one last careful pull he made it, at last. Carefully, he took a blanket out of the wagon, unfolded it and spread it on the ground near the bubbling fountain. Then he gently lifted a fat little puppy out of the wagon, and held it against his chest. As he turned to sit down, the puppy struggled and the boy lost his balance falling onto the blanket, the puppy still in his arms.

He heard laughter. "Benjie, are you all right, sweetheart?" his mother asked.

"I'm okay, Mama. My puppy's not hurt either. I made it here all by myself!" he said proudly as he stood back up. Benjie was tall for his four years. Dark brown hair gleamed in the sunlight. Annaliese slowly walked up the incline and stood next to her son.

She reached out and patted his shoulder. Her light skin was such a contrast to his olive complexion. He was a handsome boy, and when he smiled, Annaliese' heart turned over – no longer with fear but with a love so strong it consumed her.

Benjie stood straight and tall and took his mother's arm helping her to the blanket. Her tummy was getting big with his baby sister. Daddy told him to watch out for her. Auntie Linda and Grace had packed a lunch for them to eat together here at his favorite place.

"Let me lay out the lunch while you play with your puppy. Have you thought of a name, yet?"

Benjie thought for a moment, "Yes, I'm going to call him Ranger. He's going to be my soldier and we will be guards at the ranch and protect you and my baby sister when Daddy goes to town or out on our land with Uncle Ray." His little chest puffed out with pride. "This ranch will be mine someday. Daddy said if I give my pony to my baby sister, I'll get to ride a big horse like him," he smiled at his mother.

"I think you have a while before that happens, darling," she laughed.

Benjie and the puppy came back to the blanket. He stood next to his mother and put his arms around her shoulders. He laid his face against her silver hair, hugging her against him, "You're so beautiful, Mama. I love you so much, and my baby sister, too. We will always take care of you both – me and Daddy."

Annaliese felt tears fill her eyes as she gazed up at her son. She loved this child so much. He would grow up a part of this land. Someday, they would tell him about his biological father – but, not for a long, long time. Jackson Kendrick was his father. A good man, a leader Benjie emulated already. Yes, Benjie would someday inherit this land along with his siblings – for there would be more babies after this one she carried near her heart.

As Benjie hugged her then walked back to his dearly beloved wagon, she looked out over the landscape. Thank you, God, she silently prayed, for the peace and love, and new life I have found here. She watched as Benjie pulled his wagon over to the puppy and struggled to pick him up and place him in the wagon.

"Careful, Benjie, he's a little heavy for you," she cautioned as the puppy squirmed.

"I know, Mama, he's my precious cargo." Annaliese smiled with pride.

The End

Juliann Dorell grew up always having stories in her head. While spending time with her mother during hospice, she urged her to write her stories and get them published. After her mother's death, that is just what she did.

Juliann lives both in southern California and Minnesota where she enjoys writing, reading, fishing, and crafts. Her husband, children, grandchildren and two wonderful dogs complete her family.